Thinking About Her

Thinking About Her
Copyright © 2020 Ophelia Alexander

All rights reserved. This book or parts thereof may not be reproduced in any form, stored in any retrieval system, or transmitted in any form or by any means—electronic, mechanical, photocopy, recording, or otherwise—without prior written permission from the publisher, except as provided by United States of America copyright law.

This is a work of fiction. Names, characters, places, and incidents are either products of the author's imagination or are used fictitiously. Any resemblance to actual persons, living or dead, businesses, companies, events, or locales is entirely coincidental.

The author acknowledges the trademarked status and trademark owners of various products, bands, and/or restaurants referenced in this work of fiction, which have been used without permission. The publication/use of these trademarks is not authorized, associated with, or sponsored by the trademark owners.

ISBN: 9798664526387

Thinking About Her

Ophelia Alexander

If even one wayward soul finds comfort in the words within the pages of this novel, I will consider it a monumental success.

Thank you.

1

The Last Party of Summer

Each word my friends spoke on that picturesque Illinois night dug into my mind like a crown of thorns. Instead of buzzing around the party and chitchatting, I chose to sit alone on the sidelines, watching Max, Devon, and the rest play basketball and get drunk. The solitude was a welcome distraction—don't get me wrong: I did my share of polite socializing before following Max into his backyard. The masqueraded speech and feigned smiles were made all the worse because Max had acted like there was nothing wrong between us.

As if he could read my thoughts, Max shot me a warm smile, giving me a look. His cocksure bravado made my body tighten. I could see the deep hope in his eyes.

I smiled back, even as my conscience fought with my guilty feelings. I owed Max everything, and breaking up with him that morning right before his big party was probably the worst thing I could have done. Everyone knew my name, freckled face, and long brown hair only because I had begun dating Max during my freshman year. There must have been something wrong with me, because Max was a great friend—just not a great boyfriend. Tragically, by the way he acted like nothing was different, I assumed that my prayers asking for him to move on had gone unanswered.

Instead of looking for a conversation to join, I flicked through some advanced settings on the camera app. As I framed the beautiful sunset in front of me, an eerie stillness came over the backyard.

I followed the gazes of my classmates over to the driveway just in time to catch the foot of Max's broad silhouette striking a basketball. The orange sphere rocketed toward the backboard but hit the rim with a loud *clang* and ricocheted wildly off course, momentarily disappearing in the bright shine of a floodlight.

I shrieked as the basketball reappeared, speeding toward me. As I raised my arms to shield my face, a voice in my head screamed, *God punishes the sinner, Clarissa!*

FUH-THWAP!

My heart raced as I cautiously looked around, confused that I wasn't in pain or sprawled out on the ground.

A loud hissing noise stole my attention, and my mouth dropped as my eyes came to rest on the punctured remains of the basketball, impaled on the end of a tree branch.

Shouting erupted, and I recognized Max's and Devon's voices, but I was distracted by my savior. I opened my mouth to thank him when a gust of evening air brought with it the smells of floral perfume.

A tall, gorgeous girl walked into view. The left side of her head was shaved down, but the right was still long. The punkish undercut meshed nicely with her near-gothic levels of makeup. She wore a ratty shirt that hung down off her left shoulder and exposed the strap of her black sports bra for the world to see. Everything about her seemed as confident as it was sinful.

"Whoa, I-I like your outfit." Saying the words out loud made the cross dangling around my neck feel slightly heavier.

"Uh, thank you," the girl said in a strange accent, and I couldn't tell if she was asking a question or taking the compliment. "Is this style uncommon in America?"

"Uh, not really. I mean, it is at Saint Mary's."

She scoffed. "I guess I need to set the trend." Then she glanced down at my church-approved button-down blouse and dark-wash blue jeans. "I like your outfit, too."

"Thanks."

The new girl tilted her head, probably wondering why I was so intimidated by her, but that was when the light from the sunset caught her eyes.

"Your eyes!" I gasped. "Are they s-silver? How are they—"

A smile began to tug at the corner of the girl's mouth as she continued to watch me with a quaint curiosity.

"Sorry. I don't mean to, uh—"

"Don't be." The girl shrugged coolly. "I know they're weird."

"They're beautiful," I said, then cleared my throat again. "Are those contacts or something?"

The girl opened her mouth to speak, but then Max walked between us. He was wearing his football jersey, because of course he was.

"Hey, sorry about that, Clare," my ex-boyfriend said, slurring a bit. "Is everyone okay?"

"Yeah," the girl and I said simultaneously.

"Jinx," she said with a smirk. "You owe me a drink."

My stomach clenched in embarrassment, although I couldn't pinpoint exactly why. "I'm fine, Max. Really."

Devon, my best friend since we could talk, walked over holding the deflated basketball in his dark hand. "I think you're gonna need a new ball, Max."

Max inspected the deflated basketball, and then we all looked over to the tree, back to the basketball, and finally to the girl standing in front of us. "How hard did you punch this?"

"Hard enough," she replied.

"Forget about the stupid ball," Devon urged. "You Bruce Lee'd it right out of the air. I don't think I've ever seen anyone move that fast. Or look that good doing it."

Forgetting about myself for a moment, I narrowed my eyes with annoyance. *Really, Devon? Mr. "I want Veronica back" Deville? One minute you're complaining about breaking things off with her on the car ride here, and then you're hitting on the new girl!*

The proverbial devil who had been lurking on my shoulder leaned into my ear and whispered, *Then again, Devon wasn't the one to ruin Veronica's life forever, was he, Clare? So much for "judge not, that ye be not judged."*

Seeing Max and Devon giving the new girl the least subtle once-over in human history, I cleared my throat.

Max blinked and asked, slurring slightly, "Sorry, who are you?"

"Brünnhilde Bernhardt?" the girl replied as if she had expected us all to know already. "But you can call me Hilda. You're Max, ja? Thanks for putting this together."

Max hesitantly shook Hilda's hand. "Uh, you're welcome, I guess." He winced a little as Hilda squeezed his hand. "That's some grip you got there."

"I'm Devon, and wow, they sure make them tall where you're from. I mean, God, how tall are you?"

"A little under two meters," Hilda said as if she'd rehearsed the answer.

Max snorted. "What's that in a real measurement system?"

Hilda thought for a second. "Uh, about six feet, three inches?"

I couldn't believe she was that tall, but she was certainly taller than Max and Devon. My eyes fell to her shoes. I assumed she had heels, but she was wearing well-worn running shoes.

"I think you might be the tallest person I've ever met," Devon said, clearly impressed.

Hilda sighed. "I'm getting that a lot tonight." Then she turned to me and held out her hand. "I didn't catch your name."

My stomach leaped into my throat. "I'm, uh, sorry. I mean, I'm Clarissa Huffington. It's a pleasure to meet you, Hilda." Her hand was softer and warmer than I thought it would be, and it struck me that she didn't squeeze my hand as she had with Max. When she let go, it suddenly felt like something was missing, as if I should be holding—

My phone!

Hilda picked up my cell and checked it out before handing it back to me. "I think it's okay."

I wheezed in relief. "Thanks."

Max chuckled as he took a seat, expecting everyone else to follow his lead. "Damn, Hilda, if you hadn't just popped my basketball, I would have invited you to play . . . Wait! You're the girl Coach Taylor talked up all summer, aren't you? Didn't you set some kind of track record in, uh . . ."

Hilda somewhat rudely stayed silent, making a fool of Max as we all sat down.

"Germany," I guessed, trying to save Max from future embarrassment.

"It was two records," Hilda added. "But they're nothing to brag about."

Devon leaned forward and picked up the can of soda he'd left on the table. He was my designated driver, after all. "Don't be so modest. Two records are two records. Germany clearly lost a great runner when you moved."

"Actually, I was born in Grand Forks," Hilda said. "So technically, America lost me when I moved to Germany."

"You're American?" I gasped.

Devon chuckled. "She just said she was, Clare. Come on, you're not that drunk yet. Wait! I got it. Let's toast to Hilda's return to Grand Forks. I'll go grab us some new drinks."

As Devon collected empty cups and cans off the table, I muttered, "Who in their right mind would want to celebrate a return to Grand Forks? The only thing this town ever contributed to society was Saint Mary's. 'The highest class of education for the faithful and the virtuous.'"

I heard Hilda scoff next to me but didn't dare turn and face her. Something about her was putting me on edge.

Devon rolled his eyes. "Psh, what about that photographer you're in love with? Ripley Gray?"

"Ridley Gracy," I retorted. "And he doesn't count. He got out of Grand Forks. I'm going to be stuck here forever."

Devon shrugged and glanced at Hilda, who was already sitting back with a relaxed demeanor like it was just a normal Saturday evening for her. "What's your poison, Hilda?"

"Gin," Hilda said without any hesitation.

"I, uh— I'll see if we have any."

When Devon left, Max asked, "Not a beer fan?"

"The opposite actually," Hilda replied. "American beers don't even come close to anything I drank in Germany."

"You must drink a lot then," I said, sounding more prudish than I would have liked.

Hilda waved her hand in the air dismissively. "I guess, but unlike your friend here, I can hold my liquor."

Max nearly stumbled out of his chair as he leaned forward. "You did not just say that! Was that a challenge? I'll drink you under the table. Anytime. Anywhere."

"Not tonight," Hilda said, "I pray you do not fall in love with me, for I am falser than vows made in wine."

Max blinked, trying to understand what Hilda had just said, and I admitted that I was a bit lost, too. *Did she just ask him not to fall in love with her? Have I been misreading her?*

I couldn't help but feel Hilda's waves of confidence as they seemed to press into me. There was something aggressively admirable about how she acted. Each word and gesture seemed so . . . strong. I wasn't sure why, but it felt nice to have another woman around, especially one who wouldn't bring up relationship drama, be it mine or Devon's.

Speak of the devil. Devon returned and set two plastic cups on the table, one in front of Hilda and the other in front of me.

I took a curious glance into my new cup, not having expected Devon to bring me another one. When I saw the eerily neon-blue liquid, I scoffed. "This isn't water."

Devon grinned. "It's vodka. Hey, Hilda, did you know vodka means 'water' in Russian?"

Hilda was already lifting the drink to her lips, but she stopped before she took a drink and cocked an eyebrow. "That's not true."

"Uh, yeah, it is," Devon said. "I read online—"

"I've *been* to Russia," Hilda interrupted. "If you ask for vodka at a restaurant, you're not going to be given water."

I gasped. "You've been to Russia?"

Hilda nodded. "It's not hard. I just took trains up through Poland, Lithuania, Latvia, and Estonia. It doesn't take long if you plan it right."

My jaw dropped. "Wait, you've been to all those countries?"

Hilda shrugged. "If you count sleeping on train station benches or layovers, then yeah, I guess so."

Hilda's lying, right? There is no way—

"Devon! Max!" Ryan, one of Max's football friends, shouted from the back door to the house. "You're missing the worst game of beer pong ever! Get in here. I need a real team. Lin, Michelle, and Kate are destroying us, and I refuse to lose to girls."

"Ah! Duty calls." Max grinned as he pushed away from the table. He turned back and saw that Hilda and I hadn't moved. "Come on, everyone inside. It's time to watch me do what I do best."

Act like a total jerk? Embarrass me by acting like we're still dating? Both, I decided.

Hilda and I glanced at each other, and oddly, I could tell we had the same thought. I turned back to Max to talk, but Hilda spoke first. "Watch you vomit all over the floor? Nah, the sunset is too nice to ruin by being indoors."

"What if I ask you to dance with me after our game?" Devon suggested.

I scowled at him, one straw away from snapping at him about Veronica, but Hilda downed the rest of her drink in one massive gulp. "It's not good," she said, pronouncing it like *goot*.

Devon hesitated. "The music or the drink?"

"Both," Hilda replied wryly.

"Guys!" Ryan shouted. "Come on. What's the holdup?"

"Well?" Hilda said as she waved her hand and shooed Max and Devon toward the door. "Don't you two have women to lose to?"

Max snorted. "You're new here, so I'm gonna let that slide. But I don't lose to anyone."

Naturally, I reached out and touched Max's arm. "It's really nice out tonight. Plus, there are only so many ways I can say 'Oh, my summer? I spent it being a junior counselor for a Bible camp in the Grand Fork's hills' before I die of embarrassment. I'm going to stay out here, at least for a little while longer."

Max sighed heavily but turned and walked to the door.

Once the boys were gone, I found my fingers nervously tying themselves into knots as I struggled to think of a topic that Hilda and I could mutually relate to. *Catholicism? Nope. Clearly, Hilda had strayed far from that subject. Max? She wouldn't care about all my relationship drama. Veronica, a girl Hilda had obviously never met? My summer at Bible camp? Ha. She probably did more exciting things than that before she ate breakfast every day. Travel? We clearly had no common ground there.* I felt pain in my fingers as I pushed them together harder. My heart was beating fast, and a voice started to chastise me for not being a better conversationalist.

Occasionally, our strange game of silent chicken would break when one of us looked up only to catch the other doing the same. We shared a giggle, but neither of us could find words.

"So," I finally started, finding the liquid courage I needed halfway through my drink, "uh, what grade are you in?"

"I'm going into my senior year. Technically, I skipped a grade."

"You skipped a grade?" I blinked. Hilda didn't strike me as the kind of person who could. Then I kicked myself for continuing to think like my mother.

"It's not like I wanted to. It's just that the German and American school systems aren't really comparable, so Saint Mary's gave me a test to do over the summer."

"Wait, how old are you?"

"Sixteen."

I gasped. "I'm older than you?!"

Hilda laughed. "I don't know. Are you?"

"Yeah, I just turned seventeen." I ran my hand over my face, feeling my cold fingertips against my burning cheeks. Not knowing what to say next, I noticed Hilda's empty cup on the table. "You finished that pretty quickly."

Hilda snorted. "We were racing and you didn't tell me?"

"No, I mean, you drink fast."

"Should I slow down for you next time?"

"You don't know me. I'm not even that buzzed."

"Oh, is that so?" With a sudden burst of speed, Hilda plucked the drink out of my hands.

"What the hell?!" I exclaimed. Hilda raised a finger to my face while she gulped down the rest of my drink. She exhaled deeply and set my empty cup inside hers. "Oops."

"What the hell is your problem?" I huffed. "Don't think just because you're tall and"—the word "hot" popped into my head, and I caught myself before I could say it—"whatever that you have any right to take things from me."

Hilda just laughed at me, and I turned away, trying to get my thoughts under control. I mean, I almost called another girl "hot." Not that it wasn't true. Devon and Max had tried to make passes at her. Or did they? *Argh, why is tonight so strange?*

When I looked around, there weren't many people in the backyard after Max left. I caught a wave of red hair and the emerald green eyes that went with it. The warm blood flowing through my face chilled as Veronica Lancer and I locked eyes. She was standing in a small circle of people who had just walked outside. Her familiar crimson turtleneck, blue jeans, and hair pulled back into a ponytail gutted me. *That's what she wears when—*

My thought was cut short as Veronica smiled sympathetically at me, but I couldn't return the friendly gesture. I swallowed my guilt and turned in shame. After a few seconds, I chanced a glance up, praying Veronica had looked away from me. She hadn't and was staring at my phone. I needed to escape the situation.

"I, uh—"

"It's a genetic disorder," Hilda interrupted.

"W-What?"

Hilda smiled, but there was something hidden behind it. A deep regret, maybe? "My eyes. You asked about them before, remember? *Monochromatic ocular hypoplasia.* Don't worry. It's not contagious or anything." She brazenly kicked her feet up on the table and looked at the stars. The act conflicted with the sudden softness in her voice. "I'll be blind before I'm thirty. That's what the doctors in Germany told me. There's always a chance I won't, but it could also happen sooner. It could be any day, really. The only nights I sleep well are when I'm too exhausted from working out to think about it."

I was caught between my guilty conscience regarding Veronica and my new curiosity about Hilda's sudden shift in personality. "I'm sorry," I said. I wanted to get up, but my manners compelled me to stay.

"Don't be sorry." Hilda sighed, her gaze still skyward. "It makes me see the world like I'm taking photographs. That way, when I go blind, I'll have, um, things to remember. What's the word? Snapshots? Oh . . . Sorry if this is weird."

"No, it's-it's not weird at all," I stuttered, awed by how Hilda's words spoke to me. "Actually, I, uh—even if you go blind at thirty, you've probably seen more of the world than I ever will."

Hilda hummed curiously.

"I mean, I see beautiful photos of all these places around the world, but I see more. Framing, lighting, focus depths that would improve most of them. I don't know how to explain it, but I guess I kind of see the world in photographs, too. But it's not like it matters in my case. I don't even have a real DSLR."

"DSLR?" Hilda asked, clearly unfamiliar with the term.

"Um, like a Nikon or a Canon." Hilda gave me a blank expression. "Like a real camera a photographer would use."

"You're a photographer?" Hilda swung her feet back to the ground and leaned forward. "That's so cool!"

Hilda's sudden enthusiasm pushed me back into my chair. "I don't know about that. Other than my phone, the only camera I own is an old Polaroid Spectra. I usually carry it everywhere, but I forgot it tonight. Plus, my mom might have suspected something if she caught me leaving with it. The Spectra makes me feel like a closet hipster, but I do love the way polaroids turn out. I have a whole wall of my room completely covered in pictures. I'm talking floor to ceiling. It's really cool."

"Whoa!" Hilda gasped. "You must either have a tiny room or take a lot of pictures."

"It's the second one," I assured her, feeling a spike of excitement. "Most of my allowance goes to ordering film refills off Amazon. The only problem is, it's a little awkward to take selfies with my Spectra. But my new phone has a camera on the front, solely for taking selfies. I haven't used it much, but I suspect once school starts—"

"Let's take one right now!"

"Huh? Oh, uh, sure. I guess." I picked up my phone and started down the checklist of photography I'd drilled into my mind through hours of YouTube tutorials.

"Is something wrong?" Hilda asked after a few seconds.

"No," I lied and drew my phone back, tapping on the screen. "I'm not sure."

Hilda bit her lip and looked away. "It's because I'm so different, isn't it?"

"What? No. Not at all. You look great," I spluttered and cleared my throat. "I was just overthinking it. Sorry, I do that a lot when I take pictures. Wait. Turn your chair a little. No, like this." It took a few seconds to reposition us how I wanted. I couldn't help but feel the attention from our classmates as I set up the shot, but I was too in the moment to care, and Hilda didn't seem to mind at all either. "Okay, there. Now say 'cheese!'"

"Käse!" Hilda grinned as the camera flashed.

"Hey, I said say 'cheese.'" I shoved her playfully with my shoulder. A sober me wouldn't have done that.

Hilda giggled and nudged me back. "I did, but you never said what language."

Unlike the rest of the socializing I did that night, the playful banter genuinely made me happy. Conversations with Hilda felt like God had answered my prayers, because she didn't seem to ask the same tired questions that everyone else did at the end of every summer. Did I travel? No. Did I do anything fun? No. The one thing I had to gloat about was my new phone, which wasn't much because all my friends had also upgraded. Hilda, on the other hand, seemed to want to get to know me first. To say it was refreshing would be a massive understatement. It was downright . . . attractive. I shook my head to clear the thought, but with Hilda studying the photo on my phone, I couldn't.

It's just the drinks. I bet I would be thinking this way about anyone right now. Still, I felt myself smiling as I asked, "So, what do you think?"

Hilda's silence lasted just long enough for my inner critic to nearly pull all of my hair out. "I like the way you put the porch light behind you but kept me in darkness by using the shadow of the table umbrella. It makes you look very . . . angelic and me very, um, what's the word? Evil? It's really good. You made it look like you used a filter, but you didn't. You should post this somewhere."

"Ha, that'll be the day." My sarcastic words betrayed my feelings as my heart skipped, and my mouth started moving of its own accord. "I-It's weird. I usually don't like telling people I'm a photographer because everyone with a camera phone thinks they're the next Ridley Gracy. Don't get me wrong, I'm guilty of taking the occasional vapid photo here or there, but I always try to include something special." I flicked and thoughtlessly scrolled through my camera roll. "You have no idea how many hours I've wasted online learning about things like shutter speeds, depth of field, and aperture settings. But here I am, no closer to being a photographer than anyone else."

Hilda giggled. "Not with that attitude."

"What's that supposed to mean?"

"You think Ridley Whatever gets up every morning and thinks he's not a photographer?"

I rolled my eyes. "Of course not, but—"

"Exactly!" Hilda slapped the table with her palm, attracting the attention of everyone in the backyard. "You can't compare your work to his, but you can compare your passion. If you keep telling yourself you're not close to being a photographer, then it won't matter how talented you obviously are. Don't be the best for someone else. Be the best because that's what you are. That's what my mother said."

"I, uh . . ." I struggled to think of words to express myself in the wake of Hilda's passionate and empowering speech.

Hilda turned her head sharply to stare at me, and I could nearly feel the fire that burned within her. "You're a photographer, Clarissa. Say it."

My eyes darted away. I didn't know if it was because I was drunk or intimidated or completely in awe that people like Hilda actually existed, but I muttered, "I-I'm a photographer."

Nervously glancing up, I could tell that I hadn't convinced Hilda. "Well, that's a start, I guess. We'll have to work on it."

I blinked, still trying to figure Hilda out. "Huh?"

Hilda dismissed me with a wave right as Devon, Max, and a few others returned to the table with new drinks for everyone.

From there, the night blurred into a tapestry of conversations, group photos, and starlight. I knew it was a little rude to ignore everyone else and only talk to Hilda, but everyone else would have talked about what they did over the summer, which would have either made me bored to tears or jealous. Speaking with Hilda was a hundred times more pleasant than those dull conversations ever were.

Somehow, even as Devon and I said our goodbyes and departed

the party, I still had dozens of questions for Hilda. I nearly asked if she wanted to come over to my house so we could keep talking, but it would have been too out of character, so I settled for "goodnight" and a wave.

* * *

The stained-glass cross above the door weighed down on me as I drew near and laid a hand on the doorknob. The door flew open, and a looming shadow fell over me.

"No," I gasped involuntarily.

"What?!" my mother bristled. She was dressed in an evening muumuu adorned with holy crosses and appeared about three hard breaths away from blowing down a brick house. I half-expected her to be holding a crucifix, but she clutched her Bible instead. Her meaty index finger was wedged into the middle of the ancient text. She had probably found the perfect verse to guilt me for being out so late.

"What did you just say!?" she snapped.

I locked my eyes on the ground and tried to swallow the lump in my throat.

My mother's hand shot out, locking my upper arm in her vice-like grip, and pulled me into the house. The door slammed behind me as I tried to catch my breath.

"You!" my mother sputtered. "Start talking! Now!" She thrust me into the wall with a *thud* and held the Bible up like she was about to strike me with it. "Where were you?!"

I covered my chest with my arms and cowered into the corner of the door. "I was—"

My mother sniffed the air. "Have you been drinking, too!?" she shrieked.

"I-I can explain!" I said, my eyes darting to the thick tome in my mother's shaking hand.

"Start explaining this instant! If you lie, so help me God, I will ground you for the rest of the year!"

I swallowed, feeling tears well at the corners of my eyes. "Max's brother gave us a few beers, and then he brought out some vodka we all shared. I only had a sip I swear. And Devon didn't drink anything but soda. He and I stopped at the Taco Bell downtown on the way home. That's why I'm so late." I struggled to keep my voice from shaking.

My mother thrust out her hand, palm up. "Let me see the receipt."

"I don't have it," I said as I looked down to the floor. I didn't dare to bring any attention to my throbbing upper arm or aching shoulder. "We ate in the parking lot and threw out everything before we left because Devon didn't want trash in his car. You know how he is." I cautiously looked up, praying my mother remembered that Devon took a near-religious pride in keeping his fancy Mustang in top condition.

"Convenient." My mother's nose flared, but I could tell she was calming down because she had stopped screaming and lowered her Bible. "For drinking, you're grounded for a month. And I don't care how much it was. I raised you better than to give in to peer pressure. Now, your father and I are going to discuss further punishments in the morning when he gets home. Go to your room and pray."

"I'm tired, Mom. Can't I just sleep?"

"You'll pray until the sun rises! Then you'll help me with breakfast for your father and start your chores. That's the last I'll hear about it!"

I tried to pretend that I wasn't scared to death as I nodded and walked up the stairs to my bedroom. Being inside my room brought me some comfort, but knowing that my mother wouldn't let me close my door meant I had no privacy.

I wiped tears away from my eyes as I took to my knees at the foot of my bed. With my hands clasped, I began to pray for God's forgiveness at the large wooden cross that hung above my headboard.

I might have still been buzzed, because once I ran out of things to ask God's forgiveness for, my thoughts strayed to Hilda. What was it like to move to Germany as a kid? What were her friends like? Where did she live? Some divine intervention must have occurred to produce someone so seemingly unburdened by the world's expectations.

I opened my right eye, glancing to my open door. Thankfully my mother wasn't looming in my doorway and waiting to catch me. With a heavy sigh, I looked up at the wooden cross above my bed. "I bet Hilda never had to deal with anything like this. I bet she would just jump out her window and . . . leave."

2

The First Day of School

I groaned as I scrolled through Twitter for the fifty-sixth time. *House arrest, for a whole week!* I glanced over at my photo collection and the homework that Devon had left behind from our study session the night before. *The only three things that've kept me sane this entire week.*

I bit my lip and threw my hands up in the air. My bedroom window and social media were the only ways to keep in contact with the outside world. Even that was getting boring. I pushed away from my desk and rolled my office chair over to my collage. I smiled, once again reliving all of my best memories.

There was something cathartic and calming about trying to make all of the photos of my life work together. I controlled it. It was small in the grand scheme of things, but its seemingly random layout made sense to me. I frowned as I meticulously scanned the photos. *No more space on the wall, and some of these just don't belong anymore. Time to make room for the new year!*

My eyes fell to the photo of me and Max as a couple, and I cringed. It was special, or at least it *had been* special at some point. Max's goofy expression, my genuine smile, and our hands wrapped around each other's waists. It was all iconic of a typical high school couple. Looking at it felt too perfect, like it had been manufactured in a stock photo lab. *There's no way those two people were ever a couple. He's too handsome to go out with someone like her. And she's too stuffy and prudish to consider going out with a wild jock like him . . . That one is definitely going in the box.*

As I filled an old shoebox of freshly archived photos, I wondered how best to replace the coveted spot nearest to my pillows. It would be the picture I fell asleep to each night. Thinking back on Max's party, I wondered if anything I took then would work. Or would I have to suffer a blank wall until the first day of school?

Clicking idly, I passed the selfie I'd taken with Hilda. Then a few photos later, my brain registered what had happened, and I quickly went back. Even with my phone locked away somewhere in the house, it still uploaded all my pictures to the cloud—not that my parents knew that. The selfie was better than I had remembered, and seeing Hilda flooded my mind with pleasant memories from that evening.

Yet when I went to print it out, my mouse cursor just hovered over the button. *What if Mom sees this? She'll think that Hilda and I hang out. Not that I wouldn't hang out with Hilda. She's smart, cool, and more worldly than anyone I know. She's—*

I stopped myself and just stared at the picture for a few seconds, trying to figure out what it was about Hilda that made me think such wild thoughts.

Shaking my head, I told myself that I needed to get a grip. After all, Hilda and I had nothing in common. She probably wouldn't even want to hang out with me at school once she found her own clique of friends. This picture was a one-time thing.

After a satisfactory press of a pushpin into the drywall, I stood back and admired the printed selfie near my pillows, even if it wasn't going to stay there for very long.

* * *

The cold hung in the morning air as I stood on the freshly cut grass of Saint Mary's Catholic Academy. It was the largest, most prestigious private school in the state—and expensive to attend. The metal pulleys of the three flag poles shifted as they waved their banners. My attention was drawn to the lowest flag, a simple burgundy affair with a golden otter holding a white cross. I never understood why such a religious school had an otter for a mascot. A sacred heart or rosary would have been more appropriate. I supposed it was easier to make a costume and cheer for an otter.

I couldn't help but take a picture of the flagpole with my Spectra. Hearing the familiar camera gears churn out the Polaroid film filled me with joy. I had already decided where I would put it on my wall when I got home from school.

The old school was a featureless, square, three-story structure made of brick. Its corridors were narrow, and the classrooms were claustrophobic. I debated taking another picture but decided against it as I squeezed my way through the front doors. I wasn't shy about my hobby; I just didn't want to bother everyone who was rushing to find their names and homeroom classes on the sheets of paper pinned to noticeboards around school.

Seeing large groups of people crowded around the noticeboards of the main hall, I took a quick turn to find one of the less popular ones. I didn't want to talk about what I had been doing since Max's party. *Escape,* I promised myself for the hundredth time. *This year is all about keeping a 4.0 GPA so I can leave Grand Forks and never look back.*

Matilda had texted me. She asked about how Max's party was and gave me my new locker number, padlock combination, and homeroom class number. I gathered my things and ran for homeroom before the late bell rang, only to be stopped a dozen or so times by people wondering how my summer went. Having spent nearly all summer as a Bible camp counselor, at church, or grounded in my room almost made me forget who I was.

Sister June pointed to the whiteboard at the front of the class, where she had written her name. She looked down at the stack of papers in the crook of her arm and began calling names. A moment later, a boy I didn't recognize handed my paper to me. I mustered a quick thanks and took the paper from him. *Please be easy.* I prayed as I flipped the sheet of paper over like I was revealing a lottery ticket.

I almost swore out loud when I saw the first line. Stantin was the only teacher I didn't want to see on my schedule. He was the worst teacher at Saint Mary's, and I got him first thing in the morning. *So much for winning the lottery.* At least everything else on there looked simple enough. Both of the honors classes would be challenging but nothing a few late-night study sessions with Devon wouldn't solve. World History would be a cakewalk because Hallberg was artsy, and his definition of "due dates" was lax, to say the least. I hadn't expected to see PE on my schedule, but even seniors couldn't have more than one free period. Having an extended lunch would be worth an hour of physical effort at the end of the day. Plus, it meant that I'd either arrive at religious studies with Sister June or at home freshly showered.

* * *

My shoes dragged up the metal ramp to EVA-04-1, and when I opened the door, the portable was as bad as I remembered it being in my freshman year: cramped, stuffy, and smelling of dry-erase markers and depression. It was hard for me not to turn around, but my mother would throw a fit if she ever found out I switched.

The excuse of "the teacher is really mean" wouldn't be enough to satisfy her.

Stantin's vigilant gaze fell on me as I walked through the doorway of his classroom. His worn face, broad shoulders, and stocky build made him look like a buff penguin. Max's older brother had taken to calling him "Sergeant Satan." I had never liked the mean nickname, but it did seem to fit him.

"Clare! Fuck yeah," Ryan whispered as loudly as he dared. The heavier-set boy then pushed the backpack across from him and onto the floor. "Got your seat right here."

"Uh, hey, Ryan." I hesitated. "Wasn't that seat taken? I could have just sat over one."

"Nah." He chuckled. "We need to sit together so I can cheat off you."

"Yeah, okay." I felt bad for taking the seat but felt obligated as well.

As I looked to the backpack in the aisle wondering whose it was, Ryan said, "I bet Max is going to be fucking jealous when he hears about this."

"*Swearing is for whores and the uneducated,*" my mother's voice called out in my mind. "I wouldn't be so sure. Max's brothers still tell horror stories about Stantin."

Stantin's hawkish eyes fell on us and held for a long moment before he moved back to reading something on his desk.

I cleared my throat and pulled out a notebook that I had written "English" on. When I opened it to the first blank page, it reminded me of my future. I swallowed as I tapped my pen on the paper. *This is what I wanted, though, right?* I dreamed of leaving Grand Forks forever and starting my photography career, but the world was so big, and I would have to quickly make so many choices that could change my life forever.

A sixth sense prickled the back of my neck, and I looked up to see Lin Cho was standing in the doorway, exuding her signature resting bitch face and dangerously aggressive attitude. Her critical eyes were staring daggers directly at me. Her gaze dropped to the backpack on the ground next to me. With her lip curled into a snarl, she marched down the aisle.

As Lin reached down for the backpack, I started to apologize. "Sorry, I—"

"Shut up, Huffington. Nobody cares. I leave for the bathroom, and you just take my spot? Fuck both of you."

"Miss Cho!" Stantin roared from the head of the class. "Take a seat immediately, and if I hear you swearing again, you'll be sent to the dean's office."

The late bell rang, and Stantin stood up, silencing the class with the smack of a metal clipboard against his hand. "When I say your name, raise your hand. Bernhardt, Brun—Brunnhilde?" His eyes scanned the classroom.

"What!?" I gasped in disbelief. *How could I miss her?!*

Stantin scoffed something about there "always being one" while he marked at the clipboard.

He has no right to judge Hilda so harshly! The portables weren't really labeled properly, and despite the fact that she's a senior, it's only her first year.

After roll call, Stantin slammed his clipboard on his desk, making sure he had every student's undivided attention. "Did anyone not receive the reading instructions over the summer?" When nobody raised a hand, Stantin nodded. "Good. Pull out your books and open them to chapter five."

The unzipping of backpacks and fluttering of pages was the only noise until the door to the classroom opened with a loud creaking of hinges. Bathed in sunlight, Hilda stepped through the doorway, looking a bit lost. She was wearing tight-fitting ripped blue jeans and a black Slayer pullover hoodie with a pentagram made of swords on it. Her dark pin-up eyeliner elegantly covered her eyes but made her platinum irises stand out and seem piercing. I was amazed that she hadn't burst into flames on the spot.

Hilda awkwardly adjusted her backpack—which looked fresh off of a World War II battlefield—before she cleared her throat. "I can explain."

"I don't care," Stantin said. "I've heard every excuse before. And if you ever feel like arriving late to my class again, kindly escort yourself to the dean's office instead. Do I make myself clear? That goes for everyone. Unless you have a note from the school nurse, I do not accept tardiness. If you're in my class, you need to take your seat and open to chapter five."

Hilda crossed her arms. "I don't have a book."

"So," he said, nostrils flaring, "you had all summer, and you still couldn't find the time to get a copy? Is that right? Too busy with all that makeup, I presume. You're setting a fine example for what someone who wants to fail my class on the first day looks like. Strike one of three for the year."

To my surprise, Hilda didn't seem embarrassed at all. In fact, she just kept her eyes locked on Stantin as if she were sizing him up.

"What now?" Hilda offered so brazenly I swore I heard several jaws hit desks. Hilda had just signed her own death warrant and didn't even know it.

Stantin finally released all of the air in his lungs through his nose and pointed to the shelf next to Hilda by the door. "Grab a copy of the textbook and take a seat. If there's even a page out of place, I'll know it, and you'll be out of my class."

In utter shock, I watched Hilda walk over to the bookshelf, take a copy, and sit in one of the few remaining seats—the one next to me in the corner, which Lin had opted to leave open.

"Name?" Stantin called back.

"Brünnhilde," Hilda answered back confidently with the full brunt of her German accent.

Stantin made a mark on the clipboard. "As I was saying, chapter five . . ."

Anxiously, I tapped my desk, waiting for an opportunity to present itself, and once Stantin's back was turned, I poked Hilda on the shoulder with the butt of my pen.

Hilda glanced over and then did a double-take as her eyes lit up. "Clarissa!?"

Hearing her say my full name with her unique accent made my stomach tighten.

"Strike two, Miss Bernhardt!" Stantin roared. "One more word and you'll have set the record for the fastest drop from my class. Do I make myself clear?"

Hilda turned to face our teacher. She touched an index finger to her temple and smoothly saluted him with it. "Jawohl."

Anxiety gripped me, and I hardly even moved for the rest of class; if I did one more thing, I could get Hilda kicked out on the first day.

* * *

As Hilda and I walked out after class, I realized how many students were either openly gawking at her or actively looking away. A bad feeling crept into my mind. *No, it's okay. They just don't know her like I do.* Then I realized that I'd only known Hilda for a total of four hours. *Should I just excuse myself and head to the bathroom or something? How would I explain needing to do that every morning for the next year? What if she asks to come with me?!*

"I can't believe we're in the same class," Hilda said, completely oblivious to or apathetic about everyone looking at us. "What are the odds?"

"So where are you off to next? How crazy would it be if we had more than one class together?"

"I'd like that," Hilda said as she unfolded her class schedule and held it between us. "Looks like chemistry in SCI-04-01."

"That's on the first floor of the main building. We're pretty close, but I could walk you there if you want."

"Is that your next class, too?"

"No, I'm heading off to geometry in the math wing. It's across the quad from the main building, which is also pretty much straight ahead."

"Ah, at least we can walk together every day, Ja?"

I snorted. "I guess so. Why does that matter?"

"I know it may not look like it, Clarissa, but this is all new to me." Hilda's smile softened. "I haven't . . . It's just nice to already have a best friend who knows everything."

Best friend?

3

Lunchtime

My phone lit up as I finished grabbing my pudding dessert out of the cafeteria cooler. I was long overdue for a particular text. I sighed, knowing full well what Matilda wanted to talk about.

Batty Matty: *You broke up with Max AGAIN?! Why didn't you tell me?*

Me: *It's complicated. I don't want to talk about it.*

Batty Matty: *"It's complicated" should be the title of your autobiography. And we're SO talking about it.*

With a sigh, I put my phone away. *Max is the last thing I want to talk about right now. Then again, I haven't seen Matty since I got grounded.* With none of my friends in sight, I left through one of the side doors, sidestepping any confused first-year students. *Now, what am I going to say to Matty this time?* I rounded a hallway corner and tripped on a person kneeling in front of one of the lower lockers built into the wall. Two hands shot out and helped steady me while I focused on keeping my tray flat.

"Are you okay?" a familiar voice asked.

My whole body stiffened as I looked up. Veronica was standing in front of me, looking worried, both of her hands still holding my shoulders. I opened my mouth to speak, but Hilda stood up, rubbing her leg.

"Clarissa?"

"Oh, uh, morning, V."

"It's lunchtime, Clare," Veronica said politely. Then we both looked down at my tray.

"R-Right," I said, feeling a lead weight in my stomach shift.

Hilda curiously glanced between us. "Is something wrong?"

Veronica responded first. "It's a very short, very tragic story. Do you need any more help finding your way around, Hilda?"

"No thanks," Hilda said, but she still seemed skeptical about our interaction. "Clarissa has already promised to show me everything I need to know."

"Clarissa?" Veronica ran her eyes over me, knowing only my mother ever called me by my full name.

Feeling caught off guard, I cleared my throat. "That's not exactly what I said, Hilda."

Veronica smiled. "Well, in either case, I can see you're in good hands, Hilda." She nodded and walked around us to the lunchroom.

Once she was gone, Hilda raised an eyebrow at me. "What was *that* about?"

"I, uh . . . We got drunk and . . . I don't want to talk about it." I forcibly changed the subject. "Do you need to pick up lunch?"

Hilda held up a finger, then bent back down to finish whatever she was doing with her locker. After a second of shuffling things around, she stood back up while holding a brown paper lunch bag in her hand.

"What's in the bag?" I asked as we set off down the hallway.

"Just some healthy snacks."

"You know they have salads in the—"

"Sorry, what I meant to say is, I like to make my food." Hilda smiled, but there was something behind it I couldn't read.

"So you can cook? That's good to know." I wasn't sure why I said it, but the words just came out naturally.

Hilda giggled. "Cooking is pretty far from what I do, but I can set a microwave timer like you wouldn't believe. I was going to eat here." Hilda stopped at an empty hallway bench between a set of lockers right before we exited the main building. "Want to join me?"

"Oh, no, are you kidding me? Only weirdos and freshmen who don't know any better eat in the hallways, Hilda."

"Ah." Hilda scratched the side of her head and looked around for another place to sit.

"Wait." I reached up and touched her shoulder, surprising both myself and Hilda. I quickly brought my hand back to my lunch tray. *Awkward.* "Uh, sorry, but, uh, do you want to come and eat with me? I'm sure Max and Devon will want to say hi, and you'll get to meet Matilda and everyone else who missed Max's party."

Hilda looked down at herself, then to me. "Okay. If you think it is a good idea."

"It's the best idea! Come on. I'm sure Matty will have a hundred questions for you." *And hopefully none for me.*

* * *

Hilda stuck out like a sore thumb among the cheerleaders, football players, and upper-echelon students at our table. I felt inconsequential, which was nice; I had someone to be an outcast with. Devon had brought me into the group because I wasn't cool enough to join on my own. It felt good to be Devon for once. Matilda had, of course, saved me a seat across from her, and I couldn't help but notice it was conveniently next to Max, too. She was wearing a posh fitted shirt and a pleated skirt to match. Her dirty blonde, shoulder-length hair was perfectly cut and highlighted with platinum streaks.

Devon gestured grandiosely as Hilda took the open seat next to him. "Welcome, Hilda, to our table of wonders. We have all of the amenities you'd come to expect from a table, plus some of the best company Saint Mary's can offer . . . And Max."

For better or worse.

Hilda smiled. "Good afternoon, I'm—"

"Soooo," Matilda interrupted. "Is anyone going to introduce me?"

"Sorry, that's my cue," Devon said with a flashy wink. "To everyone who doesn't know, this is Hilda. Hilda, this is everyone and Matilda."

"Matilda is our student body president," Max mumbled with his mouth filled with pasta.

"Or unchecked social tyrant," I poked playfully, "depending on what side of the bed she wakes up on."

Matilda rolled her eyes. "Pleasure to meet you, Hilda. They sure make them tall in . . . wherever you're from."

Hilda shrugged and raised her eyebrow playfully. "Actually, I'm from here, and you're pretty short, so I think together we make a good average, ja?"

I watched Matilda's eyes narrow and felt compelled to explain. "Hilda, Matilda's actually pretty self-conscious about—"

"No, don't." Max interrupted. "It's about time someone said it out loud. Matilda's short. But there's nothing wrong with that."

I looked at Matilda and said, "So how was South—"

"Hey," Max said as he nudged Hilda with his elbow," sometimes an inch is all it takes, right?"

Hilda was about to take a bite out of a sandwich which didn't even look like it had anything between the pieces of bread, but she paused to consider. "I guess?"

Max leaned forward and attempted to whisper, but he had all the subtlety of a diesel engine turning over. "What do you mean you 'guess'? Oh my God, Hilda. You're not a virgin, are you?"

"Max!?" I gasped loudly. With my cheeks flushing with embarrassment on Hilda's behalf, I looked at her, mostly to tell her that she needn't dignify Max with a response. To my surprise, Hilda looked bemused instead of offended.

"My V-card was punched a while ago," Hilda said, "but I'm getting the feeling you're covering for something. Could it be that—"

"He is," Devon interrupted. "He just keeps telling everyone that he's saving himself for the right girl."

"Duh." Matilda snorted and then waved at me. "The right girl is sitting next to him, as I've been saying for years. After you two are married, of course."

That's not even . . . Argh! I fought to keep my mouth shut because Matilda knew that wasn't even one of the top ten reasons I had broken up with Max. *Not the best way to start my senior year. It's okay. I can turn this around. All I have to do is not say anything else about—*

"Having sex is excellent cardio," Hilda interrupted. "If you find a willing partner, I would highly recommend it, especially if you're an athlete."

My wide eyes darted from face to face as I tried to gauge if Hilda was making some kind of strange joke. "Hilda, maybe we shouldn't—"

"Is that how you see it?" Matilda interrupted. "Like a workout?"

"It's true," Hilda said earnestly. "As long as you're doing it right and it's not over in ten seconds."

"Given your physique," Matilda said, "one might assume you do a lot of working out."

My whole body lurched. *Did Matilda just call Hilda a slut?*

Hilda grinned without missing a beat. "Maybe. Maybe not." Then she leaned forward. "Maybe it's none of your fucking business."

There was at least one sharp inhale, which might have even been from me. Nobody made fun of Matilda, not even Max, the king of cursing. That was like the unspoken rule of our clique.

Matilda's shocked expression contorted into an insincere smile. "I'm going to assume that's a yes."

"Assume whatever you want, Miststück," Hilda said with a smirk as she took another bite of her sandwich.

Forcing a change of subject, I asked, "So, Hilda, what part of Germany did you live in before you moved back here?"

"Schöneiche," Hilda replied, "It's a small town just outside of Berlin. My parents both worked in the Marzahn-Hellersdorf borough of Berlin. Are you familiar?"

Max piped in. "Berlin, that's the town that had that big wall after World War II, right?"

Hilda seemed to shift uncomfortably at the mention of the Berlin Wall. "Ja, but Schöneiche is quite beautiful. I used to bike with my mom to school. Then after classes got out, I would ride to where she worked in Berlin. There was this long road that cut through a small forest, and after about five or six kilometers, it would open into these big fields of wildflowers. In the winter, when it would snow, my parents and I would make Schneeleute, snow people. Then we would take turns tackling them over. My father always built the most durable ones. I could never knock over the ones he made. After that, we would all go out to dinner, where I would get hot chocolate and roasted chestnuts from the street vendors." Her voice took on a suddenly forlorn tone as she looked down at her half-eaten sandwich. "Those were the best days."

I smiled as Hilda's words painted a vivid picture in my mind. *I wonder if she has pictures on Facebook.* Matilda pressed her glossy lips together and widened her eyes. Hearing Hilda laugh again pulled my attention away from Matilda. It was getting bothersome that everything Hilda did pulled me away from the normal flow of conversation I was accustomed to.

"I live much farther away from school than I used to in Germany," Hilda said. "My legs are still a little sore from my run here this morning."

Aghast, I asked, "You ran to school this morning?"

Hilda nodded. "Ja, and I will for the rest of the year. It's only about eight kilometers. It helps wake me up, like a big cup of coffee."

Matilda took a deep breath. "I'd rather have a coffee, honestly. I mean, eight kilometers? What is that? Like, two miles?"

"It's not a big deal," Hilda said. "My family never owned a car, so I got used to running everywhere."

Devon nudged Hilda with his elbow. "No wonder you broke all those records then. You should join our track team."

"I know!" Hilda suddenly slammed both of her hands on the table, making nearly everyone jump. Then she looked directly at Max. "Do you know someone named Veronica? She told me that you would—"

"Wait, which Veronica?" Matilda interrupted. "Veronica Lancer? Red hair? About Clare's height?"

"Uh, ja, why?"

Matilda crossed her arms and took up a stern tone. "We don't talk about her at this table."

I couldn't stop myself from pressing into Max, trying my best to hide from all the looks from everyone at the table. My phone felt dangerous as it sat next to my lunch tray like I had a loaded weapon out for all to see.

Hilda broke the odd silence, looking directly at me. "Is whatever happened why you were acting so weird a second ago?"

Matilda cleared her throat. "I said we don't talk about it, and if you want to keep sitting there, you'll stop talking right—"

"You know what?" Hilda interrupted, holding up a hand. "I take it back. I don't care. As I was saying, Max, Veronica told me to talk to someone named Lin Cho after school today. Do you know her?"

My body tightened upon hearing Lin's name. Max wrapped his arm around my shoulder in response, causing me to cringe internally. I shifted uncomfortably as Hilda seemed momentarily confused, and the look she had given me made my stomach churn.

Devon spoke first. "Well, I think you're a sure win for the team if you try out."

"A what? Do you know Mrs. Cho, Devon? Could you introduce me?"

"There's no 'Mrs. Cho,'" Matilda corrected, emphasizing her annoyance with air quotes. "Lin is a senior, like the rest of us. Also, she's a total bitch. Ask Clare."

I nearly choked on a bite of pasta. "Oh, um, yeah, Lin's kind of . . . Well, she's in first period with us, Hilda. She sits near the front. She's Chinese, I think."

Max shook me a little and chuckled. "Actually, Lin's Korean. She did a whole report about it last year for history. I'm shocked you didn't know that, babe."

I don't like Lin, or rather, I'm not supposed to like Lin. Why would I have her genealogy memorized? Bothered by Max's presumption, I leaned forward and rolled my shoulder back, knocking his arm off me. Max recoiled in shock, then nervously glanced around the table to see how many people had noticed. I immediately regretted being so mean to him and felt a stab of guilt for embarrassing him in public.

"Hey," Max whispered, "I'm sorry. I was just playing. I didn't mean to—"

"Max, don't. Okay? I'm trying to think." *Plus, I'm not your girlfriend anymore. Stop acting like I am.*

"I'm faster!" Hilda shouted excitedly, pulling me back into her conversation with Devon. "I swear it."

"Whoa! Calm down, crazy," Devon laughed. "Lin's the one you need to impress. As I was saying, she's the captain of the varsity track team. Actually, she's right over there." He pointed kitty-corner to a small round table on the other side of the cross-shaped quad. "Next to, uh, Veronica."

Hilda nodded. "Oh ja, I do recognize her from English." She turned and gave me an acknowledging smile. "I'll be right back." Then, just like that, she abandoned her lunch and started to make her way across the quad.

Matilda muttered under her breath. "I really hope she doesn't come back."

"Don't be that way," I whispered. I glanced up and found Devon bluntly checking out Hilda's butt as she walked away. *Would Devon and Hilda be a couple? If they got together, would Max and I start dating again so we could go out on double dates?* I grabbed a lock of my long hair and pulled it down, straining to figure out what the hell was going on with me. For reasons I didn't understand, I wanted to hide my face, but my eyes never quite left Hilda.

Seeing how uneasy I was, Matilda asked, "What the hell is wrong with you today? Did something happen over summer break you haven't told me?"

I shook my head. "No, I just . . . I don't know. I'm having a really strange day."

Matilda cocked her head to the side. "Want to talk about it?"

"I've just been grounded ever since Max's party, and going from literally no social interaction to the first day of school is a bit much. That's all, I think."

Matilda giggled. "That's such a 'you' answer."

As I told Matilda about Max's party, I made sure to severely limit how much I talked about Hilda. Still, I couldn't stop myself from glancing over to Veronica's table where Hilda had taken a seat and seemed all too comfortable.

* * *

As we walked toward the student parking lot, I wanted Devon to ask if I had taken any exciting photos earlier. I had—mostly of hallways filled with students, the bustling quad at lunch, and various welcoming banners and things. All too soon, those photos would be all I had left of Saint Mary's, which was simultaneously scary and exhilarating.

"What's that look for?" Devon asked, reading my mind.

"I'm kind of already done with school. Can it be graduation yet?"

Devon chuckled. "Says the girl who's scared out of her mind about 'what she'll do with her life after high school.'"

I rolled my eyes. "You're one to talk. The second Max made you quarterback sophomore year, I don't think I've seen you read anything that wasn't for homework. All that talk about becoming the next world-famous journalist and 'exposing the corrupt society we live in' has all vanished."

"Hey, just because I'm a jock doesn't mean I'm not smart. That's a hurtful stereotype."

"Oh, I'm sorry." I flippantly flicked some of my hair over my shoulder. "Who had a perfect GPA last year out of the two of us? Because I'm pretty sure it was me."

"Three-point-five," Devon sighed. "I got a three-point-five, and you're lording that over me until the day I die, huh?"

I scoffed. "You must have done something in a previous life to deserve it."

"You don't believe in reincarnation," Devon rightly pointed out.

I shrugged. "What can I say? In your case, I feel that the evidence is overwhelming."

"Do you have any homework yet?"

"Yeah, I think we might need to start our usual study sessions early this year."

"Good, because I got into AP bio, and my teacher might as well have been speaking German the whole time. So did you get any good shots today? I saw you standing on a bench between fourth and fifth period, acting like a complete nutcase."

As we walked, I handed Devon polaroid after polaroid, talking him through how I shot each one. Once I was finished, I looked up and something unusual caught my eye.

"Is that Hilda?" I squinted, trying to see better.

Devon mimicked my posture, shielding his eyes. "Yeah, Lin too. Hilda's probably trying out for the track team. Remember?"

"Want to go watch?" My sudden rush of excitement seemed to confuse Devon, so I quickly added, "I mean, if you have time."

Confusion changed to curiosity as Devon handed my stack of photos back to me. "Sure, but I'm not the one who's going to get in trouble if I'm a few minutes late getting home."

"I think we can spare a few minutes."

Devon put the keys to his Mustang back into the pocket of his varsity jacket. "Okay, but don't blame me if you get grounded."

We stopped at the fence that surrounded the track, watching Hilda and Lin line up. Coach Taylor held a stopwatch and a clipboard and wore a gruff expression. The squat woman always reminded me of a panda—a very loud, very aggressive panda.

I couldn't ready my Spectra in time and huffed as I hustled past the bleachers, feeling like I missed my chance at a good picture. Mentally, I counted down as the two girls turned the corner and came into the straightaway. *Three. Two. One!* I slammed the shutter button down and was rewarded with the soft whirring of gears as my Spectra fed out an undeveloped polaroid. I had prayed that framing the setting sun behind them would silhouette their figures.

I looked up just in time to catch Hilda sprinting past me—and also to gasp at her loose-fitting burgundy and gold jersey. As it flapped in the wind, there were points where the entirety of her black sports bra was exposed. My breath caught in my throat. Seeing her racing made my stomach feel light. My hand tightened on my Spectra. *Why am I feeling this way?* When I looked up, Hilda was on the far side of the track. I began to take a step back when Taylor blew her whistle.

"Hell yeah!" Devon shouted, nearly giving me a heart attack. I hadn't even realized he was standing beside me. "Great job, Hilda!"

Hilda looked up and gave us a snappy three-fingered salute between heavy breaths. My throat felt dry, and I wrapped my hands around my torso to pretend like I was shivering from the brisk breeze. *Had Hilda noticed me? Had Devon noticed me gawking?*

"Come on." Devon ushered me forward. "I'm pretty sure they're done. Let's go congratulate Hilda on her win."

I couldn't take my eyes off of Hilda despite my best efforts—and Lin's death stare. Sweat glistened on Hilda's skin, and she looked a bit strange without the sinful eyeliner I had come to expect. There was a freedom about her; she seemed unbeholden to anyone or anything, and it was a little intoxicating. As Devon and I drew closer, I looked down at my developing polaroid and smiled.

"Hilda, look what I—" I froze as Hilda lifted the bottom of her top to wipe the sweat off of her forehead. She had abs. They weren't like Max's or Devon's, which merely hinted at their physical aptitude. No, Hilda's were cut in a perfectly soft way that worked with her lithe, feminine figure. As I closed my mouth, my hands began to sweat around my Spectra.

Hilda's breath was still labored, but she brushed the hair out of her face and smiled at me. "Hallo."

I opened my mouth but found myself unable to form words anymore. Part of me wanted to run away. Another part of me justified the somewhat forced interaction: Devon liked Hilda and I was there to support him while he hit on her. Clashing thoughts made me anxious and unsure of what might happen next.

"I was about to give Clare a ride home." Devon put his hand out for a low five, which Hilda indulged. "But we thought you might like a cheer team."

Coach Taylor slapped Lin and Hilda on their backs. "These two are going to make us famous. Mark my words. Hilda broke our school record on her first lap this afternoon. Couldn't believe it, so I made her do it again."

Hilda laughed. "And again."

Coach Taylor nodded. "At this rate, we're going to need to repave the track."

"She barely beat my time," Lin spat, still recovering from the race.

Hilda grinned. "Still, I beat it."

"I like you better when you're running, Bernhardt," Lin sneered. "Because you don't talk. Also, it takes more than a few impressive laps to make my team. I need endurance racers, not sprinters. Kate and I already have that covered." Hilda shrugged as Lin continued. "What's with that shit-eating grin, Huffington? Watching us from the sidelines wasn't enough?"

My smile disappeared, and my breath hitched.

"Language, Miss Cho," Coach Taylor scolded before she left.

"Whatever. I'm going home," Lin scoffed, shoulder-checking both me and Devon as she stormed away. "I don't have time for anymore bullshit today. I hope you enjoyed the view."

Devon snorted as he yelled after her. "Would have been better without you in it, bitch!"

"Wasn't talking to you, asshole," Lin called over her shoulder.

Hanging her head in disappointment, Coach Taylor said a quick goodbye and walked off.

"What's this?" Hilda said, snatching the polaroid out of my hand.

"Hey!" I shouted. I reached to try and swipe my picture back, but Hilda held it as high in the air as she could. Shoving my camera into Devon's chest, I jumped for it. "Give me that!" I didn't know why I was suddenly so upset, but I felt a ball of energy well up inside of me and needed to release it.

"Oh, this?" Hilda waved the photo in the air, giggling. "You're going to have to try harder than that, Clarissa."

Out of options, I looked over at Devon for some sort of assistance. "Help me, you jerk!"

"Jerk?" Devon seemed to hesitate. "You've never—" Then we both looked down to what was in his hands: my Spectra.

"No, don't you dare . . ."

As I stepped away from Hilda, her muscular arms wrapped tightly around me. "I got her!" she exclaimed. "Hurry, take the picture!"

My whole body went rigid as I whimpered. "Don't—"

Hilda flinched and immediately released me.

I drew my arms across my chest and started shaking. Hilda backed off and held her hands out in surrender.

"I'm sorry," she said, sounding as scared as I was.

"Clare," Devon interrupted, pulling my gaze to him. "What did you just say?"

I swallowed. "I, um . . ." Everyone was looking at the three of us from the bleachers. "I don't know."

"You're shivering like you're freezing," Devon said. "Did Hilda really freak you out that badly?"

"Shh," Hilda whispered. I flinched as her shadow moved across my back. My heart was racing, and I felt like I couldn't breathe. "I didn't mean to scare you," she whispered into my ear.

Clare, run! Before she hurts—

Hilda gently wrapped her arms around me again. My breath slowed, and I found myself relaxing into her. She felt like a protective shield from the world. Looking up at her gentle and concerned expression made me feel safe. The sound of my camera going off snapped me back to reality.

"Perfect," Devon said proudly, waiting for the polaroid to be ejected into his hand.

Hilda hummed curiously as she let me go and went to see the picture.

My hand reached up to stop Hilda but only touched her elbow. She didn't seem to notice. Pulling my hand back to my chest, I felt overwhelmed as a veritable cocktail of perplexing and frightening emotions squeezed against my heart. I was struck by embarrassment upon realizing that people had just watched me freak out.

"I like both of these," Hilda said, holding the two pictures. "I'm going to keep them."

"I-I'd like my things back," I said meekly, not daring to look either of my friends in the eyes. "Please."

"You want them so bad? Come and get them." She shoved them down her jersey, revealing her empty hand a second later.

My stomach churned, and my fists clenched.

Devon raised his hand with a playful smirk, wiggling his fingers. "Don't worry, Clare. I got this."

"I wasn't talking to you," Hilda said, batting his hand away.

Something inside me suddenly snapped, and I sprang forward, thrusting my hand down Hilda's jersey. Hilda's face flushed as I felt the sharp edges of the Polaroid film, along with something cold and hard. I dismissed it as an exposed wire in her bra before triumphantly producing my stolen photos.

"Ha!" I shouted, proving to myself and all onlookers that my facade of normality was still intact. Devon raised a curious eyebrow. I panicked, shoving the polaroids down my shirt. Once I realized what I had done, I took a shallow breath and said, "There, now neither of you can have them."

* * *

"Two times now. Two!" my mother shouted as I opened the front door. "I raised you better than this. What's your excuse for being late this time?"

I took a deep breath. Having anticipated her rage, Devon and I had brainstormed a relatively good lie. "Sorry, I stayed late helping a transfer student. We're in that AP lit class you signed me up for." I attempted a nervous laugh as I looked away and pushed some hair behind my ear. "I mean, she didn't even have a copy of the book we're reading. Stantin totally chewed her out for it, too."

My mother narrowed her eyes and said, "You're lying."

I flinched but managed to stutter, "I'm . . . I'm not lying, Mom. Her name is Hilda, and she just transferred from Germany." Nervously, my eyes locked onto the staircase. *I need to reach my room. Once I'm there, I'll finally be able to breathe.*

"Did I hear someone say something about a transfer student?" my father asked as he stepped out of his study, looking every bit like the overworked politician that he was. He had his glasses propped up on his head and wore a thousand-yard stare as if he had only just unearthed himself from the stacks of papers that littered every flat surface of his office.

I cleared my throat, trying to remember what little I knew about Hilda. "I only met her—I mean, Hilda—today. Well, technically, her name is Brünnhilde." I put a hand on my upper arm, trying to think quicker. "She broke some track records in Germany, but, uh, we didn't get time to get to know each other very well. Like I was telling Mom, I was mostly helping her get around and stuff. She's got a really thick accent and, uh . . ." *All the confidence I don't.*

"Well then," my father said, rubbing a hand over his chin, "it shouldn't be a problem to invite Hilda and her family over for dinner. Always good to welcome new neighbors, right? After all, Grand Forks isn't as small as it was when your mother and I grew up." My father chuckled. "Your mom could even make her famous welcome-to-Grand-Forks roasted ham. We haven't had that in ages."

The idea seemed to sit well with my mother, and she uncrossed her arms. "You did the godly thing by helping your classmate, but call next time."

"Or even a quick text," my father added with a look that told me I should have known better in the first place.

My mother held out her hand. "Speaking of phones, hand it over."

I instinctively reached for my back pocket, but to guard it, not give it up.

"I wasn't asking, Clarissa," my mother ordered, but something about her venomous tone felt weaker than it had in the past.

"Sorry, today has been really strange." I did my best to force an apologetic smile, and reluctantly, I gave up my phone. My mother plopped the phone into her apron. I kept my eyes locked on the rectangular square as my mother turned to leave. *I bet my phone is going to be caked in baking soda. Again.*

My father was also returning to his study, leaving me standing there. Of course, I was expected to head upstairs and start my homework. If I finished before dinner, then I would start my chores: laundry, trash, and anything else my mother could think of. In retrospect, I was glad Stantin assigned me a book report; it kept my mind occupied.

In my room, I opened my English book. That was when I saw the two polaroids I had randomly stuffed inside. Slamming the book shut, I involuntarily stared at my door, waiting for my mother to burst in. Fear started to well up inside my body as I slowly slid my hand between the cover of my textbook and pulled out the two photos. Without looking at them, I threw them into a drawer next to me, then closed it. *It's okay, There's nothing illegal or sinful about these pictures. They're just like any of the others. Just my friends at school. Nothing new. Nothing even interesting.* I kept my eyes on my door, my hand still holding the drawer closed.

I didn't even know what the photos looked like. Slowly, I peeled back the drawer and cautiously looked inside. I pulled out the photo Devon had taken and clicked on my desk lamp as if something about the dim light of my computer screen was playing tricks on my eyes. The photo had me looking up into Hilda's face as she beamed down at me. I had both of my hands resting gently on her arms. If I hadn't known any better, it looked like I was pulling her closer to me.

For a few minutes, I just stared at the polaroid in my hand, not believing the reflection of the world it was showing me. I wasn't sure why, but I found myself running a finger across the photograph, trying to feel the warmth of Hilda's skin through the photo. "Darn you, Devon," I whispered. *This is the best photograph I never took.*

4

A Hesitant Invitation

Friday came more quickly than expected, and I had spent the better part of the last few nights working on my book report, studying with Devon, or texting with Matilda. What I had not been doing was figuring out a way to invite Hilda to dinner, and with my mother quickly growing tired of my excuses, Friday felt like my last chance.

I walked into my first period and spotted Hilda talking with Ryan in the back row. A pang of jealousy hit me. It didn't seem fair that Hilda was able to make friends with everyone so easily. I had tried hard over the years to simply keep my head down and pass by mostly without notice. Yet here Hilda was, a week into school and acting like she owned the place.

Someone cleared their throat behind me. "Anytime, Huffington." Lin gestured for me to get out of her way.

"Sorry—"

Lin shoved past me. "I don't want your worthless apologies."

"Sorry," I repeated weakly to Lin's back.

As I took my seat, I noticed Hilda had a strange-looking copy of the class textbook. It even had a different cover picture. Then I noticed the words "Property of Grand Forks Public Library" stamped boldly along the spine.

"Morning," I said as I pulled out my textbook, only realizing then that everyone else in the class had the revised edition. Still, Hilda's bright smile made my stomach feel light and got me excited for the day ahead.

"Morning to you, too, Fräulein."

It felt wonderful but also made me want to shrink into my textbook and disappear. Some part of me wanted to ask Hilda what the word meant. "Did you do your homework? Stantin always collects it first thing in the morning." I pulled my perfectly presentable book report out and thought about a Bible verse. *Well done, good and faithful servant.*

"Ja." Hilda reached into her backpack and produced a bunch of loose college-ruled sheets, some of which I swore were slightly different colors. "Got my report right here." Seeing my perplexed expression, she quickly moved the handwritten report under her elbow, trying to shield it from my unintended scrutiny. "Don't look at me like that, please. I don't have a printer, and printing at the library costs money." She seemed hesitant to continue. "I'm kind of on some scholarships, and I've never had a computer of my own. Also, I am very slow at typing. It's faster for me to do it this way."

"Hey," Ryan whispered across my desk, startling me slightly and upsetting me with the fact that he had clearly been eavesdropping. "You could come over to my house. I got an extra laptop and everything. Or we could just 'exercise,' if you're down."

My gut lurched into my throat, but without missing a beat, Hilda snorted. "By the look of things, the only exercise you're currently getting is with a fork and knife."

"That's what I'm saying." Ryan chuckled. "We should swap numbers."

Hilda scoffed. "Someday I'll give someone my number, but it won't be today, and it certainly won't be to you."

Once Stantin turned his back to the class to write on the whiteboard, I prepared to slide my note to Hilda across the aisle. *One . . . Two . . . Three!* My hand didn't move. *Argh! Why is this so hard?!* Desperation began to take hold as I started feeling like I was overthinking the entire thing. I batted the note at Hilda's desk with the back of my hand.

The paper hit Hilda's elbow and dropped to the floor. Raising her eyes at me, she stealthily moved her foot over to it and dragged it under her desk. My hands tied themselves into knots as I watched Hilda unfold and read the note. The episode was made all the more stressful by the fact that I couldn't look at her directly and had to keep my face forward.

I have a strange favor to ask you. Please don't think I'm weird.

Before I knew it, Hilda was sliding the note back onto my desk.

I snatched it only to realize afterward that I needed to chill a bit. *Play it cool, Clare. It's just a silly note, not a letter from God.* Doing my best to be nonchalant, I unfolded the note.

Do you want to invite me over to use your printer, too?

My breath hitched. I shook my head and began to write, feeling a smile stretch across my face.

No, but my mother is forcing me to invite you over for dinner at my house this Saturday. Sorry for the short notice, and it's totally okay if you can't make it. Obviously, your folks are invited, too.

This time, I confidently placed the note on the corner of Hilda's desk. I waited as she unfolded it and scratched away with her pencil. I kept trying to ask myself why I felt hyper-aware of my surroundings. My eyes, when they weren't focused on Hilda, were darting around the room wildly, scanning for anyone who might have caught onto what was happening in the back row. I peeked over to see if I could preview what Hilda had written.

I'd love to come over for dinner. But I don't think my mother will make it. She's dead.

Whatever feeling was welling up inside me came to an abrupt and morbid halt as I looked up to Hilda's face. What—

"Miss Huffington!" Stantin snapped, gesturing to Lin. "What do you think about what Miss Cho just had to say?"

"Uh . . ." I cleared my throat, realizing that most of the class had turned around. "Honestly, I think what Lin said was kind of, um, shallow." I prayed that being as vague as possible would be enough.

"Is that so? Then please"—Stantin swept his hand across the classroom—"Miss Huffington, enlighten us all with *depth*."

My breath caught in my throat. Of course Sergeant Satan would call me out; he was the Lord of Lies, after all. "What I—"

"What Clarissa meant was," Hilda interrupted, "Lin's basic summarization of the chapter wasn't really useful. I mean, we all read what happens, right? Now, what I think—"

"Miss Bernhardt!" Stantin barked. "Next time I want to hear your voice, I'll call on you. As for you, Miss Huffington, if I catch you looking at another student's desk again, I won't hesitate to send you to the dean's office. If we had been taking a test, I would've had you suspended on the spot. Do I make myself clear?"

"Yes, sir." My voice nearly cracked as I replied.

As Stantin turned to continue his lecture, I caught Lin whipping back to sneer at Hilda and me. I didn't know what it meant, but I was sure I just got Hilda into trouble. Wanting to whisper an apology, I glanced over at Hilda, but she had covered her face with her textbook, and the piece of notebook paper we were sharing had vanished.

* * *

After my elective, I started down the familiar path home, remembering with annoyance that my mother was probably waiting for me with our old station wagon out in front of the school; after my recent tardiness, she no longer trusted me to walk the three blocks home.

"Clarissa! Hey!" Hilda's familiar voice called from my right. When I looked over, she was jogging toward me in her Saint Mary's PE uniform. She said something in German that sounded like "what's up," but there was no inflection like that of a question.

"Yup, I still don't speak German, Hilda."

She held up a finger as she caught her breath. "Sorry, what I mean to say is, what are you doing here?"

"I was in my elective class," I said, grinning unconsciously. "What are you doing here? Have you been running this whole time after school?"

"Ja! I still need to catch up with Lin."

I raised a skeptical eyebrow. "Didn't you beat Lin on Monday?"

"That didn't count. Also, I need to keep my energy up!" Hilda's excitement was infectious, and I caught myself thinking about when she wrapped her arms around me.

"Why?" I asked, focusing on the present. *Had Devon asked her out? He must have, because what else would make someone so happy?* I kept a bright smile, though I felt a sinking feeling in my chest. *The two of them could end up dating for the rest of the year.* "Well? Out with it already."

Hilda grabbed my hands and my heart skipped a beat. "I got a job interview tonight! If I get it, I can save for a phone! Then we can text like you do with Matilda and everyone else."

Am I on my phone that *much?* I gulped as confusion overtook my other thoughts. "Hilda, if it's really that big of a deal, you can get a little prepaid flip phone for like less than forty bucks. You don't need a whole job just for that. It was probably different in Germany, but things are probably cheaper here."

Hilda gave me a perplexed look. "Way to sound really ignorant, Clarissa. I don't want a cheap phone." She paused, brushing hair out of her face. *What a cute nervous tic. Not that Hilda has anything to be nervous about, ever.* "I want a phone like the one you have. It feels like everyone at school has that same model."

I broke eye contact and blushed. *What am I thinking?! Focus. Of course, Hilda only wants to fit in, and here I am, judging her like Matilda or Mom. Argh. Maybe if I beg Dad for a few advances on my allowance, and if I promised to be good, I could help Hilda save up. She could easily just pay me back later.* I physically ran a hand down my face to try and get a grip. *Stop! We're not even that close. I'd sound like a crazy—*

"Is everything okay, Clarissa?"

"Yeah." I laughed, sure that it sounded as awkward as it felt. "Sorry, just spacing out."

"Oh. I didn't mean to stop you, if you have somewhere else to be. It's not like a phone is all I need, either. I could use a new backpack and some clothes. I'm almost out of makeup, too." The smile she was holding faded as she stared at the track. "I left a lot behind in Germany."

I sidestepped, making sure I could look into Hilda's sparkling eyes. "I—" Something stopped me. As a gentle breeze kicked up, I felt myself wanting to draw her close to me. My emotions felt like they had been thrown into a blender. "I, uh . . ." I gasped, feeling how hot my cheeks were as I tucked a strand of hair behind my ear. *What were we talking about? Her job. Right!* "Well, that's great news about the job then. I really hope you get it."

My cell phone going off cut me short. *Mom, shoot.* "Hold on a second, Hilda." I tapped the answer button and turned away.

"Clarissa Huffington!" Mom spat through the receiver immediately. "Where are you?"

I put my hand over the phone, praying that Hilda couldn't make out how upset my mother was. "Sorry, Mom. I got caught up talking to Sister June. You know how she can be. I'll be right there, okay?" I didn't know why I lied, but it was the first thing that came out of my mouth.

"Why are you whispering?" my mother growled. "Clarissa Huffington, if I don't see you in the next two minutes, I'm coming to find you."

"I'll see you in a second, Mom. Promise."

"You better," my mother spat before hanging up.

"Sorry, Hilda. I need to go."

When I finally looked at her, Hilda had her arms crossed. There was a concerned expression on her face. "Everything okay?"

"Please don't look at me like that. I'm fine." Seeing Hilda begin to ask a question, I added, "My mother is kind of, uh, strict." A flash of concern crossed Hilda's face as she caught me rubbing my arm. Immediately, I dropped my hands to my sides. "Um, yeah. Like I said, I need to go or I'm going to get into trouble. Or something. See you tomorrow for dinner?"

"Ja."

5

Dinner Introductions

I buzzed around the house on Saturday as I prepared for Hilda's arrival. Neither chores nor changing my outfit for the fifth time could quell my anxiety. I didn't own anything to try and match Hilda's punky aesthetic, so I settled on a long-sleeve gray button-down blouse and a black floor-length skirt, both of which I had exclusively worn to church and never together.

I tapped my foot at my desk, trying to study but not really being able to digest a single word written on the textbook in front of me. Instead, my mind kept running over the evening's game plan. I knew my mother would pull her usual passive-aggressive questions, so I would need to counteract that with all of Hilda's strengths. Then I would casually mention how she skipped a grade and was an ace athlete. I hoped that would be enough.

My thoughts strayed to Hilda's father. I pictured him being somewhat debonair, a thick German accent, and a great bushy mustache. He had the looks of a Hollywood actor who could play both the slick spy and the gruff action hero. That was the only kind of person I could see raising someone so equally charismatic and confident as Hilda. It made me partly excited to meet him, but also a bit scared that my own family wouldn't measure up.

It was a quarter past five in the evening when the doorbell rang. I practically flew down the stairs a few seconds later and flung open the front door.

"Welc—" My mouth hung open in horror.

Hilda was wearing a mini tube top that might as well have been a bra, a faded black hoodie, and tight blue jeans. Her sterling eyes were encircled by black eyeliner, and her hair looked like she'd just got it trimmed.

Hilda adjusted the backpack looped over her right shoulder. "Good evening, Fräulein."

"Hey," I wheezed. There was no way Mom wouldn't comment on her outfit, but asking Hilda to keep her hoodie zipped up for the entire meal would be equally awkward.

"Did you do your nails?" Hilda asked and grasped my hand. "They're beautiful. I like the color."

"It . . . It reminded me of your eyes," I sputtered.

"I wish my eyes did this." Hilda moved my wrist so the pearlescent gray shimmered in the porchlight. "I'm totally going to steal this from you."

"Uh, you can just have the bottle. My mother doesn't let me paint my nails very often anyway." Hilda tilted her head to the side, but I changed the subject before she could say anything. "Isn't that the same backpack you use for school?"

"Ja. I needed to pick up some things for work, and I only have the one. My mother would have said I'm overly efficient. She liked that about me."

"So, uh, that means you got the job then, right?" I smiled, feigning ignorance. "Where do you work?"

"It's a small gym downtown called Mick's. Do you know it?"

"No, but now I'm going to randomly drop in to make fun of you."

Hilda smiled, but there was something restrained about it. "Ja, well, I think I only got the job because the owners know my father. Once I dropped his name, they gave me a very unorthodox interview and . . ." She rubbed her shoulder with the palm of her hand. "I'm still a little sore."

"What do you mean?"

Hilda pulled her hoodie down to reveal a huge purple and black bruise on her left shoulder.

I gasped and stepped back. "Oh my God, Hilda. What in the Lord's name did they do to you?"

Before she could answer, my father called from the dining room, "Is that your friend, Clare? Why don't you invite her inside?"

Right. I cleared my throat and stepped aside as Hilda covered the bruise up. "Welcome to Casa de Huffington. Ah! Watch your head!"

Hilda ducked, narrowly avoiding the stained-glass cross above the front door. The piece of art lowered the clearance of the door by about six inches, which wasn't usually noticeable.

"Thanks," Hilda said as she looked up at the cross. "You really like crosses, don't you?"

"Yeah." I smiled, remembering the days when Veronica, Devon, and I played games in the prismatic light cast by the stained glass. "My mother actually wouldn't move into this house until that was installed. Apparently it's a family heirloom or something."

"That must be nice." Hilda reached up to touch the glass but seemed to think better of it and lowered her hand. Then she turned to me with an expectant look on her face. "So . . . ?"

"So, what?" I asked, feeling that I had forgotten something.

Hilda giggled. "Shouldn't you be showing me around?"

I blushed at my forgetfulness. "Yeah, sorry. Come on."

As I led Hilda into the dining room, I swelled with pride at my father's composure. Dad didn't even give Hilda a second look as he stood up from the head of our dinner table to greet her. "Ah! We finally meet. You must be the infamous Hilda. We've heard a lot about you. You're all Clare talks about these days."

Hilda shot me a worried look as she reached out to shake Dad's hand. "Oh, ja?" she said, recovering with a smile.

After a quick exchange of names, I said, "My dad's on the city council."

"Your humble public works director." He bowed slightly. "At your service."

"Oh? Are you the person I should talk to about all the uneven sidewalks?"

"I suppose." My dad chuckled. "You sound like you take uneven sidewalks very seriously."

Hilda nodded. "I run a lot."

"Well, I'll see what I can do. Take a seat. You got here just in time. Mary will be out with dinner in a moment. She likes to taste everything before she serves it. Maybe a little too much." He winked at the two of us, and his ability to make anyone feel welcome made me happy.

My mother cheerfully called from the kitchen, "I heard that, Roger!"

My dad made a cartoonish face like he'd just been caught stealing a cookie, and we all laughed.

Hilda moved to the other side of the table, and I wanted to grab her shoulders and spin her around just to tell her she'd already made a great first impression, but she didn't even look remotely out of her element. If our roles had been reversed, I would have been anxious—maybe even a little scared—to meet someone's family for the first time.

Once we were seated, my father asked, "Are your parents out parking?"

"Oh, no." Hilda seemed to struggle to find the right words. "My father had work to do."

"I'm sorry to hear that. What does he do?"

"He's taking online college courses," Hilda said, but she seemed more focused on taking in her surroundings than the conversation.

"What's he studying?" my dad and I asked simultaneously.

Hilda sighed. "Who cares?"

The jovial atmosphere was dampened as a hesitant look passed between my father and me, but he recovered first and gave a slight chuckle. "You don't care what your father is studying?"

Hilda rolled her eyes. "No. It's his business."

A smile appeared on my father's face, but I could tell it was forced. "I suppose that's one way to look at it. Well, let him know dinner is a standing offer, okay?"

"Sure." Hilda nodded, but the gesture seemed dismissive. I wanted to press her for information about the relationship she had with her father, but the other half of me wanted to avoid the subject altogether because that was what polite dinner etiquette dictated.

There was a sudden clattering of plates as Hilda shot up from her seat. "Can I help carry something?"

My mother had stumbled over her own feet and was staring at Hilda. "No, I do this all the time. Please don't get up. I'm sorry. Clare hadn't mentioned you were so . . . tall." My mother gave me a telling glance as if the way Hilda dressed was somehow my fault. *If only I hadn't been such a coward and warned Hilda this might happen. Now Mom is going to badger her.*

Once my mother had set down dinner, she smiled at Hilda. "Where are my manners? I'm Mary, spelled like Mary Magdalene. Clare's mother, if you hadn't guessed that by now."

"Brünnhilde," Hilda replied with a warm smile. "Like the Norse Valkyrie. But I'm sure you know that everyone calls me Hilda."

My father cleared his throat and said, "Well, I hope you're not a vegetarian, Hilda. Mary spent all day on this ham, and it's been making my mouth water all afternoon."

Hilda shook her head. "I'm not, and if it tastes half as good as it smells, you may not have leftovers by the time I'm done."

"Clare tells us you don't eat the normal school lunches and that you only eat vegetarian sandwiches and granola bars," my mother said. "I'm just so glad you're not one of those strange vegans I've heard so much about. Otherwise, we might not be able to feed you much. Even our salad has bacon bits in it." My mother's ignorance perturbed me, but I was trained to only speak when spoken to at the dinner table, so I bit my tongue. "Can I get you something other than water, Hilda?"

Hilda casually replied, "What kind of beer do you have?"

My mother looked appalled, and my father furrowed his brow.

This was not part of the plan! Quick, Clare, think! I wanted to laugh and pretend that Hilda was just messing with everyone—anything to deflect the sudden tension in the air.

My mother curtly raised an eyebrow as I felt her eyes dart between Hilda and me. "I'm sorry, Hilda. We don't serve any alcohol to teenagers here in America. We take underage drinking very, *very seriously* in this household."

"Sorry, I didn't mean to offend. Water is fine. Thanks."

My parents shared another critical look before my mother disappeared into the kitchen to fetch our drinks.

My dad leaned toward Hilda and whispered, "Sorry about that. Mary isn't too used to the whole 'rock-n-roll lifestyle' you kids are into these days. I know Germany is a little lax with their drinking laws."

Hilda curiously lowered her volume to match my father's. "What? Did I say something wrong?"

My dad leaned back and shook his head. "No. In fact, forget I said anything."

Moments later, my mother returned with drinks and began to set them on the table. "Do you drink a lot of beer, Hilda?" she inquired in an apathetic tone.

"I guess?" Hilda replied carelessly.

I gritted my teeth in frustration. My plan was crumbling before my eyes, and all I could do was physically bunch up my skirt and watch it happen. *Why can't I just say something? Anything. I'd settle for a single word at this point. I'm such a coward.* Hilda unfolded her napkin and placed it on her lap. *Wait, that's good, right?*

After a drink of water, Hilda continued. "My father keeps some beer in the fridge at home. Sometimes I have one or two with dinner, but not much other than that. They're not very healthy, and I'm a bit of a . . . snob when it comes to beer. To be honest, Mrs. Huffington, I'm still getting used to America. It's a lot of 'the same but different,' if that makes sense."

My mother scoffed. "You must have had to try a lot of beers if you're a self-proclaimed snob."

Hilda shrugged. "Ja, but I've never thought about it like that before."

After that, an odd silence fell over the room, and my unusually warm blood ran cold as I realized why. Guests *always* said grace, and I didn't even know if Hilda believed in God.

Mom took a deep breath as she prepared to speak but then paused and looked at Hilda, who was already pulling a piece of ham off the platter. "Hilda, do you have a favorite Bible verse we can say for grace?"

Wide-eyed, Hilda snapped her cutlery back down on the table, leaving a slice of ham hanging halfway off her plate. "Ja, sure."

I gasped in disbelief. "Wait, you do?"

Hilda grinned while shaking her head at me. "We go to the same *Catholic* school, Clarissa. Of course I do."

The rolling ball of anxiety in my stomach lurched itself into my throat when Hilda grabbed my hand with a forceful clasp. I jolted a little and flicked my eyes over to my mother, wondering if she saw how badly Hilda had startled me. Luckily, it seemed like she hadn't noticed.

I relaxed just long enough for my whole body to seize back up as Hilda took a deep breath and started to speak. "I looked, and behold, an ashen horse; and he who sat on it had the name Death; and Hades was following with him. Authority was given to them over a fourth of the earth, to kill with sword and with famine and with pestilence and by the wild beasts of the earth." Her German accent gave a grim edge to the passage—and also a hint of credibility—which was a nice change from what I was used to.

My mother nearly coughed "amen" when Hilda didn't correctly finish.

Dad chuckled as he reached out for some salad. "That's not really how we usually thank the Lord for our food. It's a nice change of pace."

Hilda nodded. "It was my mother's favorite verse. She had it tattooed in Latin down her arm."

My mother sat back in her chair. "Does your mother have a lot of tattoos then?"

"Not as many as my father. I feel that each time I see him, he has a new one. His whole chest, arms, and back are mostly covered now. It's getting to the point where it's hard to tell where one starts and one ends."

The image of the man who was Hilda's father shattered in my mind. Worse, I got the inkling that Hilda was hiding something. Tragically, so did my mother.

"Do you have any?" my mother asked.

"Not yet, but Olympians commonly get tattoos to celebrate their participation, as both of my parents did. So if I get to go, that will likely be my first tattoo. I also want something to remember my mother by, but I haven't given it much thought yet."

My parents shared surprised looks. Then my mother's voice grew more restrained. "Oh, has your mother passed then?"

"Ja." Hilda kept her focus on cutting her ham, like nothing was wrong. "I don't like talking about it."

The air seemed thin until my dad spoke. "Did I catch that *both* of your parents were Olympians? That's quite impressive."

Hilda's smile finally returned, and I wanted to give my father a thousand hugs. "That's how they first met," she explained, "and why we moved back to Europe. They both wanted to train and compete for Germany in 2012. Germany is also closer to London and more centralized. I'm training, too, but I don't think I'll make it to Rio. I'll probably have to try for Tokyo."

I nearly dropped my silverware in surprise. *Why didn't Hilda ever talk about this before? If I were training for the Olympics, that would be the first thing out of my mouth when I met someone.* "Hello, I'm Clare Huffington, seventeen-year-old Olympic photographer in training. Nice to meet you."

"Wait," I said, "You're training for the Olympics? Like, for the actual *real* Olympics on TV?"

Hilda grinned, her brilliant eyes not giving anything away as she took another bite of ham.

"What sport are you training for?" my mother asked before I could.

Hilda seemed to mull over her thoughts for a few moments before she spoke. "Well, my mother wanted me to follow her in the hundred-meter dash, but I . . . I didn't do very well at the German nationals. There was a lot against me."

Hearing Hilda sound so vulnerable made me curious. "What went wrong?"

Hilda raised an eyebrow at me. "You really want to know?"

I nodded.

"My mother had just died the month before, even though she had promised to make it until I competed."

"Maybe she did." I swallowed. "You know . . . from Heaven."

"Maybe," Hilda said evenly. "But the morning of the race was the day my dad decided to tell me we were moving back to America. So even if I won, it wouldn't have mattered. Also, I had just broken up with someone and started my period a few days before, so . . ." She shrugged. "Basically, it felt like God kept kicking me while I was down."

Period references and blaspheming were irredeemable offenses in my household. I glanced at my mother to see her reaction, and though she had the outward appearance that nothing was wrong, her smile had curdled like old milk.

Thankfully, my father spoke before anyone else. "You made it to nationals, though. I'm sure your father was very proud."

"I'd like to think so. He didn't show up, either, so . . . who knows."

"Remember how I told you Hilda's on the Saint Mary's track team?" I chirped. "She's amazing."

My dad nodded. "Yes, I recall. Maybe you'll see nationals again, Hilda. Saint Mary's commonly goes to the state-level meetups."

Hilda sighed. "Well, I'm off to a bad start. I already missed my first big practice because of a job interview."

"Where did you interview? I know a lot of people. I can probably put in a good word for you."

"She's—" I began.

"It's just a dumb janitorial position downtown," Hilda said, "and I already got the job, but thank you for the offer."

I was a bit confused as to why Hilda was vague with my parents. Was there something special about Mick's that I didn't know about? I had half a mind to bring it up anyway. *But what if there was something sinful about Mick's?* I gulped.

My dad pointed his fork at Hilda. "You know I started out cleaning grills at EZ Burger? Best job I ever had. I keep telling Clare that having a summer job builds character, but she ends up weaseling her way out of it by volunteering with the church."

Hilda reached for what must have been her third helping of ham. "I just need money. I couldn't care less about building character."

"Clare also tells us you're in honors English with her," my mom said. "Do you find it hard to be in such an advanced class? It being your second language and all."

Hilda smiled, but there was something snide about it. "Despite my accent, English was my first language. Plus, I've already read most of the books."

"You have?" I asked.

"Ja, there's a surprising amount of overlap with the literature class I took last year in Germany. Should be an easy A for me. I can't wait for—"

"Is that so?" my mother interrupted. "Clare has told us you were struggling."

I acted like nothing was wrong and kept cutting up my ham. When I glanced up, Hilda seemed calm, almost mischievous. I swallowed, unsure of what her reaction was going to be.

Hilda brushed the hair out of her face, looking almost embarrassed. "Ah, I think I know what Clarissa meant. You see, I got accepted to Saint Mary's pretty late in the summer and didn't realize there was summer reading required for our class. The book isn't one I had ever read before, so Clarissa is helping me catch up."

Both of my parents shared a look and nodded. Hilda, meanwhile, snuck me a quick wink. A euphoric feeling rushed through me. Hilda and I had somehow spontaneously conspired to save me from certain doom. I smiled back at her to let her know that I appreciated the help.

"So," my mother said, "have you looked at colleges, Hilda?"

"No, but it really doesn't matter," she said as she reached for more salad.

I nearly coughed up my water at what was absolutely the wrong thing to have said around my folks.

My father hastily chimed in. "Statistically speaking, a college degree is a must for your generation."

Hilda appeared confused, so I explained, "My folks haven't stopped nagging me about college since I was in preschool. I'm doomed." *But at least it will get me out of Grand Forks.*

"Huh?" Hilda seemed even more perplexed until something clicked. "Sorry. I meant it doesn't matter because the Olympic circuit is, um . . . They are separate. I want to go to university, but it doesn't really matter which one. My Olympic competitions and tryouts will be mostly unrelated."

My mother scoffed. "It sounds like you haven't given it much thought. Clare, for instance—"

"You're right," Hilda interrupted. "I'm just going to wing it."

There was a split second of spite before my mother smiled and said, "You're just going to 'wing it'? I hate to break it to you, but that's not how the real world works."

Hilda fixed her gaze on my mother. "Maybe for you, but I'm planning on moving to California after I graduate."

I gasped. "Wait, you're going to move across the country after we graduate? All alone. Without having been accepted to a college?"

"Probably, ja, but I could always use some company if you want to come, too. My dad went to the University of Berkeley and has mentioned they have a good athletics program. I hear they also have a great art program. That's where I'll probably apply first, but if I don't get in, I'm not worried. Maybe I can get a personal trainer's license or something."

My father said something, but I couldn't be bothered to pay attention to it. I was utterly absorbed in the way Hilda moved and projected herself: the faint way she ran her hand along the shaved side of her hair when she was deep in thought or how she occasionally swept the longer part of her hair out of her face. When her silver eyes caught the crystal light, I forgot about the world around me as they twinkled like something out of a fairy-tale.

I tried several times to move my mouth and start sentences, but the words always died on my lips. Since meeting Hilda, I had become a graveyard for words.

* * *

After dinner, my father caught me talking to Hilda as she stretched for the run home. At first, he seemed confused, but then he said, "I just checked the forecast, and it's going to rain tonight. Hilda, why don't you just spend the night? I'd hate for you to catch a cold getting caught in a storm. Clare has an air mattress. You can use our phone in the living room to call your dad and tell him that I'll drop you off after church tomorrow morning."

Hilda seemed hesitant to answer, and I couldn't help but think that the reason had something to do with me. "I'd like to stay. As long as you're okay with it, Clarissa."

"O-Of course..." I stuttered. Nobody had ever asked for *my* permission to stay the night in my room before. Matilda and Veronica both always just asked my folks or assumed I was okay with it, not that I ever had a reason to reject them.

Hilda gestured toward the stairs. "After you."

I crossed my arms, making sure that I appeared responsible in front of my father. "Don't you need to call your dad first?"

Hilda shook her head. "No. I already told him I'd be home late. He'll probably just assume I went for an early jog tomorrow morning. Now come on. I want to see this 'wall of pictures' you always brag about."

I looked at my dad for reassurance, but he was already walking back into his office with his face in his phone. "Alright," I said, feeling a little bit like I was getting away with something I shouldn't have been. "Let's go."

A faint horror gripped me when I opened the door to my room. There were clothes and pictures strewn about like a tornado had just passed through. "I'm sorry it's such a mess," I said, scrambling to start cleaning. "It's usually not like this. Promise. I wasn't expecting anyone to stay over."

Hilda seemed to completely ignore the mess and walked toward my wall of photos like a moth mesmerized by a flame.

I laughed as I deposited a ton of clean clothes into my laundry basket, making a mental note to fix it later. "Yeah, I wasn't kidding. I take a lot of photos."

Hilda stopped in the center of my room and took in the whole collage as I often did. Seeing her awestruck filled me with validation. *Maybe . . . Maybe I could actually be a photographer and not starve to death first.*

Hilda murmured. "This is the coolest fucking thing."

"That's just the tip of the iceberg. Take a look in my closet."

I watched as Hilda gasped at the stacks of shoeboxes. "Are those all full of pictures, too?"

"Yup," I said, absently picking up another article of clothing.

When I glanced up, Hilda was scrutinizing my wall with a closer eye, giving each picture a few moments before she moved to the next one. At the rate she was going, it would take her all night to see everything, but that was okay with me; I needed the time to figure some stuff out.

"Ta-da!" I announced as I pulled the inflatable mattress and pump out from under my bed.

Hilda raised an eyebrow. "And here I hoped you wouldn't find it. Your bed looks so comfortable." Without permission, Hilda took two strides, leaped into the air, and landed on my bed, nearly disappearing into my puffy down comforter. "Mmmm, it smells nice, too," she said as she wiggled deeper into my sheets. "Can we share, please?"

"Oh, will you grow up?" I walked over and dropped the mattress and pump onto her chest. "My mother hasn't let anyone sleep in my bed since I was like ten. You're lucky we get to have my door closed. If you were Max, she would force us to leave the door open all night while she patrolled the hallway like a prison warden. In fact, if she catches you acting like this, she might do it anyway."

"Too bad. I'm a pro at cuddling."

I swallowed and felt my breath grow shallow. "S-Stop it. I'm serious."

"Stop what?" Hilda said as she leaned forward.

I began to move into her, but the wooden cross that hung over my headboard caught my eye, making me stand up suddenly. My whole body felt rigid, and I could tell Hilda was nearly as confused as well. "Seriously, stop being weird. I need to go get you some blankets from the hallway closet." My eyes darted around my room, and then I pointed at an open electrical outlet near my desk. "Plug in the pump and turn it on. That thing takes like five minutes to fully inflate."

Hilda grabbed the stuff on her lap and reluctantly got up. "Alright. Geez. You're so pushy when you're not in public."

* * *

I stared at my bed as I removed my shirt and made sure Hilda was out of my field of view. Typically, I would have just changed in the bathroom down the hall, but my father was showering, and it was already late in the evening. Any moment, my mother could burst through the door and scold me about how we had church and other responsibilities early the next day. The last thing I wanted to do was be disciplined in front of Hilda.

Hilda didn't seem to mind changing in front of me at all. With her being some sort of star athlete, it shouldn't have surprised me, but taking my clothes off so close to her felt bizarre. I tried to tell myself there was nothing out of the ordinary, that I had changed in front of Matilda and Veronica plenty of times when we all had prepared for parties or church. I was a bit irked because this time felt *different*. It was my room, my sacred space. I should have had a home-field advantage or something, but I just kept feeling like Hilda was constantly putting me off balance.

As quickly as I could, I changed into a pajama top, only to realize afterward that I had left my bra on. Irritated, I reached behind my back to unclasp it and take it off without removing my shirt, a technique Veronica had shown me in the locker rooms at school in our freshman year. Naturally, I turned my head to see if Hilda was watching me. Her back was turned to me, and she had just pulled off her tube top, taking her bra with it in one swoop. My body seized as I saw a flash of metal at her nipple line as she reached out for the pajama top hanging over the back of my desk chair.

A flare of anxiety shot up from the depths of my stomach and exploded in my heart, making my entire face flush with warmth. *There is no way Hilda has her nipples pierced. Right? Right?!* My imagination had clearly gotten away from me. It was probably just a strange glint of moonlight or maybe something reflecting off of my computer screen. Deciding to keep my bra on as some sort of holy protection, I began to climb onto my bed. Then I heard the descent of Hilda's jeans zipper and gasped so badly I nearly face-planted on the wall.

"Clarissa? Are you okay?"

"I'm fine. I just, uh, slipped a little," I said, wrapping myself in blankets and making sure to stare at the empty wall. Yet even while my mind raced with what-ifs, something tugged at my heart and told me to glance over my shoulder. The reasoning behind this need was too terrifying to think about, so I just closed my eyes and tried to will myself asleep.

When Hilda spoke again, it startled me. "Should I shut your laptop?"

I feigned a chuckle, confident that it was the fakest I had ever sounded, especially since I was talking to my wall. "Yeah. Sorry. I'm just, like, super exhausted." The light of the screen dimmed a few seconds later, leaving us in the filtered moonlight of my draped window.

I wanted to say goodnight, but my head was pounding. Or was it my heart? It was hard to clarify anything about my body when Hilda was around, and I was struggling to discover *why*. I couldn't tell if I was flying or falling. It honestly felt like both.

Hilda's shadow on the wall shrunk down. "Goodnight, Clarissa. And thank you."

"For what?" I squeaked.

Hilda's voice was soft and filled with embarrassment. "For inviting me over. You're the first person that has."

A storm of swirling emotions swept me up, and suddenly, my heart took over and justification for what I was about to do became irrelevant. "Hey, Hilda?"

"Huh?"

"Do you have any piercings? I mean, other than your ears, of course." There was a thick silence, and every part of me felt constricted as I waited for an answer. Did she not hear *me? Is she ignoring me? Or maybe—*

"Ja, I have both of my nipples pierced."

I nearly launched out of my bed as I flipped over to see if Hilda's expression was genuine. She was lying on the floor mattress just a few feet from me, staring at the ceiling. Her eyes flickered in the moonlight, and a sudden mix of dreaded anticipation and excitement gripped me. It was as if my heart had just led me to the pinnacle of a rollercoaster, and the chain that brought me up had just released, freeing me to whatever fate God had in store for me.

"Oh," I said as nonchalantly as I could manage. "That's cool."

When Hilda spoke, her tone was distant, and her gaze was fixed on my ceiling. "My mother told me I could get it done when I turned eighteen. We never told my dad about it because it was supposed to be a 'girls only' thing. Plus, it's the last thing I wanted him knowing. Then, right after my mom died, my father and I used to fight a lot. Actually, we still fight a lot. One night, I snapped and told him about it. That's when he drove me to this dark tattoo parlor in Berlin. I think he thought I would chicken out once we arrived. It actually worked out for me, because I had just turned sixteen and I needed his permission. I still can't believe he signed all the waivers. Having my father there, staring at me the whole time, it was bizarre. I think he did it on purpose, to make a point or something. We didn't talk the entire ride home. Or really any time after."

All I could do was try to keep talking so I didn't have to think about my own feelings, which were set to explode out of me at any moment. "Wait, aren't you only sixteen right now?" Hilda nodded, and I whispered. "Did it hurt?"

"The first one didn't, but I think I had all the adrenaline going, so that's probably why. The second one hurt so much. It felt like someone strong pinched my nipple where the needle went in, followed by a bizarre feeling, like when a doctor injects something cold into your arm and it makes your arm tingle. I cried a lot then."

"You're lying." Something as fantastical and forbidden as nipple piercings weren't for the people I knew. They were reserved for lead singers of punk or heavy metal bands. They were for people who went to Hell. Sinners.

Hilda sat up on her elbows and looked at me mischievously. "Do you want me to prove it?"

Instantly, I lifted my comforter up to my mouth as if it would stifle whatever answer I dared to give. It was outrageous of Hilda to even make the offer, and I could feel the proverbial devil resting on my shoulder and nodding in agreement.

I tried to sound apathetic, maybe even a little aloof. "Yeah. Actually, I dare you, too." Part of me also hoped that the challenge would quell the thundering of my heart or maybe make Hilda back down.

Hilda sat up and turned to face me, and as the blankets covering her chest fell to her hips, all thoughts and ideas left my mind. My eyes locked on Hilda's nipples, clearly visible through the light pajama shirt. More importantly, I saw the two extra spheres on either side of them. My heart began to beat erratically as Hilda started to lift her shirt. The feeling mixed so oddly with the immediate regret over accepting Hilda's ridiculous offer that all I could do was stare in shock.

In one fluid motion, Hilda bared her chest to me. Her breasts were beautiful, smaller than my own. It made sense since breast tissue was fat, and Hilda was mostly muscle. My scientific justification for staring only lasted until I saw the silver bars with little balls on either side pierced horizontally through both of her nipples. The silver jewelry reminded me of her eyes and had the same entrancing effect on my mind. A voice screamed in my mind to look away, but I couldn't. I was utterly frozen by awe and soul-quaking indecision. *This is beautiful and forbidden and—*

Hilda cleared her throat. I squeaked and recoiled back into my covers. Hilda had been staring back at me the entire time I was gawking at her chest.

"You weren't lying," I whispered into cupped hands while my eyes locked onto the foot of my bed.

Hilda burst into hushed laughter. "Why would I lie?"

Despite my embarrassment, I couldn't help but turn to look at her. A mix of hesitation and unexpected warmth pervaded my voice. "That's so cool." I looked down at my own chest, average and unimpressive—at least as far as I was concerned. "I wish mine were smaller, like yours."

Hilda sounded intrigued. "Ja? Why?"

"Ugh, you have no idea how many times I've caught Max or someone else with their eyes glued to my chest while I try and talk to them. It's honestly the worst. It makes me feel so awkward just walking down the hallway at school. The worst part is, I don't even wear low-cut shirts. I don't even own anything like that."

Hilda smiled. "Well, if you want to get your nipples pierced, I know a place, but I don't think that will help with people staring."

"Of course it won't help," I huffed. "It's just . . . Ugh! I used to dream of having big boobs like Matilda, but I just didn't expect it to happen so . . . quickly. You know?"

I watched Hilda look down at her basically flat chest. Then she looked up at me with an incredulous grin. "I bet yours are perfect just the way they are."

I knew Hilda wanted to see, but I wordlessly pulled my comforter up and muttered something nonsensical. Hilda must have seen my resolve break as she hummed beckoningly. I let out a strangely uncomfortable chuckle at myself, then took a long breath and tried to summon courage from deep within me. My hands moved from my blankets to the bottom of my shirt as I tried to find an explanation—any floppy excuse would do. I just needed a way to justify it to myself. When I looked over, Hilda's doe-eyed, expectant, and lip-bitten grin didn't help my performance anxiety at all. Holding on to the threshold of indecision was painful, and I needed to be rid of the feeling one way or another as I threw my shirt up.

Even as the cold air touched my freshly exposed skin, I expected to combust into flames. For almost three full seconds, I held there until common sense and embarrassment rushed through me. Hilda was still wide-eyed when I lowered my shirt and pulled my covers around me again.

"There," I said absently to my knees, not yet brave enough to look Hilda in the eyes.

"Tsk."

"What?"

Hilda was shaking her head at me with a huge grin. "It's not fair. You cheated."

"Huh?"

"You still had your bra on, Clarissa."

My eyes widened when I realized she hadn't seen everything—or anything, really. For some reason, that helped put my mind at ease. "Yeah, nice try, but not even Max has seen that view."

We sat in silence for a while as I waited for my feverish mood to subside. Once I felt somewhat normal again, I still couldn't really focus on anything other than the crazy girl staring at me from the floor.

"You're insane," I finally whispered.

"Am I?"

"Hilda, nobody else's father would literally drive to a tattoo shop to get their teenage daughter's nipples pierced! Wait till everyone hears about this. They're going to—"

Hilda's eyes snapped open. "No, please! Don't tell anyone."

The swell of indescribable emotion that I'd been holding in my chest came to a crashing halt. Cautiously, I said, "You seemed pretty excited to show me. Plus, it's not like you're going to be able to hide your piercings forever. I mean, if track is anything like football, you'll, well, you know."

Hilda kept her gaze fixed on her mattress and seemed to struggle with what to say. "I just need some time. Everything is so new. I don't want to mess up." She exhaled and looked up. "I've never been good at making friends. I always end up doing something like this, and I ruin it. This was dumb. I'm sorry. I didn't mean to make you—"

Her sudden vulnerability knocked the wind out of me. Without forethought, I threw my sheets off and jumped out of my bed. I landed on the air mattress, quickly scurried over to Hilda, and wrapped my arms around her. Hilda tensed up when I pressed against her, then relaxed into me. I couldn't help but notice how soft and warm she was. My head seemed to fit perfectly in the crook of her neck, and our bodies just fit together. I'd held Devon like this during his breakup with Veronica, yet there was something more here. Something deeper.

"I promise I won't tell anyone," I whispered into Hilda's neck as I squeezed her torso. I tried to think of what Devon would do. He probably would have made a bad joke. *Let's try my luck.*

I pulled away from Hilda and gently pulled her chin to face me. "I don't want to brag, Hilda, but I've had each of my ears pierced twice since I was like ten. We have the exact same number of holes. It's really nothing to brag about."

Tears budded in Hilda's eyes as she tackled me onto the air mattress with a hug. "Thank you, Clarissa." She sobbed slightly. "This is going to sound crazy, but you're the best friend I've ever had and I—"

A loud knock made Hilda jump off me, and we both looked at my bedroom door. "I thought I heard someone crying," my father called through the door. "Is everything okay in there?"

"It's fine, Dad," I called back, scrambling to get back into my bed. "We were just talking about school and stuff. Nobody is crying."

There was a short pause while my father waited to hear a sob or something. Thankfully, Hilda had recovered. "Alright, girls. That's enough chit-chatting for tonight. Get some sleep. Don't forget we have church tomorrow morning, Clare."

Once my dad was gone, Hilda whispered, "Goodnight, Clarissa."

"Goodnight, Hilda."

Even as I drifted off to sleep, the butterflies in my stomach never stopped fluttering.

6

The Devil's Footprint

The next morning, I sat behind the driver's seat of our old station wagon as we drove down the familiar road to church. Amazingly, my parents had convinced Hilda to come with us. I wanted to talk to her about it, but I woke up late, and everyone else was practically ready to leave when I just walked out of my room to brush my teeth.

When we pulled into the large parking lot adjacent to Saint Christopher's, I grabbed Hilda's hand and practically dragged her across the back seat as the car came to a stop. "I want to show you something. Come on." We ran past cars and trucks, the outer gardens, and the two-story apartment complex the clergy members lived in. Then we rushed up the marble stairs and into the spacious and impressive interior of the church.

"I know this is going to sound lame, but I basically grew up here. The church is actually shaped like the Star of Bethlehem if you see it from above. And those huge doors, they're actually exact replicas of the doors to the Vatican. Or that's what my uncle says."

"I've been to the Vatican," Hilda said casually.

I sighed, feeling jealous. "Of course you have. I should have expected that."

"Oft expectation fails, and most oft there where most it promises," Hilda said.

"Huh?"

Hilda giggled. "It's Shakespeare."

"We read *Hamlet* last year, but that's all I know."

Hilda shrugged, and I wasn't sure what to make of it.

"Good morning!" Sister June said.

"Good morning," Hilda and I replied.

As soon as we were past her, I led us down a hallway of large relief sculptures that depicted the Stations of the Cross. I could tell Hilda was impressed with the carvings. "This is where I got the idea for my collage wall."

"Honestly, I like yours better," Hilda sniggered. "Less naked men."

I rolled my eyes but felt proud that Hilda had favorably compared my work to these. *Maybe I really am as good as she says.*

At the end of the hall, we came to a dead end. "It's normally not locked," I said as I shook the handle. "Argh, just a sec." Standing on my tiptoes, I tried to feel the key hiding up on a flat part of the arching gothic masonry that outlined the door. My middle finger touched it but only managed to push it back farther. "Darnit—"

"Here." Hilda pressed into my back, pinning me between her and the stone as she reached up and grabbed the key easily. She stepped away from me and inspected it curiously before holding it out. "Where exactly are you taking me?"

There was a split second when I was completely lost. Having Hilda's warm body pressed up against me made me feel strangely safe. Suddenly, I was acutely aware of just how close we were—and how close her face was to mine.

I snatched the key out of her hand. "Come on, stop being weird. We're running out of time."

Three dizzying flights of spiral stairs and one featureless corridor later, we arrived at the small balcony that overlooked the whole congregation. The small space was nestled in one of the westernmost points of the star-shaped church. Some of the massive wooden beams that held up the roof converged at a junction just below, so the balcony was almost unnoticeable from the first floor. It was the best view in the house, and most people didn't even know it existed.

I turned around and found Hilda ducking through the doorway. I winced. "Sorry. There's not much headroom here. I didn't think about that."

Hilda hunched down a little and moved next to me as she gasped at the view. After a second, she muttered something in German.

"I do some of my best thinking from up here," I said, gesturing to the view. "You have no idea how many times I've just perched up here for hours on my phone. This view made me want to be a photographer. I've taken so many pictures from up here." I glanced over at Hilda and assumed she would be just as enamored. Instead, she had a huge grin on her face. "What's that look for?"

"Oh, it's nothing," Hilda said with her signature tone, that sly sarcasm that beckoned me to follow up.

"Tell me," I said, shoving her playfully.

"It's nice. But—"

"But it's no Vatican?"

"No. It's no *Frauenkirche*."

"Come again?" I giggled.

Hilda cleared her throat. "The Frauenkirche is a huge cathedral in Munich. There are two towers you can climb to see the whole city and some of the countryside. My mother took me a few times. We would wait until right before it closed and race to the top, each one of us in a different tower. Sometimes, we got there just in time for the sunset. It was one of the last things we did together before she died, and it was the first time I ever beat her to the top." She stopped and swallowed. "I wish I had thought to take a picture."

I set my hand on Hilda's shoulder. "I'm sorry. I didn't mean to—"

"Hey. Want to know a fun fact about me?"

"Uh, of course?" I said, trying to sound upbeat.

"The devil and I have the same sized foot."

"What?" I said nervously, chancing a flickered glance at the huge figure of a crucified Jesus that hung behind the altar and loomed over the general congregation. "How could you possibly know that?"

"When the Frauenkirche was being built, the architect ran out of money, or so the story goes. So he made a deal with the devil to finish construction. The devil said that the cathedral must be built with no windows to forbid any of God's light from reaching the inside. The architect agreed, but he was a very clever man. He constructed the inner columns in such a way that from the entrance, where the devil stood, there were no windows visible. When the devil discovered he had been tricked, it was too late, and light flooded into the church, forcing him to stay in the darkened foyer. The devil stomped his foot in frustration, and it left a deep mark on the floor. There's a real spot on the ground in the entrance of the church that looks a bit like a footprint. Whether it is the devil's, I don't know, but when I put my foot over it, it matched almost perfectly." She leaned on the banister and looked out over the church. "Only one other person knows that about me. Pretty silly, ja?"

Hilda's soft smile made me want to confess something, too; it was only fair, after all. "Well, I'm glad you told me. I mean, the only thing about me is that nobody knows that I have no idea what I'm doing."

There was a flash of panic on Hilda's face before she cautiously narrowed her eyes at me. "No idea about what?"

I sighed, letting my hand drop from her shoulder as I leaned over the balcony. "Life, I guess." I watched people milling around while ambient choir music faintly played throughout the church's stereo system. "I don't know."

"You seem like you're doing fine to me."

"Don't humor me," I said, rolling my eyes. "Take you, for instance. You have a job, you know what you want to do after high school, you have the body some people only dream of, and you—" I refrained from looking directly at Hilda's chest— "you just seem to know everything. I mean, I don't even know what college I want to go to yet. I haven't even thought about scholarships like you have. I'm probably just going to get pressured into attending whatever college my mother deems appropriate anyways. I mean, do you have any idea how hard it is to be a freelance photographer? I'm no Ridley Gracy. How am I going to make a living? Where am I going to live? I have to get out of Grand Forks, even if it kills me, but I've never even had a job, let alone a real photo shoot." I took a deep breath and shook my head. "You just seem to have life figured out, and I'm jealous."

Hilda laughed. "Do I now? I'm glad it appears that way."

I elbowed Hilda's arm. "Stop it. I'm trying to be serious here."

"Me too," Hilda said, then seemed to have an epiphany. "Okay, I'll do it."

"You'll do what?" I inquired a bit incredulously.

"I'll be your first client for a photo shoot. Once I get my first paycheck, I'll pay you. If I'm going to be a famous Olympian, I need a personal photographer. They all have them."

My throat tightened. "No, I don't . . . Uh, I don't do photos of my friends, and I don't even have a real camera. Plus, I'm pretty sure you're making that up."

Hilda raised an eyebrow, "It is a poor craftsman who blames their tools, Clarissa. I trust you'll do fine with what you have."

I'm sure my heart would have skipped a beat if I hadn't been so racked with guilt. *Not if you knew what I did to Veronica.* Still, something about the way Hilda spoke made everything she said feel set in stone. "Hey, how did you know you wanted to be an Olympian? How do you wake up at four o'clock in the morning just to run or do homework? It seems so impossible to me."

Hilda smiled but remained still for a moment, and I found myself relaxing, too. We enjoyed the silence together. Finally, she chuckled lightly and said something in German. "That's what my mother used to say when I was unproductive."

"What's it mean?"

"It's a saying . . . It is something like, 'The Devil's favorite piece of furniture is the long bench.'"

I rolled my eyes. "What's with you and the devil?"

Hilda grinned. "Hail Satan." She put her hands on her head like horns.

I reached out and pulled her arms down. "Stop it!" I hissed. "You can't do that here! Are you insane?"

"According to you last night, ja, I am."

I wanted to scold her further, but something about Hilda's disregard for the rules woke the rebel inside me. "Alright, Satan, what is a 'long bench'?"

Hilda hummed as she thought. "To put something off for a long time is to put it on 'the long bench.' What's the word . . . ?"

"Like procrastinating?"

"Ja! That's it."

"Well if that's the case, I feel like my whole life is on 'the long bench.' I'm not even who I appear to be."

"Oh?" Hilda mocked. "Are you a superhero? Is this your alter ego? The stunning, super-popular high school student masquerading as an amateur photographer. It's a little cliché, don't you think?"

"Hey, I'm being serious." I held back a laugh as I tried to maintain a straight face. Revealing so many of my closely guarded secrets felt dangerous, but for some reason, confessing things to Hilda was effortless. I penned a silent prayer to the Almighty and focused on the massive crucifix. I started talking to it more than Hilda. "I just feel lost, I guess. I feel like I'm someone pretending to be something that I should already be. But if I'm not me, then who am I?" I felt defeated by my inability to properly convey the foreboding, transitional feeling I'd been having ever since I knew to look for it. "Sorry, I'm not explaining this very well."

"I've felt that way before," Hilda said, much to my surprise.

I perked up. "Y-You have?"

"Ohhhh ja. When I first started secondary school in Germany, I was different. I've always been different. Even before I grew." She glanced over and pointed at her eyes. "My mother used to tell me that I just needed to be myself. It wasn't until right before I moved to America that I really found out who that was." Her voice dropped to a whisper. "I hurt someone very badly, Clarissa, and I don't want to do it again."

I blinked in disbelief. "You did?"

"Amelie and I—"

The massive pipe organ across the church rang out, startling both of us and signaling the start of mass.

* * *

My cheeks burned throughout the entire sermon, and I could hardly make eye contact with anyone around me when the Rite of Peace began. I also couldn't help but notice how many people hesitated to shake Hilda's hand or offered a patronizing "peace be with you" when they did—not that she seemed to mind.

Immediately after the sermon, my mother grabbed me by the wrist and dragged me into a hallway. "What kind of example are you setting by waltzing in late like that?" She was seething. "How could you disrespect your uncle and the Lord in that way? I swear your behavior is getting worse every day."

I was about to apologize when a loud whistle seemed to split the atmosphere like a bomb. My mother and I turned to see Hilda walking toward us, her eyes narrowed and her lips drawn into a thin line.

No. Hilda don't—!

"Can I help you?" my mother sneered when Hilda reached us.

"You can start by letting go of Clarissa's wrist," Hilda said so sharply that the words felt like razors on my ears.

"Excuse me?" my mother hissed as her grip tightened. "What right do you have to—"

Hilda's right hand shot out and grabbed my mother's wrist. I watched in silent horror as Hilda's nails seemed to dig into the fabric of my mother's shirt. "How's it feel?"

"How dare you!" my mother shouted. I nearly screamed as she twisted, her free hand cocking back to slap Hilda across the face.

Hilda blocked the blow with ease and shoved my mother by the collarbone with both of her hands, sending her reeling back.

The shock on my mother's face and Hilda's stern expression made me dizzy. The whole hallway seemed to spin, and all I wanted to do was run. I took a step back but realized my back was already against a wall.

"Hello!" a voice echoed down the hallway. I turned, pressing a hand to my chest to steady my racing heart. Reverend Nicholas James Huffington, my father's older brother, was about three hot dogs and one white beard short of a mall Santa. Not a discount mall Santa, but the good kind, like the one at Rockridge Mall in the winter. He had a belly that protruded uncomfortably over his pants and big ears that stuck out past his puffy white hair. His upbeat demeanor always elevated my mood. Nothing ever seemed to get him down. He approached us as if nothing was the matter and with no hints to how much he had witnessed. "Who's our heavy metal–looking friend here?"

Hilda never quite took her eyes off my mother, but she bowed slightly. "Brünnhilde Bernhardt." Then she seemed to take a deep breath. "That was a wonderful mass. Thank you, Father."

My uncle put a finger to his lips for a moment, then pointed at Hilda. "Dutch?"

Hilda looked a bit shocked. "No, I'm German."

My uncle smiled. "Has Clare told you yet that I studied for almost a decade in Europe?" Then he wiggled his ears like he did when I was a child. "These aren't just for show, you know?" When Hilda extended her hand, my uncle seemed offended. "Oh, no. Clearly, you haven't been briefed properly. We Huffingtons are huggers." He swung his arms open wide and fluttered his hands toward himself. "Bring her in."

Hilda hesitated, locking eyes with my mother before she accepted the hug. During the embrace, she turned back and gave me a very specific look, but I was too out of control to register what it meant.

Uncle Nick released Hilda and curiously pinched her bicep through her hoodie. "They sure do make 'em tall in Germany. And sturdy, too. Good Lord, girl."

Hilda nodded, more to my mother than to my uncle. "Ja, my mother used to say I was the finest in German engineering."

Uncle Nick laughed. "Well, she wasn't wrong. Now, how's my favorite niece?" I could tell by the look in his eyes that I was his next target for a hug. Once he was wrapped around me, he whispered, "Other than being a few minutes late, I noticed." He pulled back and gave me a wink.

I tried my best to be as polite and cordial as possible, given the fact that my head was still swimming. "Oh, you know. Same old, same old," I said, looking straight down at my feet.

Uncle Nick raised my chin up to meet his wise eyes. He clearly didn't believe a word I'd said. "Well, you let me know if that changes, okay? And if you can't tell me, God is always listening, although he doesn't often have a habit of replying." He chuckled again. Then he reached out for Hilda's hand, which caused her to flinch back slightly, but my uncle didn't let go. He nodded to her and took up a solemn and sympathetic tone. "I'm very sorry to hear about your mother's passing. Loss can be hard for someone so young. If you'd like, we can pray together for her. I know some very nice passages."

Hilda pulled her hand away and seemed troubled that Uncle Nick knew about her mother. She glanced over her shoulder at me, her eyes screaming *"Did you tell him?!"*

As subtly as I could, I shook my head, not sure what would get me into trouble anymore.

Hilda looked back to my uncle. "How did you know about my mother's death?"

"I told him," my mother said bluntly as a few of her friends began to hover just outside of the conversation. "I simply thought you could use some spiritual guidance, but I can see that you're a lost cause."

"Now, Mary—"

"You know I don't believe in all this, right?" Hilda said as she thumbed back at the nave.

Someone beyond the four of us gasped, or maybe it was me, and the sound echoed back. *Was saying grace over dinner last night an act? Was Hilda keeping the fact that she was an atheist from me on purpose for some reason? Is that why she attacked my mother?! Why wouldn't she just—*

My uncle cleared his throat, "Well, it seems we've touched on some very complicated subjects here, haven't we?" He chuckled. "Mary, there is no such thing as a 'lost cause' in the eyes of God." He turned to Hilda. "Miss Bernhardt, would it help to tell you that God listens regardless of whether you believe or not?"

Hilda rolled her eyes. "Given God's track record, I'd honestly rather talk to Satan."

My eyes snapped shut at the mention of Satan. I didn't want to see my mother's expression or feel how much trouble I was in.

"I don't think Satan is really the listening type," my uncle said. "But always remember, just because you've turned your back on God does not mean he's turned his back on you. Quite the opposite, in fact. He'll always be here to welcome you if you allow him to."

I peeled an eye open to see how Hilda was going to respond. She kept her scowl and began to speak but then stopped when she glanced at me. I wasn't sure what kind of expression I was making, but whatever it was must have changed her mind about what she was going to say. "Whatever, I'm going to walk home. See you at school, Clarissa." All of my mother's friends parted like the Red Sea as Hilda marched down the hallway.

Not daring to make eye contact with anyone after that, I quickly excused myself to use the bathroom. I hadn't realized until after I locked myself in a stall that both of my arms were wrapped so tightly around my stomach that it hurt. "Why—" I whispered but began to sob. "Why? God, why am I like this?"

* * *

No sooner had I reached for the seat belt than I felt my mother glaring at me from the rearview mirror. I could tell by the contempt on her face that I was in for some verbal scolding, so I prayed and mentally braced myself one more time. *I'm not in trouble*, I told myself. *I didn't do anything wrong. Hilda was the one who—*

"Clarissa," my mother said so suddenly that I jumped. "I forbid you from talking with that horrible girl ever again."

I gasped. "What? That's not fair—"

My mother whipped around to show me just how seriously she was. "So you think the way *your friend* treated me this morning was okay?"

"N-No, but—"

"But nothing," my mother barked. "That kind of violent behavior is completely unacceptable, and I won't have you being associated with it. As it stands, we're going to be the laughingstock of the whole town now. Do you have any idea how embarrassed I am? Can you even imagine what your father is going to have to deal with downtown now?"

My fists clenched, but I lowered my head and apologized anyway. I couldn't imagine my father, who was currently pacing outside the car while on an unrelated phone call, would see any fallout from what Hilda had done. He hadn't even been there.

Staring at my knees as my father got in the car, I noticed Hilda's forgotten backpack resting behind me on the passenger seat. I reached over and heaved the heavy pack onto my lap. I was in the middle of asking myself why I even bothered to move it when a faint floral smell hit my nose. It smelled like Hilda, so naturally, I pulled it closer to me.

I heaved a sigh of relief when I finally arrived at my bedroom. Carrying Hilda's backpack up the stairs had been rough. With a grunt, I lifted the ratty pack onto my desk, wondering what made it so heavy. Curiosity got the better of me, and I hesitantly began to unzip the main section of the backpack.

I knew it was a massive invasion of Hilda's privacy, but I had to figure her out—why couldn't I stop thinking about her? Once I learned why she was so special, I could go back to pretending like she hadn't flashed me or that she didn't ... have her nipples pierced.

Argh! I ran a hand down my face, trying to get a grip. *Stop thinking about that!*

With my gaze never entirely leaving my bedroom door, fearing my mother could burst in at any moment, I took a deep breath and opened Hilda's backpack.

The top was just clothes, which I pulled out because there was no way that was why it weighed so much. I paused, removing the two sporty crop tops and matching workout short-shorts because they all still had the plastic security tags on them. I prayed that the clerk had just forgotten to take them off as I continued to dig. Next, I pulled out two heavy sacks that velcroed to themselves. I assumed these were some kind of ankle or wrist weights by their shape. I pulled out two eight-pound hand weights, two more five-pounders, and a neatly tied jump rope with both plastic handles missing.

I looked at all of Hilda's things sitting on my desk. *Jesus, she really is serious about the Olympics. No wonder her backpack is so heavy. It literally has weights in it.*

Looking inside the backpack to make sure I hadn't missed anything, I noticed a hidden zipper pocket. I prodded it with my finger and felt something hard. Opening the inner pouch revealed the back of a flat pencil box about eight inches long and three inches deep. Curious, I pulled it out and shook it. Something shifted inside, but there wasn't any noise. Flipping the box over, I recognized Hilda's handwriting scrawled across the top in sharpie.

Frustrated that I couldn't read German, I looked up to find my laptop was sitting right in front of me.

This will be the last thing I do. Then I'll put it all away and pretend I never did any of this.

As quickly as I could, I transcribed the words from the pencil case into a translation website.

"Uneasy lies the head that wears the crown."

Something about the phrase was familiar to me, and a quick

Google search showed that it was a Shakespeare quote. I smiled, thinking about how Hilda clearly had a bit of a literary crush, although that did nothing to ease my anxiety.

When I looked back down at the rectangle sitting in front of me, the simple silver latch seemed to call out to me.

Okay. I took a deep breath. *Just a peek. Look, but don't touch.*

With sweating hands, I slowly raised the lid, half-expecting Satan or my mother to burst into my room at any moment and yell, "Gotcha!" Inside there was a note and two sets of nipple rings in little baggies. I tilted the box to get a better look at the jewelry. One was a set of bars with orbs on either end, and the other was a set of hoops. The first set was what she was wearing the night of our sleepover. My stomach lurched up as I realized she either had a third pair or didn't wear any to church, and I wasn't sure which thought had made me suddenly feel so flushed.

I picked up the note, mostly to distract my thoughts as they wandered to memories of Hilda's bare chest. It was folded in a neat square, much like the ones we commonly exchanged in class, and the front read "Amelie." The name rang a bell. *Wasn't she going to say something about whoever this person was in church before we got interrupted?* As carefully as I could, I unfolded the note.

I didn't know what I expected; the entire thing was written in German. I set the note down and leaned back in my chair.

"Um," I whispered but found myself leaning forward as my right hand reached out for my mouse. With a bitten lip, I transcribed the note and winced as I clicked the "Translate Now" button.

Amelie,

I thought I meant something to you, but you obviously never cared about me. I'm glad that I made you and that asshole end up in the hospital. *Don't try and find me. Don't try and contact me. Don't even speak my name.*

Next time, you may not walk away.

Goodbye forever,

B.B.

At first, I didn't know what to make of it. I knew the translation software wasn't exactly perfect. Still, the feeling that Hilda was *dangerous* settled into my mind. Before, when she had spoken about hurting someone badly before she moved to America, I assumed she meant emotionally, but this—along with her actions at church—indicated that it was . . . physical.

No. Hilda isn't like that. She was protecting me and then herself. She just doesn't understand how things work in my life. And now, thanks to my mother barring my friendship with her, she never will.

* * *

Monday morning came, and I was unsure of what seeing Hilda would mean to me. The weight as I hauled her backpack to class reminded me that I was forced to interact with her, regardless of how awkward it might be.

When I walked into class, Hilda was standing at a desk across from Lin and having a conversation with her. Neither of them even looked at me as I passed by. I couldn't tell if they were knowingly giving me the cold shoulder or not, but it made the storm cloud over my head darken.

After sitting down at my desk, I tried to eavesdrop on their conversation, but all I caught was that Hilda was apologizing for something. The late bell rang, interrupting their argument, which it looked like Hilda had lost as she trudged back to her desk with a stack of books and some loose papers. When we locked eyes, she . . . smiled. It was soft and filled with an emotion I couldn't place. Regret, maybe? It was hard to tell; I barely had enough time to register it before she bent down to pick up her backpack. "I'm surprised your mother didn't burn this." She giggled. "I forgot I left this in your car. Thanks, Clarissa."

I nervously squeaked out, "No, sure," which was the nonsensical difference of "no problem" and "sure" that my mind had spewed out. Hilda, thank God, either didn't notice or was too focused on unzipping her backpack and shuffling things around to care. I would have passed Hilda a note while Stantin lectured, but I had too much to say, and I didn't want anything to be taken the wrong way.

After what felt like an eternity, class ended, and she stood and pushed herself up to the front of the class. Seeing how she was going to hit some traffic, Hilda suddenly skipped and then vaulted over some boy still clearing off his desk. She landed with her back to Lin in the opposite aisleway. Spinning around on her heel, Hilda turned to face Lin and cocked her head while wearing a huge grin. I assumed the gesture must have had something to do with what they were talking about before class, because why else would Hilda be looking at Lin so . . . friendly?

Lin opened her mouth to speak, but Stantin roared, "Miss Bernhardt! My desk. This instant."

Hilda didn't even turn around to acknowledge our teacher. She gave Lin a relaxed shrug as if to convey that whatever punishment she was going to receive didn't matter to her in the least. Then she turned around and walked toward Stantin's desk.

As fast as I could, I packed up and left class, hoping that Hilda's conversation with Stantin wouldn't take too long so we could still walk together between classes.

I waited in the hallway for Hilda, praying to God that he could show me how to make my mom like her. I was interrupted by Hilda laughing. I began to step out but stopped when I heard Lin say, "I told you she'd be a stuck-up bitch, didn't I? I mean, what in the fuck made you even think that going to church with them was a good idea?"

My heart skipped a beat. *Are Hilda and Lin talking about me?! About church? About—*

"I don't know," Hilda said as the two passed at a brisk pace, neither of them noticing me. "I just thought that it would be nice and maybe she would—"

"Stop," Lin interrupted. "I already know what you're going to say, and it makes me want to vomit. I told you, I just get that feeling from her. It's not like I know."

Hilda replied, but they were too far away from me to hear clearly. *There it was*, I thought darkly. *Hilda thought I was a stuck-up bitch, which meant she was only nice to me in class because it was polite.* I wanted to cry. *No, I won't let this friendship end like Veronica. I can't.* Then, with a deep breath, I pushed off the wall and walked toward the main building.

I caught up to Hilda right as she split away from Lin to head to her second period. *Perfect.* I pulled her aside and with a knotted stomach told her that I just overheard her and Lin talking about me. Hilda laughed and said they were discussing my mother, and not me. With that weight lifted off my shoulders I asked Hilda if she wanted to go off campus with me for lunch. I knew about a coffee shop a few blocks away called Pleasant Grounds. It was a bit artsy, even for me, but students rarely went there.

7

Ryan's Birthday

I bit my tongue as Max and Devon talked about how badly they were looking forward to Ryan and Michelle's birthday party. I did not want to go, but social obligations—and Max—forced me to.

We arrived late because Max insisted that we bring a bottle of whiskey, which meant his older brother had to go out and buy one for us. Then Devon suggested we stop and get pizzas as an extra layer of surprise. Polite was polite, but it annoyed me. By the time we got to the party, I would basically have to leave.

As I walked into the open garage, which was also Ryan's bedroom, I was surprised to see Hilda standing on one of two couches in the back. She was leaning forward, trying to balance a beer can on top of a worryingly tall tower of similarly empty cans. Lin, Michelle, and Kate were all fixated on seeing if Hilda could perform the feat without knocking the stack over completely.

Max, not seeing Hilda's intense focus, loudly announced, "Happy birthday, Stone twins! We come bearing gifts of pizza and alcohol!"

Everyone jumped in surprise, and the mass of aluminum cans crashed to the ground.

"Fuck!" Hilda swore as she threw down the can she was holding.

"See." Lin crossed her arms and leaned back, mocking. "I told you you couldn't do it. Now you need to do another shot."

Hilda stuck her tongue out at Lin and defiantly slurred, "There is no more regret in me than there is milk in a male tiger." Then Hilda turned and locked eyes with me. "Clarissa!" she shouted and vaulted over the coffee table.

"Hilda, wait. Stop—!" I tried to warn her, but her foot caught on a cable, and she tripped. Dropping the bottle of whiskey Max had given me was all I could do to protect my face as Hilda's shoulder slammed into me.

The back of my palms smashed against my nose as I heard the glass whiskey bottle hit the ground with a thunderous crash, sending large shards of glass scattering across the concrete floor.

Thankfully, Hilda tripping had slowed her enough to not completely knock us both over. When she staggered backward, she swayed, and Devon reached out to steady her.

"Oh shit!" Max exclaimed, but he wasn't looking at the mess of glass or the whiskey that soaked my pants. "Clare, your nose!"

"Huh?" Something warm dripped into my mouth. With a quick sniffle, I ran the back of my hand across my upper lip, only to see it covered in blood.

Max ran over to me, pulling out some napkins from one of the pizza bags. "Here, quick."

Everything was happening so fast. People were shouting at Hilda and pointing at the mess she had made while Max quickly ushered me upstairs to the bathroom. I wanted to say something to Hilda as I passed her, but she just shouted back at Lin and Ryan.

Even with my nose corked with tissue, my entire face throbbed with each step I took on my way downstairs. *Maybe I could borrow some of Michelle's pants. No, I'm sure my mother memorized what I was wearing, and if I came home in anything else while anywhere with Max* . . . The thought made me shudder. I regretted coming to the party, after all.

Outside, Hilda was standing in the farthest corner from the door, talking to Lin in the darkness. Both had beer cans in their hands and didn't look like they wanted company. Max was doting on me like we were dating again. He led me to a metal table with Ryan, Devon, Kate, and Michelle. There was a half-eaten chocolate cake in the middle.

"Hey." Ryan nodded at me as I sat down. "You okay?"

"Not really," I said, hearing how awkward my voice sounded with my nose plugged.

"Well, you can't feel bad while eating birthday cake. It's like illegal," Max said, already cutting a slice I knew he would want us to share.

"I think I'll pass right now," I said. "Everything would probably just taste like blood."

"Y-Your nose isn't broken," Kate stuttered, "is it?"

I began to shake my head, but Max answered for me. "Nah, it takes more than that to break someone's nose. Trust me on that."

Kate looked uncomfortable and went back to her drink.

"Clarissa, do you have a second?" Hilda startled me because I hadn't even noticed she was standing behind me.

"Yeah, sure," I said, pulling the tissues out of my nose and praying that it had stopped bleeding. "Want to sit with us?"

"Actually, Lin told me about a convenience store nearby. Do you mind walking with me?" Hilda seemed more sober than she had a few minutes prior, but maybe I just imagined it.

"Actually, I'd rather stay here," I said. "At least until my pants dry off a little. I don't want anyone thinking—"

"Whatever," Hilda interrupted as she turned and stumbled her way toward the front of the house, pausing only to hold onto the door frame for a few seconds before she disappeared inside.

"Jeez, someone should go with her," Ryan said.

"Why don't you?" Max asked. "I thought you had a crush on Hilda?"

"Hell no," Ryan responded, almost too quickly. "I'm not into girls who could beat the shit out of me. I mean, Hilda's cool, but there's definitely something wrong with her. She's been drinking nonstop since she got here."

I groaned in frustration as I pushed away from the table. "Well, *someone* needs to make sure Hilda's okay."

"Wait, babe, let me finish this slice of cake. Then we can both go find—"

"I'm leaving right now before Hilda wanders into the street and gets hit by a car. Either come or don't."

Thankfully, Hilda hadn't gotten very far from Ryan's house, but as I hustled to catch up to her, she swayed from one side of the sidewalk to the other. As I approached her, I realized she was muttering to herself. It was all in German, but I caught the name "Amelie" more than once.

"Hey," I said.

Hilda flipped around and brought both of her arms up to her face like I was going to throw a punch at her. Her serious, almost frightened expression probably looked like how I did each time my mother dragged me up to my room without dinner.

"Clarissa?" Hilda said, lowering her hands as if she couldn't believe I followed her.

"Uh, yeah? Hi."

Hilda's serious expression relaxed into a drunken grin. "Hey."

My thoughts darkened at seeing her switch emotional states so quickly. It felt borderline dangerous, especially given how quickly she had jumped to physically defend herself. "Ryan said you basically haven't stopped drinking. Did something happen?"

Hilda waved in the air, turning on her heel, and staggered forward. "It'sss nothsssing," she slurred.

Swallowing my fear, I stepped around her to block her path and said, "It's clearly something. Nobody gets this drunk for no reason."

Hilda's smile thinned as tears welled on the sides of her eyes, and I could tell my worried expression didn't help anything as she yelled, "Fine. I lost, okay! There, I said it. It's not fair, Clarissa! All I've ever done since Mom died is push myself! I deserved to win! Not all the time, just . . . just when I need to." Then she seemed to snarl at a ghost only she could see. "Amelie was right. I'm just a fucking loser."

"What are you talking about? You're not a loser, Hilda." I reached out and put my hand on her shoulder.

Hilda pulled away from me. "You don't even know me."

Without thinking, I hugged her. *She's drunk*, I reminded myself as I tightened my arms around her. *She just needs a friend right now. Someone to watch over her like a guardian angel—*

My thoughts were interrupted by Hilda's hand pressing on the back of my head and pushing me into her chest. Then I realized she was sobbing into my hair.

"It's okay," I mumbled into her shirt. When I turned my face to get some air, I could feel her nipple bar against my cheek. "It's okay," I repeated for my own benefit.

After a long, somewhat strange embrace, Hilda whispered, "Thank you."

I pulled my head back and looked up into Hilda's swollen eyes. "You're not a loser. You're—" *You're my friend.* "You're great. Now come on. While we're at the store, we can get you an energy bar or something so you're not too hungover tomorrow."

Hilda nodded. "Okay."

Longing to ask what Hilda had lost, I instead said, "Can I ask you why you want to go to this convenience store so badly?"

"Walking helps me think. Tonight sucks."

I snorted. "Is it bad to say that I agree? Tonight totally sucks."

"Ja," Hilda responded lightly, seemingly losing her train of thought as the light of the store came into view. "Hey, do you have a tampon in your bag?"

"Y-Yeah, of course," I said as I blushed. "I have a few extras. Do you need one?"

"Ja, wait here." Hilda started to pull my bag off my shoulder.

"Wait. Hilda, my—"

"Your camera, I know." She smiled. "I'll be extra careful. I'm going to look for the bathroom. Can you pick me out an energy bar?"

"I don't know what flavors you like," I said as we walked into the store to the sound of an electronic bell going off.

"Pick one you like then," Hilda said as she immediately turned right and walked down an aisle.

I sighed as I walked toward the candy bars.

"Clare?" a man's voice called, and I turned to find one of my old Bible counselors standing behind the cash register.

"Oh, uh, good evening, Counselor Russell," I said reflexively.

My panicked response made Russell laugh. "I haven't been called 'Counselor' for a long time. What brings you here tonight?"

"Um, I—"

"Hey!" Hilda called from the back corner of the store. "Where is your restroom? I can't find it."

"That's because it's outside," Russell shouted back with a smile. "I got the key up here." He reached under the desk and pulled out a single key attached to a long ruler.

Hilda walked over to the counter, but there was something off about her—besides the fact that she was clearly intoxicated. She was weirdly keeping the left side of her body facing away from us, even as she took the key off the counter and said, "Thanks."

"Wait, are you drunk?" Russell asked.

"No, I'm German," Hilda replied as she began to walk out of the store.

"It's her birthday," I said, doing my best to cover. "She's had some wine."

Russell sniffed the air. "Doesn't smell like wine. More like whiskey."

"It was both." Hilda giggled. "Now, can I go?"

There was a short pause as Russell's eyes darted between us. Then he nodded to himself. "Hey, you mind if I check your bag real quick?"

Hilda's eyes widened as she placed a hand defensively on it. "What—"

"That's actually my bag," I said, assuming Hilda was too embarrassed to admit why she was shielding it so cautiously. "It's just got my camera and a few other things inside."

"Uh-huh," Russell said suspiciously, not really taking his eyes off Hilda. "Just looks a little bigger than I remember it being when you two walked in."

I looked over, and it was strange; my bag did appear to be bulging more than it should have been. "Yeah, that's probably just my camera sitting funny. You remember my old Spectra?"

Russell sighed. "You still have that? I remember the summer you showed up with that thing. You started crying when you ran out of film before we even unloaded the bus."

As Russell and I caught up, I heard the electronic doorbell go off, and when I glanced over, Hilda was gone.

* * *

Russell slammed his fist against the bathroom door on the side of the small convenience store. "Hey! Can you hear me? Did you pass out?" He turned to me. "What's your friend's name?"

"Hilda," I said as I stood beside him and fretted over what could be taking her so long.

"Hilda, if you can hear me, make a noise!" Russell banged on the door again, and then we both listened for any sound from the other side. "Shit."

"Don't you have another key?" I asked.

"No, that was the spare. The other one got stolen. Dammit. Alright, we need to call the police."

My heart stopped beating. My pants were covered in whiskey and I smelled like I'd been drinking all night. Plus, Hilda was drunk—and five years under the legal drinking age. She would surely be arrested. My thoughts jumped to what my mother would do to me if I came home in the back of a police car. I couldn't even fathom the amount of trouble I'd be in. "T-The police? Are you sure?"

"Yeah, unless you know how to pick a lock." Russell must have seen the frightened expression on my face. "Listen, your friend was pretty gone. She could be in real trouble in there." He pulled a cell phone out of his pocket and dialed 911.

I paced up and down the side of the building, berating myself about how I should have known better or done something more to help. Occasionally, I stopped to bang on the bathroom door, trying to get Hilda to respond, but nothing I did worked. I could only pray that she was okay.

Eventually, not only did a police cruiser show up, but also an ambulance and a firetruck. They all tried to get Hilda to respond, but eventually the firefighters had to break down the door with a crowbar.

I tried to see over everyone's shoulders as the firefighters rushed in, but the police officer just told me to stand back. A few moments later, a man came out with a confused look on his face.

"What's wrong?" I gasped.

"There's nobody in there," the firefighter said, more to a police officer than to me.

The police officer turned to me. "I'm going to need a description of your friend. I'll put out a missing persons for her. Don't worry. We'll find her."

I nodded and gave him a brief description of what Hilda looked like while everyone else cleared out. Russell went back inside the shop to call his manager and tell him what happened.

"She's really tall. You can't miss her," I finished nervously, making sure I played down how drunk Hilda really was.

"Yes, you've said that already." The officer looked down at his notepad. "Your friend seems pretty unique, and you painted quite a detailed picture. Now, can I offer you a ride home?"

I shook my head. "No, I'm staying at my friend's house. It's right around the corner."

"Alright. Well, let us know if your friend contacts you."

"I will. Promise."

I didn't dare go back into the store where Russell was probably getting chewed out by his boss, so I just walked back to Ryan's house, wondering where in the world Hilda could have gone. I made a mental note to never go to that convenience store again.

Hearing Max from the front of the house made me sprint through the open garage and toward the back door. I needed to get Devon and Max in the car so we could go searching for Hilda. I needed to know she was . . . sitting with Max, Ryan, and Michelle?!

I froze. My poor heart, unsure of what to be feeling, leaped into my throat. My four supposed friends each had a shot glass in front of them with what looked like a half-empty bottle of whiskey and a two-liter of soda in the center of the table.

"Okay!" Hilda announced, not registering I was standing in the doorway. "Now it's Max's turn."

"Never have I ever . . ."

"Had sex," Devon said with a grin.

Everyone burst into laughter, but Max shouted, "Hey! It's my turn, asshole!"

"I'll count that," Hilda said, pointing at Max with a familiar ruler with a key dangling from one end. "If you've never had sex, you drink."

Max and Michelle both raised their glasses. I might have been surprised to know Michelle was a virgin had I not been so furious.

"Okay, reload," Hilda announced as she grabbed the whiskey bottle.

"What the fuck, Hilda!?" I swore, shocking even myself. Everyone—and I mean *everyone*—at the party looked directly at me.

"Clarissa!" Hilda beamed at me like there was nothing wrong. "Come sit down! We're playing a game."

"Are you kidding me?!" Fury boomed through my voice. "I thought you had passed out in the bathroom and the fire department had to break the freaking door down! I had to tell the police what you look like, and now they're looking for you!"

"The police?" Hilda said. "I don't—"

"Wait!" Max gasped. He looked at the bottle of whiskey sitting on the table, then up to Hilda. "You stole this?!"

"I—" Hilda began.

"Get rid of that!" Ryan shouted.

Everyone stood up. Michelle ordered Lin to turn off the music and shut the garage door while Ryan grabbed Max and Devon to help him throw all the beer cans and plastic cups away. Hilda vanished. No sooner had Ryan picked up the first empty can of beer than a police siren blasted from the front of the house, followed by red and blue lights flooding out the back door. Everyone in the backyard froze, and I felt the blood drain from my face.

"Hello?" an adult voice called a few moments later. "This is officer John Fielder with the Grand Forks Police Department. Can someone come out here please?" Everyone's eyes fell to Ryan, who looked like a deer caught in the headlights. "Is everything okay? I repeat, this is officer John Fielder with the Grand Forks PD."

"Uh, everything's cool!" Ryan called back as he gave us all a worried look. "I'm coming out! Please don't shoot me or whatever . . ."

Once Ryan was gone, nobody said anything until Lin muttered, "Way to go, Huffington. This'll be the second time you've ruined someone's life at a birthday party."

My eyes fell to the ground, and I said weakly, "It's not like I meant to."

"Oh, you're even going to use the same excuse?" Lin scoffed. "It'd be comical if it wasn't so fucking pathetic."

I gulped and tried to explain. "I—"

"Shut up!" Lin barked. "Nobody gives a shit."

"Hey," Devon said sharply. "We should be keeping our voices—"

"Fuck you most of all, DeVille!" Lin said furiously but then looked me right in the eyes. "You sending all those naked pictures of Veronica to everyone at her birthday party was completely unforgivable. Did it even fucking occur to you that Veronica needed help?! How did you even think taking pictures—"

"That was my idea," Devon said. "Don't try to put this all on Clare. I'm equally—"

"You didn't take the fucking pictures! You don't have the fucking spine to do something so bold." Lin snarled at me again. "Now tell me, was it all because Veronica and Matilda were running against each other for class president? Did you ruin someone's life just so your fucking friend could play princess for one more year?!"

"It was an accident." My voice shook. "I didn't mean to send them to everyone, I swear. I didn't know Devon asked her to do it, either. Veronica was drunk and cornered me. She begged me to take some photos with her phone. I didn't know she was going to... Devon was the first name on the group text, and I wasn't paying attention. I wasn't thinking—"

"No!" Lin walked over and got in my face. "You weren't thinking! And because of that, Veronica's life is completely fucked. And now you're pulling the same shit on Hilda because... what? She tripped you and spilled some fucking whiskey on your pants! Boo-hoo, you're going to be grounded for another weekend. How fucking tragic. Hilda might be sent to jail! You understand that, don't you? Do you even care?"

"I do, but—"

"Shut up!" Lin shouted.

Max stepped up next to me and pounded his chest like some sort of barbarian. "Hey! Are you fucking crazy? Keep your voice down."

Lin sneered at Max. "Oh look, everyone, here comes white knight Max to save the holy coward. What are you gonna do, big guy? I don't see a football anywhere. You sure you can function without it?"

Hilda staggered out of the house and into the backyard. "Why'sss everyone yelling? Lin, we need to go, ja?"

"Lin can't drive right now," I said. "She's been—" Lin suddenly shoved my collarbone hard, and I stumbled back into Max.

"Don't tell me what I can and can't do, Huffington!"

"Hey! Don't touch Clare!" Max said as he stepped in front of me and pointed a threatening finger in Lin's face.

"Come on, big guy. Do it," Lin said defiantly. "Do it and see what happens."

Devon appeared out of my peripheral vision, attempting to sandwich himself between Lin and Max. "Hey! Did you all suddenly lose your minds? There are cops literally out front right now. Now will you both shut up and—"

Hilda suddenly clutched her stomach and hunched over a bush.

My instinct was to run over to her. "Hey, I think there's something wrong with—"

Lin caught my arm and spun me to face her. "Hey! I was talking to you!"

"That's it, bitch!" Max roared, throwing Devon off him and charging into Lin.

Devon shouted, then regained his footing enough to run at Max's back.

My heart thundered in my chest as debilitating shockwaves of fear gripped my body like I was being crushed in God's fist. In front of me, limbs blurred and grunting sounds combined into a symphony of horror.

I squeezed my eyes shut so hard that they started to water—or maybe I had begun to cry. My only thoughts were constant reminders that I was innocent, that none of this was my fault. *As long as I don't move, I'll be okay. God won't punish me if I don't do anything.* A sudden *thud* followed by a cry of pain made me open my eyes. Max had managed to throw Lin to the ground.

"Enough!" Hilda roared. She was storming toward Max, her hoodie discarded on the ground behind her. Her whole upper body was covered in dark bruises. There was a fury in her body language. It reminded me so much of my mother.

"No . . ." I whispered. "Please don't be like—"

"Shut up, Huffington!" Lin said as she scrambled to her feet.

"Lin!" Hilda barked before turning her attention to Max. "Are you going to apologize?"

Max crossed his arms. "Fuck no. She started it."

The corner of Hilda's lip twitched, but then she nodded. "Fine."

As Hilda turned to leave, I finally felt like I could get a full breath. *Thank you, God—*

Then Max put his arm around my shoulder and drew me close, nodding at Hilda. "You really need to keep your bitch on a leash, Hilda. Haha—"

I watched Lin's lip curl as she snapped and rushed Max—us—with her right arm cocked back.

Max brought his arms in to block, but his elbow hooked around my neck, slamming my face into his chest. Before I could break free and run, something hard cracked against the side of my skull. I looked up to see Hilda's hand pulling back.

I screamed, dropping to the ground and holding both of my hands over my head.

Everything was spinning as my head throbbed and the taste of blood filled my mouth; my nose had begun to bleed again. Shadows moved across me and shoes ricocheted off of my legs as war raged above me. Inescapable grunts, curses, and shouts echoed from every direction.

A deep, commanding voice split through the cacophony of sounds like a bomb. "What the hell is going on back here?!"

"Fuck!" I heard Lin gasp. "Hilda, run!"

* * *

While it was Devon's turn to get interviewed by Officer Fielder, Max informed me about what had happened. Lin and Hilda had both jumped Ryan's fence when Ryan came into the backyard with the police officer. Max assured me the two would be punished after the police tracked them down. He must have thought that would make me feel better, but it only made my guilt-ridden frustrations worse.

Once everyone had given their accounts of the evening to Officer Fielder, we were all forced to call our parents. My mother insisted that I be driven home in the back of a police car, "just to remember what it felt like." Being in the back of the squad car vanquished the idea that I'd done nothing wrong. The metal bars that separated the front seats from the back made clear that whatever sin I had committed at the party would damn me to Hell forever. Officer Fielder tried to get me to smile a few times, but I just kept my eyes locked on my knees and sniffled the whole ride home.

I couldn't remember a time when I'd been so disappointed in myself. I kept imagining how easily things could have gone differently, if only I hadn't gone or hadn't followed Hilda to the convenience store.

Yet even after all the horrible things that happened, the worst part was knowing that Hilda hit me. *The police are going to hunt her down, and she'll probably get expelled or have her scholarships revoked.* Lin was right; I ruined her life, and that was why Hilda hit me. I clenched my fists, hating those facts only slightly less than I hated myself.

Officer Fielder and I stood on the porch of my house as he recounted to my parents what happened at Ryan's party. Even without the red and blue lights from his squad car illuminating our neighborhood, I was sure everyone on the block was peering out of their blinds. I could feel their judgment on my back, knowing the situation would only further infuriate my mother.

"That's it," Officer Fielder said, closing his notepad. "If it's any consolation, despite the smell, you'll both be pleased to know your daughter hasn't had anything alcoholic to drink this evening. I breathalyzed everyone. And if I'm honest, I feel that out of all the people I spoke with this evening, your daughter is the least at fault. Seems to me like she was just in the wrong place at the wrong time."

"Thank you, Officer," Dad said as he shook Fielder's hand. "That'll help."

No, it won't.

"And the other children," my mother said, "the ones who had been drinking or ran away. They'll be properly punished, yes?"

Officer Fielder nodded. "I can assure you that all of the parents of those who stayed were contacted in some capacity. As for the two girls who jumped the fence, we'll be contacting the school tomorrow to get their records, and their parents will be notified that way."

I flinched as the knife of guilt in my chest twisted.

"Thank you, Officer," my mother said with a curt smile. "This won't happen again." The way she looked at me made all of my other thoughts stop. I felt my fists start to shake as I struggled to refrain from grabbing the officer by the arm and begging him to take me anywhere that wasn't beyond the stained-glass cross looming above my front door.

The front door shut behind me, and then I heard the click of the bolt lock as my mother slammed it into place. "Clarissa," she said evenly. "You are to go to your room and pray for God's forgiveness."

The mild treatment shocked me into speaking. "But you heard Officer Fielder. I didn't do anything—"

"You lied to us!" my mother snapped, the fury returning to her voice in a heartbeat. "And I don't care what the officer said. Do you have any idea what an embarrassment this is for your father and me!? What will people at church think!? Your father might as well kiss his bid for reelection goodbye. Do you have any idea what you've done!?" I looked to my father for some sort of consolation but found him deep in his own thoughts. "Don't look at your father," my mother barked. "Now go to your room!"

Hanging my head, I nodded and climbed the stairs to my room, not daring to look anywhere but at my own feet. Hours must have passed as I prayed on my knees, but my heart wasn't in it. My thoughts were consumed by reenactments of the party. *I should have said something sooner or pushed for Hilda to tell me what* had been bothering her. *I should have been a better role model so she didn't feel the need to steal that bottle of whiskey. Why was Lin so mean to me? I've never even done anything to her.*

It isn't fair! My clasped hands tightened as my fingertips pressed into my white knuckles. *None of this is fair!*

Suddenly, I felt a shadow in my doorway.

"I-I wasn't sleeping," I stuttered as my mother entered with an empty laundry basket. I wanted to ask what she was doing, but I didn't dare.

My mother barely even acknowledged I existed as she walked over to my photo wall and began unpinning pictures and dropping them into her basket.

"W-What are you doing?" My voice shook.

My mother shot me a sharp look that made me feel so small and helpless. It was my room. It was my space. My mother shouldn't have been allowed to make me so terrified there. Yet there I was, kneeling beside my bed, as still as a statue with my eyes locked forward, waiting for whatever came next.

I felt my mother's shadow move across my back as she went to my desk. "Clarissa." At first, I swore Hilda was calling my name, but when I looked over to my door, I found my mother glaring at me. My wall of cherished memories and the only thing in my life that I controlled was barren and lifeless. "Follow me," she ordered.

I heard crackling fire before we reached the bottom of the stairs. The cozy smell reminded me of winter days spent making hot chocolate with Devon and Veronica after we played in the snow.

My mother turned into the den, but when I followed, there was nothing pleasant or nostalgic about the blaze burning inside our stone fireplace. It was something summoned from Hell, and my mother had brought it to our home to teach me a lesson.

"Kneel here." My mother pointed to a spot I knew was too close to the fireplace, but with all my dreams in her hands, I couldn't disobey. The uncontained flames felt like they were licking the entire left side of my body. "When I was your age," my mother began, looking into the fire. "I had a collection of dolls. I loved them so much, but then . . . then I got caught with a boy. Your grandmother taught me a very important lesson, one I would never forget. I thought I could save you before we needed to cross this bridge, but I can see that you've strayed away from me."

A weak "please" was all I could manage.

My mother turned her head to look me in the eyes, but she wasn't angry or sad; she just looked disappointed. Without any warning, her arm cocked back. I stuttered forward to try and stop her, but it was too late. The first thing to crack on the back wall of the fireplace was my Spectra, followed by an explosion of polaroids and glossy paper.

There was a moment when I just watched it all burn in horrified disbelief. I blinked and came to my senses. Frantically, I grabbed at whatever hadn't fully made it into the fire or spilled out onto the stone. Flames lashed out at my fingertips and face, but I didn't care. All that mattered was that I saved as much of my life as I could. A hand gripped the back of my shirt, tightening the fabric around my neck, but I continued to scramble and pull picture after picture out of the inferno and hold them to my chest. I nearly screamed as my mother yanked me back.

"This!" my mother roared as she tore whatever I had managed to recover out of my arms. "This is just a taste of what Hell is like. It's that feeling for eternity. Do you understand?" I could hardly breathe, let alone muster the strength to reply as I lay sprawled on the floor. "There will be no further punishments, but I want you to remember this feeling, Clarissa. I want you to know what Hell feels like."

8

Hilda and a Hard Place

The Monday after Ryan and Michelle's party, I was stuck alone with Matilda at lunch, and by the look on her face as I set my tray on the table, she wasn't going to even give me a breath before she started in on me.

"Where's your camera?" she asked.

As flippantly as I could, I said, "I don't do that anymore."

"What?" Matilda gasped. "Am I hearing this right? Clare Huffington is giving up—"

"Stop. Just . . . leave it alone. Okay?"

Matilda held up her hands like I was about to rob her. "Alright, jeez. I figured your mom would have flipped when you got home in the police car, so I was just wondering if you're okay. Speaking of the police, did you hear Hilda's name get called out on the PA system last period? I heard that the police arrived looking for her. They walked her off-campus in her PE uniform. Talk about embarrassing."

I gritted my teeth in frustration but tried my best to sound uncaring. "Yeah, the police officer who dropped me off last night told my mom that would happen."

Matilda raised an eyebrow at me. "And you didn't bother to tell me that . . . because?"

Hot air shot out of my nostrils. "It's not like I could, could I? My mom took away my phone because of last night's stupid party, and it's not like we have any classes together, Matilda. How was I—"

"Whoa, calm down," Matilda interrupted. "I was just joking—"

"I don't care!" I shouted, louder and more forcefully than I intended.

Everyone around our table, including those at other tables, looked over at me.

"What?!" I barked at nobody in particular. "I'm sure you've all heard what happened by now?" Several people looked confused while others seemed unsure about what was happening. "I'm going—" *To the bathroom? Matilda would follow me. Home? I can't.* Without finishing my sentence, I stood up and walked away.

The next day each step up the metal ramp to Stantin's class made me more and more anxious. I knew Hilda would be there because we had homework due, and she skipped class entirely yesterday. She was seated when I walked in, and she barely looked up from her notebook to acknowledge me. White gauze peaked out from beneath her long-sleeved shirt as it hung off her right shoulder. It didn't look like a solid cast, just a bunch of medical gauze unevenly held in place with metal fasteners. *Oh my God! You didn't resist arrest or something, did you?*

Noticing my shocked look, Hilda mumbled something and pulled up her shirt.

I silently vowed that I would do everything I could to fix Hilda's life. *This is not going to end like it did with Veronica. I'll find something to make things better . . . because I can't deal with this tension anymore.*

"Hey." I poked Hilda in the shoulder during the morning announcements. "Can we talk?"

Hilda rolled her eyes and barely turned her head. "What do you want, Clarissa?"

Not wanting to meet eyes with her, I looked down to the notes she had scattered in front of her, only to realize what they were. "You didn't do any of the homework?" I gasped. "Stantin always collects right after—"

"I know," Hilda interrupted as she shielded her papers from me. "Believe it or not, I've been in this class all year, too."

Frustrated that I couldn't even say the right thing to her, I looked at my own homework. "Here." I slid my neatly stacked and stapled homework across my desk and turned it so that Hilda could easily transcribe it. "Copy it." I urged out of the side of my mouth. I could see the sudden conflict in Hilda's platinum eyes. "Quick."

Hilda swore under her breath and started copying frantically. Meanwhile, with a smile, I buried my face in my textbook, trying to pretend that I had no idea what was going on.

This was it! It didn't matter that Hilda had attacked me. It didn't matter that I ruined her life, because I could start reforging our friendship. Was this a slightly illegal way to go about it? Sure, but as long as nobody ever found out, we would be fine.

As the morning announcements wrapped up, I glanced over my book to see how much time Hilda had left, but our teacher wasn't at his desk. My breath hitched when I saw Stantin standing near one of the bookshelves with both of his arms crossed. He was watching Hilda copying my notes. I went to move them, but he shook his head, letting Hilda figuratively forge her own death warrant.

Completely oblivious that most of the class was watching her, Hilda dutifully copied my homework over the ending prayer of the morning announcements. Stantin's palm slammed against Hilda's desk.

"Fuck!" Hilda shouted, nearly falling backward out of her chair.

"That's it, Miss Bernhardt!" Stantin swiped his hand across the desk, collecting his evidence. "You're out of my class! Report to the dean's office immediately."

It didn't take long for Hilda to realize what happened, and instead of hanging her head or leaving the class in shame, she grabbed her backpack and stood as if she couldn't care less. At the door to the classroom, with all eyes on her, she coolly blew Stantin a kiss and flipped him an impressive middle finger. Everyone gasped.

"That's it. You're—" Stantin started.

"Suspended?" Hilda finished for him, snorting. "Wouldn't be the first time." Then, in a burst of sunlight, she was gone.

An impossibly still silence fell across the classroom. It was finally broken by Lin saying, "Holy shit."

"That's a pink slip, Miss Cho!" Stantin barked before looking right at me. "Miss Huffington, please see me after class." He marched up to his desk, picked up the red emergency phone mounted to the wall, and started quietly spewing words into the receiver as he wrote on a pink slip for Lin. All I could think was that this was Hilda's third—and final—strike. I had officially ruined her life forever.

After class, I walked up to Stantin's desk like I was on trial for murder. My heart was pounding, and I wasn't sure what I was in trouble for.

"Miss Huffington." Stantin flipped two papers across his desk so I could read them. The first was my homework, and the second was Hilda's copied version. She'd at least managed to not copy it word for word, but it was still obviously a copy. "Were you allowing Miss Bernhardt to copy your homework?"

"N-No." I stuttered as my heart choked me. "We're not even friends."

Stantin hummed, running his gaze up and down me. Finally, he gestured to the door. "Alright. You're free to go."

I gulped. "I'm not in trouble?"

Stantin narrowed his dark eyes at me. "You just admitted to not doing anything wrong."

"Right, sorry. See you tomorrow, Mr. Stantin."

The fresh air hit my lungs, and I wanted to burst into tears. I felt stuck in a loop where trying to get closer to Hilda seemed to result in hurting her. Something tickled my sixth sense as if someone was watching me. When I looked around, I found Lin glaring at me from across the walkway. She didn't say anything, but something about the way she had her arms crossed told me she wanted to talk.

I swallowed my fear and walked over to her. "What do you want, Lin?"

Lin's lips curled slightly, but she took a deep breath and said, "I wanted to say that I'm sorry." I flinched in disbelief. "Don't give me that look, Huffington. I don't want your fucking pity. I was drunk, and I'm sorry."

I stuttered, unsure of what exactly Lin was apologizing for. "I, uh . . . thanks, but—"

"This doesn't make us friends," Lin interrupted, pressing a finger into my chest. "Now, before I go find Hilda and convince her to not drop out of school, I need to know something. Were you letting her cheat off your homework?"

I glanced around nervously and then whispered, "Yeah."

Lin sighed, pinching the bridge of her nose and muttering, "Why?"

"I just . . . I wanted to try and make things right. And before you ask, yeah, I'm really pissed at Hilda for the way she acted, but that doesn't mean I want to see her . . . drop out." I gulped. "You have to understand, I didn't mean to get her suspended or anything, either. I was just trying to—"

"You know I got suspended, too, don't you?" Lin interrupted. "Whatever, I gotta go."

"Wait," I said as Lin turned. "Can you please tell Hilda that . . . that I'm sorry. For everything. And that I don't want her to drop out." *I miss her.*

Lin hesitated as she ran her eyes over me. "I'll think about it."

9

Fazerrati's

The empty seat beside me in Stantin's class had become a constant reminder that my friendship with Hilda was likely damaged beyond repair. Still, I caught glimpses of her in the hallways, so I knew she hadn't dropped out. Had Stantin made true on his promise and actually dropped her from his class? Was she skipping first period again? Had she lost any of her scholarships? All I knew for sure was that Hilda was avoiding me. Now, when I arrived at the lunch table, conversations died down and topics quickly changed. Matilda was cordial enough, but I always got the hint that she was placating me.

On Friday night, Devon managed to get me over to his house to study. Not that I needed to, immersing myself in homework was the only thing that took my mind off of my self-loathing. I knew that leaving the house unannounced was wrong, that taking my mother's car without asking was wrong, and that taking my phone from my mother's hiding place would get me in trouble, but there was nothing left for her to take from me.

I could hear the rain and hail crash against Devon's window as

I lay on his bed and transcribed his notes onto flashcards. The atmosphere would have been reminiscent of when we did sleepovers as kids had it not been for the strange silence between us. It was awful, like we didn't even know each other.

After nearly an hour of that, Devon sighed heavily. "So are you ever going to talk about what's been bothering you? I mean *really* talk about it. Not just pretend that everything's normal like you've been doing at school for the past week. I mean, I don't think I've seen you take a single picture. What's up?"

I gulped. Devon deserved to know about how my mother destroyed my Spectra and all of my photos, along with . . . everything else. Right as I built up the courage to talk, I was interrupted by my cell phone ringing.

"Who is it?" Devon asked.

"I don't know," I said, looking at the caller ID. "It's our area code. Should I answer?"

"It's probably a spam call. Gimme." Devon excitedly gestured for me to toss him my phone. Once I did, he answered pompously, "Hello, you've reached God's cell phone. He's not in right now. This is Jesus speaking on behalf of the Holy Ghost. How may I direct your call?" I cracked a smile and tried desperately to eavesdrop, but all I heard was muffled speaking on the other end of the line.

Devon's face contorted in confusion. "Hilda?" I sat upright. "No, it's Devon. Clare's at my house. No, we're studying. How did you get this number?"

I heard Hilda say "Veronica," but everything else was too mumbled to discern. All I could do was watch Devon grimace while Hilda continued to speak.

Once Hilda finished talking, he leaned back and looked up at his ceiling. "I don't know. Why would—"

Probably knowing that I was struggling to keep seated, Devon held up a finger for me to wait as he spoke. "Alright, fine. But if this is just some weird prank or—" A few agonizing seconds passed until she stopped speaking. Rubbing his temple with one hand, Devon said, "Alright, I'll have her leave right now."

The second Devon hung up, a cascade of questions flooded out of my mouth. "What did Hilda want? Why did she call me? What's going on?" Devon didn't answer right away, keeping an annoying grin plastered on his face. "Stop looking at me like that and say something."

Devon seemed deep in thought as he eyed me with concern. "Hilda needs a ride home, and I told her you would do it, but if you want, I can."

"Why don't we go together?" *That way, it won't be so awkward.*

Devon shook his head. "I need to finish this paper. I was only offering to be polite."

"Alright," I said, standing up and grabbing my mother's keys off of Devon's desk. "I'll be right back."

Sheets of rain cascaded across my windshield and sounded like a hurricane. The wipers were on their fastest setting and hardly kept up with the downpour. When I pulled up across from the address Devon had entered on my phone's GPS, I saw Hilda right away. She was standing under a long awning with a group of leather-jacketed bikers. Each of the men looked more intimidating than the last, and I couldn't believe Hilda was laughing along with them.

Nervously, I pressed my palm against the steering wheel, trying to summon the courage to announce my presence. I didn't know why, but my hand was trembling, and I couldn't move until the largest man seemed offended by something Hilda had said. He swiftly made a step toward her. In a jolt, I slammed my hand down, honking loudly.

Everyone across the street from me stopped and looked over. I quickly rolled down my window and yelled, "Hilda, I'm over here! Come on!"

Hilda said quick goodbyes to the bikers as I rolled up my window. A few seconds later, she was opening the passenger door and getting inside.

"You're soaked," I said, adjusting the vents to blast the heater toward Hilda.

Hilda giggled. "Uh, ja, it's raining outside, Clarissa."

"I hadn't noticed," I sassed back. "Who are they?"

"The guys?" Hilda didn't even look over. She was more focused on warming her hands on the heater vents. "Or Richard?"

I was slightly concerned that she said "the guys" like she was part of a gang or something. "Was Richard the guy who was about to punch you?"

Hilda tilted her head at me. "What are you talking about?"

My stomach clenched with worry, but I had to ask, "That's not your boyfriend or something, is it?"

Hilda blinked hard. Then she burst into laughter. It felt great to hear her laugh again, but I didn't allow myself to enjoy it fully.

"It's nothing like that," Hilda said, waving the thought away. "He's like my boss most of the time. You think I would be into older men? Very wrong." She paused. "Do you mind if I . . . ?" She flipped the bottom of her shirt up.

"I'd rather you"—Hilda peeled her shirt off—"didn't." I said the last bit weakly, feeling my breath get sucked away. Seeing the bruises all over her body reminded me why I was supposed to be mad at her. I huffed. "Fine, don't listen to me. It's like Ryan's party all over again."

Hilda's shoulders dropped as she draped her shirt over the air vents in front of her. "Sorry."

Luckily, the car was still in park, because it took several seconds for me to pull my eyes away.

Hilda cleared her throat, setting one of her arms across her chest.

Then her stomach growled so loud I heard it over the rain and the heater. Sighing, she admitted, "Sorry, I haven't eaten today."

I did a double-take. "Excuse me? You haven't eaten today?"

"I had a granola bar this morning."

My hands tightened on the steering wheel. I hit the rim of the steering wheel lightly with the palm of my hand.

"Is everything okay, Clarissa?" Hilda asked cautiously.

I looked over at her, feeling overwhelmed. "No! Everything isn't okay. I'm pissed at you, for one." I hit my blinker, put the car into drive, and pulled out onto the street.

"Do you know where I live?" Hilda rightly asked.

"No, and I don't care." I stopped at a red light, trying to get my bearings. "We're stopping to get you some dinner."

* * *

I held the door open for Hilda as she ran into Fazerrati's, the best pizzeria in Grand Forks. The warmth of the heated interior brought with it the smell of fresh pizza dough and garlic breadsticks.

"Ah, if it isn't my favorite customer!" Mr. Fazerrati said jubilantly from behind the baking counter as I stepped in front of Hilda. "Please seat yourself. I'll be right out with breadsticks, yeah?"

"Thanks," I said as I reached the small podium and grabbed some menus like I'd worked there for years. I led Hilda to a table near the long kitchen window, one of my favorite seats. It was close to the brick oven, so I figured we would dry off faster.

Hilda looked around quizzically as we sat. "I remember seeing pictures of this place on your wall. Do you come here a lot?"

I felt a smile begin, along with a familiar lump in my throat. "You remembered that?" Hilda nodded. "You're right. I had this shot of Mr. Fazerrati spinning a piece of dough in the air with flour spraying everywhere and the oven behind him. It was perfect."

"Had?" Hilda asked curiously. When I shook my head, she sighed and put a hand on her chin. "There was a restaurant in Berlin like this. I only got to go once with Amelie. It was very expensive."

There's that name again. "Well, tonight is my treat." I forced a polite smile but found it came easier than I'd expected. I peered up and found I was shielding my face with the menu. The night of Ryan's party flashed before my eyes. *She attacked me. I can't just forgive her for that.*

Mr. Fazerrati approached our table. "Buonasera," he said with his signature Italian accent. "The breadsticks will be out shortly. I know you like them fresh." He gave me a friendly nudge. "So! Can I get you started with some drinks?"

I said, "Water's fine for me. Thank you."

"Water is fine," Hilda echoed.

The burly chef chuckled. "I should just give you two empty glasses. Plenty of that outside tonight." Then he walked away to fetch our drinks.

After a few minutes of flipping through her menu, Hilda set it down and looked as if she had just resigned herself to say something difficult. "Can I talk to you about something, Clarissa?"

"Sure," I said, hating that Hilda got to start the conversation, although that was better than sitting there in awkward silence all night. "What's up?"

"It's about Ryan and Michelle's party. I know I said it in the car, but . . . I'm sorry, and I owe you an explanation. Something happened the night before the party. Something I wanted to forget about. I guess sometimes I want to forget about a lot of things." She swallowed, breaking eye contact with me. "I didn't mean to—"

"To use my bag to steal that bottle of whiskey? Yeah, believe it or not, I didn't like that much, either. Or are you apologizing for leaving me alone at the convenience store? Or are you talking about when you tackled me right when I got to the party and shattered the whiskey Max brought for everyone?"

Hilda recoiled, pulling her arms across her stomach. "All of it." There was a long pause, and then she looked up at me with narrowed eyes. "There's something I don't understand. Why did you tell everyone at school I was the one who punched you?"

I blinked before cautiously saying, "Because you did?"

Hilda shook her head. "No. Lin was the one who hit you, although she was aiming for Max. I was trying to stop her. I reached out to grab you, to pull you away from them, but you dropped to the ground. Then the police officer came back, and Lin told me to run, so I ran."

I was at a loss for words. "Wait, if you knew you didn't hit me, why didn't you say anything after you heard all the rumors?"

Hilda pursed her lips. "I was scared."

My body tensed up. "You . . . You were scared . . . of me?"

Hilda scoffed. "You're one of the most popular people at school, and it was your word and Max's against mine. Who would ever believe me, even if I told the truth?" Hilda looked at me earnestly, but we both knew the answer. "So, what's good here?"

"The food," I answered sarcastically, realizing then that Hilda was still hiding so much from the world, maybe even from herself. *I get it.*

Hilda caught my gaze and cocked an eyebrow. "So that's how it's gonna be?"

I leaned back, smirking. "That's how it's gonna be. Listen, since we're laying all our cards on the table, I need to get something off my chest."

Hilda batted her eyelashes at me. "But your shirt is completely dry."

It took me a moment to get the joke, after which I rolled my eyes. "God, you're worse than Max. But seriously, I didn't know all that stuff would happen. I didn't mean to ruin your life. I was just worried about you."

"Y-You were?"

"Hilda, the police were called in the first place because Russell thought you had passed out in the bathroom. I thought you were dead or something. Also, I've been dying to ask what happened with the police. There have been a lot of rumors."

Hilda sighed. "I bet, but it's really nothing. I got taken down to the police station, where my father was called. I wasn't even put in a jail cell or anything. Once my dad showed up, the officer explained what happened, and I went home."

"That's all?" I asked, flabbergasted that Hilda didn't get in more trouble.

She eyed me suspiciously. "Clarissa, I got drunk in a backyard and stole a bottle of whiskey. I wasn't stealing the *Mona Lisa*, although my dad drove me back to the store, apologized for the trouble, and forced me to pay for the bottle and damaged door. That really cut into my savings, but my dad said it would teach me a lesson."

"You're not grounded or anything?"

Hilda shook her head. "No. My dad doesn't really do that, and it's not like he could take anything away." Her voice softened as she looked down at her menu. "I really don't have anything."

The similarity of our predicaments took my breath away. We were so different but we . . . We hurt the same. I couldn't take it anymore and said, "You have me."

Hilda's head jerked back as her eyes widened. "What?"

I nodded, and all my hopes that finally confessing everything to Hilda would clear my head vanished in her silver eyes. "I accept your apology." My heart pounded in my chest so loudly I feared the whole restaurant could hear it. Light, fluttery feelings filled my body as the world around me seemed to melt away.

When Hilda smiled and told me that she accepted my apology, too, I didn't really hear her because my eyes were resting on her lips, and I started to realize why.

* * *

Rain continued to pour from the heavens as the headlights on my mother's station wagon struggled to pierce the downpour. The muck and mire of the dirt road leading up to Hilda's house made the tires struggle to grip the ground. Several times, the car nearly stalled out in the mud, but God must have been watching over us. Thankfully, by the time I drove home, all of the evidence would be washed away, and my mother would be none the wiser.

The ominous feeling of the night intensified as we approached what looked like a real-life haunted house. I couldn't believe someone like Hilda could live in a place so cold and detached from the rest of the world. The farmhouse looked like a place that teens went to get murdered in cheap horror movies. Worse, there was a single light coming through one of the downstairs windows. Someone, or something, was awake inside, waiting.

I pulled up alongside a rust-covered pickup truck as Hilda started unwrapping her bandages. "Shouldn't you keep those on?" I asked. She ignored me, stuffing the strips of white gauze into her backpack. That was when I realized the knuckles on her right hand had all the skin torn away. They weren't bleeding, but they were raw and must have stung when she exposed them to the cold air. "Hilda, your hands."

"What's that saying you like so much?" she said with a slight smile. "It's complicated, ja? Well, it's complicated. Clarissa, I—" She turned, and I nearly jumped out of my skin when my eyes were pulled up to meet her own.

"Yeah? What's up?" I swallowed. *Act casual, Clare.* This night had brought us closer together than a thousand outings to the coffee shop could have. Everything about the way I connected with Hilda was different. Even the simple way she laughed made my life a little brighter.

Sounds of rain pattered on the top of the car as we both sat and looked into each other's eyes, neither one of us probably daring to—

Hilda leaned forward ever so slightly. Her gaze fixed on me.

In a fit of panic, I moved away. *Is she—?*

Hilda cleared her throat and broke eye contact, awkwardly pulling her backpack from the floor onto her lap. "Thanks for dinner. Now that I know that pizza is your kryptonite, I'll use it against you."

My mouth found words before my brain could process what almost happened. "For the record, this date was *my* idea. Er, sorry, I didn't mean to call tonight a date. I mean, it was, kind of, but not like—"

"What's in a name?" Hilda interrupted, looking up as rain cascaded down on top of the sunroof. "A rose by any other name would smell as sweet."

I tilted my head. "Okay, I gotta know now. What's with you and Shakespeare?"

Hilda hummed. "Amelie once talked me into auditioning for Viola in *Twelfth Night*. She was in an after-school club, which she also convinced me to join." Hilda reached up, touching the sunroof, and left an outline of her warm hand on the cold glass. "I think we were both surprised when I got the part. At the end of my first performance, I saw my father standing in the back of the auditorium. He wasn't clapping or anything, and he's never spoken about it, but I'd like to think he was proud of me. After that, I fell in love with Shakespeare, and I did as many plays as I could get parts for."

"Oh, that's, uh, cool. I didn't know you could act," I fumbled, trying to think of something equally as profound. "I like Shakespeare, too, although I've only read *The Tempest* outside of school assignments." After a minute of silence, as the rain drummed out its song on the car, I summoned up the courage and asked, "Who's Amelie?"

"She was a friend, and . . . and we got into a big fight before I moved here." Still looking up at the heavens, she whispered, "Amelie was special."

An awful tension pulled at every fiber of my being. I wanted to ask a question, but I couldn't focus. *Reach out to her.* My hands tightened on the steering wheel, anchoring themselves in place.

My mouth opened and I began to speak so softly that it might have been inaudible against the rain. "Hilda, I—"

"I should have enough money to go shopping soon," Hilda interrupted, finally looking at me. "I was going to talk to you about it a while ago, but since I had to dip into my savings, it set me back. A few people have mentioned a large mall close by. Do you know about it?"

"Um, yeah. Rockridge Mall. It's one of the largest in the state." I did my best to talk casually, but my thoughts were resting gently on Hilda's lips or her starry eyes or the shaved side of her head. My heartbeat skipped as my eyes made their way to her chest and then her hips.

Swirls of buttery emotions shifted inside me, making me feel dizzy. It all felt right. Like, of course Hilda was attractive, yet black hooks and guilty chains anchored themselves to all of the warm feelings.

Hilda, her head slightly cocked, waved a hand in front of my face. "Clarissa? Did you hear what I said? Do you mind driving me to this mall? Lin doesn't like shopping very much, and large crowds make her anxious."

I blinked, realizing suddenly how sinful my thoughts had become. Harder than ever, I focused on being casual and polite. "Y-Yeah. Of course I will."

"Perfect." Hilda nodded at me with a huge grin. "It's a date."

It's not a date. "Alright, it's a date."

"I guess I'll see you next weekend, Clarissa." Hilda moved to open her door.

Not wanting her to leave, I blurted, "We'll see each other at school, too."

"Sure," Hilda said as she stepped into the rain, but before she closed the door, she turned. With rain pouring over her, she stood there, looking back at me. "Goodnight, Clarissa."

"Goodnight, Hilda."

10

Goodbye, Grand Forks

The weekend passed more slowly than frozen molasses after I took Hilda to Fazerrati's. My mother, of course, grounded me, but with my homework finished and as much studying as I could take, I found myself pacing my room and trying to figure out what Hilda meant to me. Devon was upset that I never returned to his house to help him study, which meant I had no one to talk to, no one who would understand if I told them. I didn't even know what I would tell them. That I liked Hilda? That we went on a date and it was like a dream? That I was risking damning my soul to Hell just because I secretly wanted her to kiss me? That Hilda and I shared so many unspoken parts of ourselves?

By the time Monday arrived, I wasn't sure what to do with myself. I lumbered through the hallways, constantly scanning for Hilda. I wasn't even sure what I was going to do when I saw her, but I made a promise that I was going to do . . . something. Each day that passed without sight of her made me feel more paranoid. *Has she finally dropped out? Did she do something that got her expelled?* I wanted to ask Matilda if she knew anything, but Hilda had become a touchy subject ever since I made it one.

By Saturday afternoon, I'd worked myself into such a fretful ball of stress that I almost texted Veronica to ask if she knew anything about Hilda. Instead, I planned to try and corner Kate before I had to leave Max's birthday party.

"Tell me again, why am I the point of contact for this party?" I asked Matilda as we sat in Max's large kitchen while waiting for more people to arrive. "You know if my mother finds out I'm not studying with Devon today, you'll never see me again, right?"

Matilda scoffed. "Duh. Why do you think we're having a party in broad daylight? Also, don't pretend like you don't love every second of this. We all know Max is like a literal caveman when it comes to social media."

"That great insult to cavemen." Devon grunted like a Neanderthal as he shuffled by with two cases of soda. "Me tweet good. Have many follower."

Matilda and I both giggled, and then she said, "I hear Max has something special planned for you this afternoon."

Her tone made my stomach lurch. "W-What? Why would Max have something special planned for me?"

Matilda rolled her eyes. "Why do you think, Clare? I mean, at this point . . . Is it *really* not obvious?"

I sighed heavily. "For the last time, Max and I are done. He'll always be my friend, but I will never date him again. No amount of special surprises is going to change my mind." It felt good to say those words aloud. It made me feel in control of something—myself, maybe.

Dismissing my feelings with a wave, Matilda said, "Uh-huh, we've all heard that before."

My phone buzzed before I could reply. I glanced down at the lock screen and gulped. "Veronica, Lin, and Michelle are coming."

I looked up at Devon. "That reminds me, don't you have to go pick Kate up soon?"

Devon nodded. "Yeah, but we technically have an hour to kill until the party starts. Plus, ladies like it when you make them sweat a little."

Matilda and I shared a skeptical look at my best friend's assumption.

"At least Hilda's not coming," Matilda said, sounding relieved. "She's worse than those three combined."

I scoffed. "What are you talking about? Hilda could show up. You know her habit of crashing parties."

"*Crashing*," Matilda repeated with air quotes. "Also, you didn't hear?"

A lead ball dropped in my stomach. "Hear what?" I asked, trying my best to sound like I didn't care.

Matilda raised an eyebrow at me. "Hilda's been in the hospital all week. I assumed you knew."

My heart leaped into my throat, and I stuttered, "I didn't know. Do you know what's wrong with her?"

"No." Matilda shrugged. "If I'm honest, I really wasn't paying attention when Veronica was talking about it at the last student council meeting. I think it was something to do with those weird contacts she—"

Her eyes! I pulled out my phone and tapped the only contact information I had for Hilda—her work number.

Matilda gasped. "Excuse me, I was talking to you."

I gritted my teeth. "Just a sec, Matilda. I need to call Mick's." *They might know something . . .*

"Mick's?" Matilda asked.

As the phone started to ring, Devon said, "It's where Hilda works downtown. Clare got their number because Hilda needed a ride home the other night."

Matilda looked at me. "You . . . Why didn't you ever tell me about—"

"I can't hear anything," I interrupted, throwing open the door to the backyard and barely avoiding a collision with Max.

"Whoa!" Max struggled to balance some large bags of chips and jars of salsa. "Where's the fire, babe?"

"Stop calling me that. Also, did you know Hilda was in the hospital, too?" My tone was harsher than I had intended.

Max opened his mouth, but just as he began to speak, someone answered the phone.

I pressed a finger to Max's lips as I listened. "Hello, this is Mick's Gym," a man's voice announced.

Breathless, I asked, "Good afternoon, is Hilda there?"

"Hilda?" The man seemed unsure who I was talking about. "Sorry, I think you got the wrong . . . Wait, y'mean Bernhardt? Yeah, she's out front. Who's callin'? This ain't the doctor's office again?"

Relief flooded through me. If Hilda was at work, it wasn't likely she was blind, although the mention of the doctor's office made me anxious. "No. It's Clare. Clare Huffington. I need to talk to her." Then, as I moved around Max to have some privacy, I added, "It's important."

"Alright, kid. Hold your horses. Jesus. Bernhardt, get your ass in here! You got a call!" There was a short pause, then the man continued to shout, "Nah, it ain't the hospital!"

Seconds felt like hours as my heart raced and I waited to hear Hilda explain herself. Fear and frustration mixed as I pushed my phone into my ear.

"Hallo?" Hilda's said, and I finally exhaled.

"Where have you been!?" I demanded, emotionally wrecked.

"What? Clarissa?"

"Yes, oh my God! Matilda just told me you were in the hospital all week! Are you okay?"

"Ja, I'm fine."

I nearly tore my hair out of my skull. "People don't get sent to the hospital for a week without any reason, Hilda. What's wrong?"

There was a long pause before Hilda said, "I . . . I need to talk to you." An unexpected jolt of adrenaline ran through my entire body. "When I was in the hospital, I had a lot of time to think, and I think . . . We need to talk. But I'm in a rush right now. I need to be outside to make sure I don't miss the next bus."

"Why are you getting on a bus? Are you coming to Max's birthday?"

"No, I'm trying to get to Chicago before five. I have the bus schedule printed out, but it's very confusing. It's not like the trains in Europe at all, and my first bus is already late, so it could be coming any minute. I'm sorry, Clarissa, but I need to go."

Quickly checking my phone to see the time, I said, "Hilda, even if the bus showed up right now, I don't think you'll make it."

"Fuck," Hilda swore under her breath. "Then I need to—"

"What if I drive you?" I asked, sidestepping any rational thought. "We could talk the whole drive, too. You know"—I swallowed—"because you wanted to talk to me anyway, right?"

Hilda gasped. "Are you serious? You're not busy? Didn't you say something about a birthday party?"

I hadn't even realized that I'd been pacing Max's long backyard patio. Looking over to the kitchen window, I watched as Devon poured some salsa into a mixing bowl and Max popped the top on a beer can.

The familiar sight made me smile, not because it was funny, but because it was so . . . normal?

If I leave now, there is no way I would be back in time for whatever plan Max has concocted, but I would be back in time to catch the end of the party. Then I could head home without my mother knowing anything. The timing is almost too perfect . . . but I have to leave now.

Smiling, I said, "I can pick you up in ten minutes. Is that okay?" Hilda jubilantly cheered a bunch of words, which I suspected were German. Then again, she sounded so excited it could have been anything. "I'll take that as a yes," I said, feeling my spirits lift. "I guess I'll see you soon?"

"Clarissa! Ahhh!" Hilda squealed. "I can't believe you're doing this for me! You're the best! I'll see you soon."

My heart soaring, I gazed at the sky as I hung up. The summer afternoon was perfect for a drive through the countryside. I was already feeling excited for all of the different conversations we were going to have. Is that cheesy? Because I totally was.

"What was that about?" Matilda startled me. She was standing in the doorway, her eyes narrowed at me. "Who are you going to 'see soon'?"

"I'm going to pick someone up," I said with a tight throat as I did my best to hide my phone.

"Is it Hilda?"

I tried to laugh off my growing anxiety. "Yeah. How'd you guess?"

"Maybe because you practically sprinted out here to call her. Seriously, what's with you and her recently?"

I froze. "What do you mean? Matilda, she was in the *hospital*. I just wanted to make sure she was okay."

"To my knowledge, the last time you and Hilda were together, she punched you, Clare. Although, I guess you two went out to dinner recently, which you didn't bother to tell me about. You know that nobody else likes her, right? In fact, I don't even know why you still do. It's getting a little weird, honestly."

My mind raced, trying to come up with something to say. "I just . . . I happened to mention Max's birthday, and she invited herself." I wasn't proud about throwing Hilda under the bus, but it was all I could think of.

Matilda ran her hand down her face. "It's like—gah! I can't

even with you right now, Clare. Why would you even tell her about the party?"

"It just kind of slipped, but personally, I think we owe Hilda this for spreading that rumor that she was the one who hit me at Ryan's party, and not Lin."

"No," Matilda said, crossing her arms. "I'm not going to apologize. I don't care what Hilda might have told you, but Max told me that he saw Hilda grab you."

"Yeah, she did, but—"

"So you admit it," Matilda interrupted, her smug attitude beginning to drag across my last nerve. "I'm going to be honest," she continued. "I don't think you should go get Hilda. Or hang out with her in general. It's not just me, either. Max and Ryan both agree."

Do they? Nobody's mentioned that to me. Certainly not Max or Ryan.

I shook my head. "You're crazy. Hilda's just . . . I think you never even gave her a chance."

Matilda put a hand on her chest. "I'm crazy? Clare, you want to be friends with someone who punched you in the face, cheats on her homework, gets way too drunk for fun. Are you listening to yourself? It's like I don't even know you any—"

The window to the kitchen slammed open, and Max leaned out. "And on the third day, God created salsa! Whoa, am I interrupting something serious?"

"I don't know," Matilda said to him, then slowly turned her head to glare at me. "Is he?"

Summoning everything I had left, I said, "I'm sorry neither of you like Hilda, but if you knew her like I did, then you'd know she would never hit me."

Max gasped. "Whoa, I never said I didn't like Hilda. Who told you that?"

It was my turn to glare, but Matilda shook her head and sighed.

"Max, you told me the other day how you didn't think Hilda should hang out with us anymore."

"Well yeah," Max said with an uncertain tone. "But that doesn't mean I don't like her. She just doesn't like . . . fit with our group, you know? She's all 'punked' out, and like, she's got those . . ." He raised a hand to his nipple line and shot out his index finger.

"God, Max." Matilda sighed. "Can you not be gross for like two seconds? Hilda punched Clare. How dare you just pretend that didn't happen?"

Max seemed offended. "No, I don't know who hit Clare. I told you that. I told everyone that."

"How do you not know!? You were there."

Max scoffed and rolled his eyes. "I don't know if you've ever been in a fight, Matilda, but stuff happens fast. Devon was like choking me while I fought off Lin and Hilda. There were a lot of fists flying. Anyone could have accidentally hit Clare. It might have even been me."

The sudden admission made me want to hug Max and lift him aloft as a beacon of justice.

Matilda rubbed her temple. "So we're all going to believe the psychopath when she says she didn't do it?"

"I don't understand why you two are still stuck on this," Max said earnestly. "It happened like ten years ago. Can't either of you just, like, let it go?"

"You're right, Max," I said, keeping my eyes locked on Matilda. "Even *if* Hilda was the one who hit me, I forgave her. I like the idea of just moving on."

Matilda's lip curled. "Fine. But when this all ends in flames, don't come crying to me. I'm just going to say, 'I told you so.'"

As Matilda and I walked back into the kitchen, the tension between us was palpable. I could tell by the way she stood across the room from me that the argument was far from over, but I didn't have time to dwell on it. Reaching into my pocket to grab my keys, I gasped. "Crap." Devon drove here because I didn't want my mom driving by his house and not seeing our car out front.

"Did you just curse?" Devon asked curiously.

I shook my head but then regretted it and confessed, "Yeah, listen. Can I borrow your car?"

"Why? It's practically party time," Max said, a bit miffed. "As soon as my brother gets home with drinks, I was going to have you sound the Horn of Gondor."

"Wouldn't it be 'Light the Beacons of Gondor'?" Devon said a bit smugly.

I didn't have time to explain that technically both of them were correct. "Sorry, Max. I kind of promised Hilda I would pick her up just now."

Max glanced at Matilda. "Wait, what? I don't—"

Matilda interrupted. "Why doesn't Devon just pick her up?" She gave me a look that made my blood run cold. "I mean, he needs to go pick up Kate soon anyway, right? Save the gas."

My mouth felt dry as I tried to formulate a counter to Matilda's perfect solution. "Because I said I would?" The awkward tonal quality as I turned the statement into a question at the last second wasn't lost on my three friends, who all shared skeptical looks.

Matilda cocked her head to the side. "Why does that matter?"

I gritted my teeth, trying to think, and then said, "I'm sure Hilda doesn't want to sit around while she waits for Devon to get Kate or vice versa. Also, talk about awkward."

Matilda leaned forward. "Why would it be awkward?"

Getting the third degree from Matilda was as infuriating as it was frightening because I didn't have any answers until I talked to Hilda. I didn't know what we were, or if we were anything. "Well, you know, Devon kind of had a crush on Hilda, right? Wouldn't having Kate in the car—"

Devon cleared his throat. "Point taken." He reached into his pocket and pulled out his keys. "You might as well fill it up while you're out. The premium stuff, too. None of that other garbage."

I nodded. "Full tank. Got it."

Just as I reached out, Devon pulled the keys away. "Not a scratch. Say it."

"Not a scratch," I said, hopping up and snatching the keys from his hand.

Once I had the keys in hand, Max said, "Hey, if you're quick, you'll probably be the first ones back."

I cringed slightly. "Oh, yeah. But I bet you won't even notice I'm gone."

When I turned to leave, my sixth sense sent a shockwave through my body, and I flinched. At first, I thought it was because I remembered that taking Devon's Mustang meant he would need to find another, not-so-glamorous way to pick Kate up. But when I glanced over my shoulder to try and find the cause of my discomfort, I caught Matilda with her eyes narrowed at me and her fist pressed against her mouth.

* * *

Hilda wasn't outside on the sidewalk, so I swallowed my fear and pushed open the old rusty door to Mick's Gym. I silently prayed that she hadn't given up on me and got on the bus. A few large men glanced at me as I stood in the doorway. There was a man shadowboxing while someone shouted numbers at him, and another, heavier-set man was jumping rope as he breathlessly counted to himself.

Being ogled as I walked up to the receptionist's desk made my body start to shake. I felt like I'd walked into a biker bar or some clandestine meeting. There was a secret language happening around me, but it was foreign and scared me. Everyone around me was large, loud, and dangerous. It wasn't a place I felt welcomed.

The wiry-haired man I'd seen Hilda with when I picked her up a few weeks prior set down his newspaper as I approached him. "Can I help you, kid?" he said with a strong southwestern accent.

"I'm . . . Um, no. I mean yes." I gulped and got my thoughts in order. "I'm looking for Hilda."

The older man cocked an eyebrow. "Hilda? Oh!" He clapped his hands together, causing my flight response to make me jump back. The man chuckled. "My, you're a nervous one, ain'tcha?" Then he turned his head and roared, "Bernhardt! Your ride's here!" To my surprise, nobody else in the gym minded the volume. "If you're here for Bernhardt, that must mean you're *the* Clarissa. We just spoke, actually. Y'know, she talks about you a lot. Maybe too much." The man walked out from behind the desk to greet me properly. "Richard Longstreet, co-owner." A warm smile crossed his face, and I felt a little bad about judging him so harshly.

"Pleasure to meet you, Mr. Longstreet. Does Hilda really talk about me?"

"'Course she does. Y'know her father and I used to train together? That was many years ago now. Maybe too many." He rubbed his chin and chuckled again. Then he gestured at a small trophy cabinet near the wall. "See for yourself."

I walked over to the tall case and peered through the glass. "There," Richard said, pointing to a particular photo. It was of two men, one holding a belt above his head and the other standing by his side and holding a much smaller trophy. The one holding the trophy was Richard, in his late twenties, if I had to guess. The man holding the belt had a stern look on his face like he wasn't happy he'd won.

The taller man in the photo looked nothing like Hilda. His straight black hair was the only indication that they were related at all. He looked cold and . . . heartless. This man was *not* who I imagined Hilda's father to be at all. "Are you sure that's Hilda's father?"

"Sure is," Richard said proudly. "He was the best. Then he met Megan. 'Course you know all 'bout that, I reckon, although she was no slouch herself. Both of them competed in the Olympics twice, if memory serves. Shame Megan was taken from us when she was. Only the good die young," he said, itching his chin. "But that's life, I suppose."

"Do you know how Hilda's mother died?" I asked softly, looking for any pictures of women in the trophy cabinet and not finding any.

"Even the fastest woman on Earth can't outrun cancer, kid, though that didn't stop her from setting a few records. Just like all the greats, she was never truly satisfied. Then . . . she got diagnosed. It was the aggressive kind. The kind there ain't no coming back from. Why'd'ya think Bernhardt's so obsessed with running everywhere? I've offered her my old bike twice. She keeps saying she'll take it and fix it up, but we both know she ain't gonna. So, you and our little champ have any plans after? Chicago's big. Lot of trouble two young ladies can get into."

"I'm actually just dropping Hilda off. I'm not staying."

Richard frowned. "Too bad. You're gonna miss out. Ain't nobody as driven as Bernhardt, and I don't say that shit lightly. She gets it from her parents, no doubt. I ain't never met a stubborner pair of people. They were perfect for each other."

I gulped nervously because I was starting to get the feeling that whatever Hilda was involved in wasn't entirely legal. "You know, I've been meaning to ask—"

"Clarissa!" Hilda cheered as she walked out of the back. She was wearing a dark-blue loose-fitting band shirt and black sweatpants and had a large overstuffed duffle bag slung over her shoulder. It was a rare occasion where she hadn't done her makeup, but even still, she was—

No, I can't think about that until I find out if she tried to kiss me or not.

"H-Hey," I muttered, stopping myself from hugging her by wrapping an arm across my chest.

"What? No hug?" Hilda said as if she could read my mind. "So much for 'all Huffingtons being huggers.'"

I rolled my eyes but felt my cheeks flush all the same.

Outside, Hilda looked up and down the street and then asked, "Where's your mother's car?"

"Oh," I said, feeling a smile stretch across my face. "I pulled some strings." I hit the button on the key fob that unlocked Devon's Mustang.

Hearing Hilda wolf-whistle as we walked over to the car made me regret making fun of Devon for constantly showing off his car. *I get the appeal now.*

* * *

Hilda had been oddly silent, and by the time we pulled onto the freeway, I couldn't take it anymore. "So, uh, did you . . . I mean, why were you hospitalized?" I kicked myself for chickening out and not asking if Hilda had tried to kiss me or if I had just misinterpreted it.

"Fatigue," Hilda replied simply.

"That's it? You were hospitalized for a week because you were tired?"

Hilda giggled, but it was soft. "Sounds pretty lame when you say it like that, but ja."

"I didn't mean it like—"

Hilda waved, interrupting me. "I didn't eat for almost twenty-four hours, and then I decided to go for a run home at night to clear my head. Because of the stress I put my body under, my monochromatic ocular hypoplasia flared up, and . . . I kinda ran right into a parked van." I gasped, not even knowing where to begin. Then she added, "But the best part is that I set off the van's alarm. It was the only reason someone found me before the morning."

"You didn't eat for a whole day?" I asked.

Hilda shook her head. "I've been too tired recently."

"Too tired to eat!? Hilda, that's like . . . I don't even know."

Hilda sighed, watching the countryside go by for a while before she spoke. "I just want to be the best like my mom was."

I snorted. "I'm pretty sure your mother would have wanted you to eat. Also, your father was famous, too, right?"

"Ja. How did you know that?"

"Mr. Longstreet showed me a picture of your dad. He told me your mom held the world record for the fastest mile. That's pretty amazing." Hilda didn't say anything after I finished speaking. When I glanced over, she was looking at her knees with a frown. "I'm sorry. I—"

"My father thinks I'm going to make the same mistakes he did. When he first met my mom, he took some time off. Then I happened. I don't think he ever wanted kids. It's hard to be a father when you're spending your whole life traveling between matches or self-promoting. He lost a lot of his edge for us. For me. When he went back, he pushed too hard, too fast, and hurt his arm. After that, he always found an excuse to do something else other than spending time with me. I had Mom, so I didn't mind much. But now, after the hospital and everything else at school, I'm sure he thinks I'm worthless." She dropped her shoulders and hung her head.

"You're not worthless. You're the best runner—"

"I don't want to be a runner. I want to be a boxer. My mother and I promised each other that one year we would both win Olympic medals. After she died, I swore to do it anyways. But at every turn, I just make the same mistakes my father told me I would. He knows I'll fail. He knows everything I do fails. I . . .

I'm afraid to fall asleep, Clarissa. Scared more than ever that I'll wake up in complete darkness, but the doctors said not sleeping is bad for me, too. They tell me my eyes need time to rest, but I'm failing so many classes that I have to stay out late for work and wake up early. I'm trying, but it's so hard. I'm just fucked, and it's not fair."

I took a deep breath, and then I reached over and grabbed Hilda's hand. "Please don't curse around me."

"Clari—"

"There's still plenty of time to get your grades up before we graduate. I mean, Devon and I have probably taken most of your classes, so I'm sure we can help."

"Clarissa—"

"And maybe I can work something out with Devon where we can swap picking you up from your house in the morning. Then we can all finally leave Grand Forks, and I can have my own—" *Life.*

"Clarissa," Hilda gasped, gritting her teeth. "You're hurting my hand."

"Huh?" Then I realized that my knuckles were turning white as I squeezed tightly. "Oh my God! I'm so sorry. I hope I didn't hurt you."

Shaking out her hand, Hilda giggled. "Who knew such soft and delicate hands could be hiding such a strong grip? I'm jealous."

I snorted.

After several miles of unusual silence as I tried to come up with a rational reason for why someone would be willing to subject themselves to such a violent sport, I finally said, "Why boxing?"

Hilda sighed. "It's funny. You sound like my mom. She also hated the idea of my boxing. But as much as we don't get along now, the few times when I was younger that Dad and I sparred were some of the best times I remember. I couldn't wait to grow and match him.

The monkey's paw did its work on me, ja?" I smirked, and she continued. "My mom thought I would be a better fencer, but I think she liked that you wear armor in that sport."

"So why aren't you a fencer?" I asked.

"I don't like how fast matches are in fencing. I like boxing because you get to learn a lot about the person across from you as you fight. It's more fun."

I scoffed. "Fun? You call getting punched in the face fun?"

"Well," Hilda snarked, "you're really supposed to avoid getting punched in the face."

"Still. I bet it happens. Lots."

"Not to me," Hilda countered.

When I glanced over, Hilda was grinning at me like an idiot. I couldn't think of anything to do but huff and say, "Don't make me turn this car around, young lady." I'd nearly forgotten how natural being with Hilda could be. "Is boxing how you get all those bruises all over your body?"

"Ja," Hilda said, "How'd you get yours?"

My foot pressed down on the brake, and Devon's Mustang jolted before instinct took over and I started accelerating again. Nervously, I checked all my mirrors, but the few cars around us hadn't seemed to notice. "What did you say?" I gasped, feeling my throat start to close.

"Your bruises," Hilda clarified, but I already knew what she was talking about. "Sometimes I see them on your arms."

"It's . . . It's not what you think," I said, feeling my shoulders tighten as I pressed my back into the leather of the driver's seat.

"I didn't think it was anything . . . until now." Hilda leaned forward, trying to see my face better, and her tone grew worried. "Clarissa, how do you get those?"

I shook my head, doing my best to hide my faltering smile from her. "You wouldn't understand. It's . . . It's complicated."

"Clarissa," Hilda said as she softly set a hand on my leg. "Pull over."

"N-No," I stuttered, swallowing my fear and making up an excuse. "Don't be ridiculous. You'll be late—"

"You're more important than my match," Hilda interrupted. "Now, pull over and talk to me."

I tried to shake my head again but found my neck too stiff. "Hilda, I—"

"You're shaking," Hilda said, moving her hand on top of mine. "Clarissa, what's—"

"Stop!" I barked, feeling Hilda's hand flinch. "Please. I can't talk about it."

My eyes locked on the freeway in front of me. I only felt Hilda move back to her side of the car. I wanted to slam a door or scream out my frustrations. *That wasn't what I wanted, Hilda. I didn't mean to push you away, but I'm not strong enough to—*

"When you're ready to talk," Hilda said softly, "I'll be here to listen, okay? You can trust me."

I rubbed away the tears welling up in my eyes as I said, "That sounds good. Thank you."

We sat in awkward silence until Devon called. I put him on speaker and set my phone in the cupholder between us.

"Where are you, Clare?" Devon shouted over loud music. "The party started, and I'm starting to feel bad that I haven't picked up Kate yet."

"Um, yeah . . . About that." I swallowed, praying for Devon's forgiveness. "Hilda and I are—"

Hilda cut me off by snatching my phone and shouting, "I'm holding Clarissa hostage for the night! If you want to see her or your car again, I demand one million dollars in cash and an airplane fueled to take us to Berlin." Then, without warning, she ended the call.

"Hilda!" I gasped, trying to grab my phone. "What are you doing?! I needed to tell Devon—"

"Psh." Hilda laughed, holding my phone just out of reach. "Don't pretend you didn't love that."

I did love it, and it brought some levity, which I had previously killed. After a few seconds, my phone buzzed and Hilda read the message to herself as it appeared on my lock screen.

"Well?" I gulped. "What's it say?"

Hilda smirked, hiding my phone under her leg. "Nothing that can't wait until after you drop me off."

"But I—"

Then the robotic voice of the Mustang's GPS called out. "Take your next left, and the destination will be on your right."

The building we pulled up to appeared to be another gym, though it was much more substantial and nicer than Mick's. A square street display that looked like it should be outside Fazerrati's with the night's special chalked on it read, "Closed for Private Event."

A group of thuggish, tattooed, and cigarette-smoking bikers was milling around a line of motorcycles parked next to the large double doors of the Angry Scotsman's Boxing Club. Each man looked more intimidating than the last, and just looking at them made my blood pressure rise.

"This is it. Can you open the trunk?" Hilda asked, unbuckling her seat belt.

I opened my mouth to tell Hilda there was no way I was dropping her off with those people watching us, but she was already getting out of the car.

It wasn't until Hilda knocked on the trunk that I registered she'd asked me to open it at all. I fumbled for the key fob and nervously pressed every button on the darn thing but the one that opened the trunk. My eyes never left the men across the street. "Come on," I muttered. "Just—" Finally, with a *pop*, the trunk rose, and I breathed a sigh of relief.

Telling myself to relax, I reached over to my phone sitting on the passenger seat. *Okay, how do I explain this to Devon while also apologizing for keeping his car? Then how do I explain to Max that I would miss his—*

The sudden *slam* of Hilda closing the trunk startled me so badly I dropped my phone, which landed right in between my seat and the parking brake. "Darnit." I bit my lip, blindly fishing for it with my fingers. "Almost—"

A sudden knock on the driver's window made my heart nearly burst out of my body. Thankfully, it was only Hilda.

Placing a hand on my chest and taking a few seconds to recover, I rolled down the window. "God. You scared the bejesus outta me."

Hilda snorted and leaned down. "I did what?"

I opened my mouth to respond but realized I could see directly down Hilda's shirt. Glints of steel flashed me because the bra she was wearing appeared to be a cup size too big for her. Unable to pull my gaze away, I just held there until Hilda cleared her throat. Panicking, I looked up, praying Hilda hadn't noticed my ocular foray down her shirt.

A devilish look appeared on her face, along with the slow rise of an eyebrow. "Ready to talk yet?" she asked.

I cleared my throat and turned to look out the windshield. "Sorry, I didn't mean to—"

"It's fine, Clarissa. I was just messing with you." Then she reached into the car and ruffled my hair, saying, "Mein kleines Bibelmädchen."

"Don't do that," I chided as I pulled her hand away and flattened my hair back down. "What does that even mean?"

Hilda grinned. "You should learn German."

I blew air out of my lips. "Don't tempt me, Hilda. I can—"

Flirt just fine in English, thank you very much. "Be just as weird as you can."

"Oh, ja? I can't wait to see it."

I rolled my eyes. "What are you even doing here? Shouldn't you be getting ready to 'not get punched in the face'? Go. Fight. Win."

With a strong nod, Hilda looked both ways before she crossed the street. Once she was inside the building, I sighed and pressed my forehead on the steering wheel.

Staring at my knees, I muttered, "What the hell is wrong with me?" I tapped my head against the soft leather. I hit my head against the wheel so hard the horn honked. I gasped, rubbing my forehead. My sixth sense tingled, and I looked up. All the men across the street were staring at me. "Oh, no," I whispered. As quickly as I could, I put the car in drive and slammed on the gas pedal.

11

The Complications of Friendship

While sitting at a red light and pointedly ignoring the wall of increasingly aggressive notifications from my friends, I reversed the GPS directions from Chicago to back to Grand Forks. As the light turned green on the empty street, it dawned on me that I could just stay. *It's not like I'll make it back in time for the party anyway.* Gripped by unholy indecision, I sat at the light until it turned yellow. *I'm staying.* Flipping a quick u-turn, I sped back towards the Angry Scotsman's Boxing Club. *I just hope I haven't missed anything!*

The narrow and sterile corridors made each step I took through the gym feel heavy. The directions the receptionist had given me seemed straightforward enough, but I felt lost, both physically and emotionally. I nearly jumped out of my skin as a roar erupted from one of the doors to my left. The cacophony swelled as I pushed it open and walked into a large arena with a raised boxing ring surrounded by rows of bleachers on three sides. The side bereft of bleachers had a raised ringside table with three people taking notes and talking among themselves.

I had no idea what to do, surrounded by people who appeared as if they stepped foot in a church they would burst into flames, until I saw Hilda the ring. She was sitting on a stool in the furthest corner from me with Richard. The pink boxing gloves she was wearing made her stand out, and helped calm me down enough to find a seat. I only realized as the bell for the next round began that her opponent was a man.

The rounds flew by as time's relative nature moved at lightning speed. Not being able to hold it in a second longer, I shouted, "Kick his butt, Hilda!" She obviously didn't hear me, but it didn't matter. I heard me, and it felt amazing to shout along with everyone, to be able to get excited because I wanted to be excited and not because I was expected to be. "Hilda! I . . . I love you!" I shouted right as Hilda connected a powerful uppercut into her opponent's chin. The man named Warren, I knew was his name by almost everyone around me shouting it multiple times throughout the match, staggered back and dropped to a knee.

The referee dropped next to Warren and pointed for Hilda to go to her corner. A few seconds later, the referee stood and made an X with his arms toward the judging table. After that, the ringside bell rang three times in rapid succession as the crowd exploded into cheers and claps. When I looked back at the ring, the only thing I saw was Hilda. *I said I loved her—out loud—and nobody cared.*

After the fight, the door to the locker room opened, and I immediately heard Hilda's voice cut through the evening air. She was wearing a long-sleeve black hoodie and matching sweatpants, and I could tell she was freshly showered.

Then, like something out of a movie, Hilda froze once our eyes met. "Clarissa?" she gasped.

"Uh, surprise?" I ventured, fanning my fingers outward in a display of jazz hands that would make Bob Fosse jealous. I hoped it would help ease the tension in my chest.

Hilda dropped her duffel bag and bounded forward to scoop me up in her arms. She swung me around in a circle before setting me gently back on my feet. "What are you doing here?!"

Being literally swept off my feet and spun around made me feel so wonderful. Before I responded, I found my hands hesitating around Hilda's hips. Instead of letting go, I just left them there. "I turned around right after I dropped you off," I explained. "I tried to catch you before your match, but it was too late, so I, uh . . ." Biting my lip, I said, "Kinda stayed and watched."

Hilda's eyes widened. "You . . . what?!"

"Yes! Oh my God! I saw everything! You were amazing! I still can't believe you! The way you just . . . And when he was trying to corner you . . . And you went all . . . God, Hilda, I've never seen anyone move as fast as you did when you were like—" My overly animated retelling of the fight was complete with fake punches and swooshing noises and ended with the epic punch that put her opponent out of commission. "You were right in his face, then . . . BAM!"

Hilda's jaw fell open, but her confusion soon curled into a huge smile.

"Bernhardt," Richard grumbled, scratching his chin. "Yer fired. Huffington, when can you start?"

There was a long pause before he and Hilda burst into laughter. I just turned rosy with embarrassment.

* * *

I pulled Devon's Mustang onto the long country road that led to Hilda's house. It handled the uneven dirt much better than my mother's station wagon, but it was still a bumpy ride. I made a mental note to take it through a carwash before giving it back to Devon. Hilda watched the countryside pass by with her chin on her fist. We hadn't spoken much, due in some part to how embarrassed I was when we left the event. I assumed Hilda was either deep in thought or maybe just recovering mentally from her fight. Either was completely understandable. I was simply amazed she hadn't passed out altogether.

Hilda eventually broke the silence. "Hey, Clarissa?"

"What's up?" I asked and risked a quick glance, complete with a smile.

Hilda peeled her gaze away from the passenger side window. "I want to apply to the same colleges you do, but I don't think I'll be able to get in."

My breath briefly abandoned me. "Don't talk like that. I don't even know where I want to apply to yet. Plus, you can do anything you put your mind to. I learned that tonight firsthand."

Hilda sighed. "At this point, with Golden Gloves coming up, I doubt I'll even graduate this year."

I tried to keep my voice soothing and gentle. "One thing at a time. Let's start with, what the heck is Golden Gloves?"

Hilda perked up a little. "It's the best national boxing tournament. My father says that's where people get scouted for Olympic teams. That's why I've been practicing so much."

"Also, you'll graduate," I declared triumphantly. "And you'll win Golden Gloves. I'll come to Mick's with you every day after school to help you get your grades up. In fact, I could probably pull some strings and drive us there, too, occasionally. Afterward, I can even drive you home, and we can spend all night studying here if we need to. We could even go to Pleasant Grounds more often at lunch. Then, when you're out at your matches, I can collect your homework for you. If you're gone too long, or you're too stressed, I'll even do it for you and turn it in. I owe you that for getting you kicked out of Stantin's class." My mind was racing at a thousand miles an hour, and even as I pulled up next to the rusted truck out front of Hilda's house, I couldn't stop. "We can do this. I swear to God I'm going to get out of Grand Forks, and I'm taking you with me."

Hilda looked as if she were on the verge of tears, emotional weight falling every which way. "Clarissa, I—"

Without thinking, I reached over and ran my hand across the shaved side of Hilda's scalp. Her short hair prickled the tips of my fingers. The warmth of her body, her silver eyes budding with tears, it all made my heart yearn for something more—more than gentle caresses and comforting words.

As my hand reached the back of Hilda's head, I gave her a gentle, encouraging tug. I nervously beckoned her toward me until our lips finally met. The soft and surprised moan that escaped Hilda's mouth made all the tightness I held in my body for so long surge into silky ribbons of delight. I didn't care about how awkward it was or that we were both women or that God was probably shaking his head in shame. All I cared about was being there for Hilda when she needed me, and I needed to show her that it wasn't just me being polite for someone else. I was doing it for me.

An immeasurable amount of time passed as we kissed and held each other. Finally, Hilda eased out of our embrace, wiping tears from her eyes. "You have no idea how long I've been wanting to do that. The crying I could do without next time."

The thought of there even being a next time made my whole body feel pillowy. "Yeah?"

"Ja. I just can't believe it happened. I was so scared you didn't . . . well, you didn't like me—like this. I feel very silly now." Hilda looked away bashfully, but I could tell she was still watching me out of the corner of her eye.

"So you're—" I couldn't bring myself to say the word.

"Gay?" Hilda finished with a smirk. "Ja."

You've done it now! You're going to Hell for sure. Mom is going to find out about this and lock you away forever. Suppressing the voice was hard, but looking into Hilda's shimmering eyes helped summon my confidence. "I guess we all have secrets." I smiled.

"It's not really a secret, Clarissa. It's just . . . When I moved back to America, my father warned me to be careful who to trust at school. He said people might not want to be my friend if they found out I was a lesbian."

The L-word made my chest tighten. *Is that what Hilda is? Is that what I—*

"Also," Hilda continued. "As I'm sure you know, Saint Mary's doesn't have any LGBT clubs or anything, so making friends has been hard for me. Not that I was good at that to start with." She grinned. "I have a history of always doing stupid things that—"

"Who else knows? I mean, about you being . . ." I swallowed, my tongue feeling like a lead weight in my mouth.

Hilda leaned back and seemed to think pretty hard. "Let's see . . . Lin figured it out first. Hard to keep anything from her for too long. Then I told Veronica. Kate and Michelle. Plus a few others figured it out."

My jaw dropped in astonishment. *So many people know and word never got to me? It's almost like someone hadn't wanted me to know . . .*

"What's with that look?"

"I was just—I was just caught off guard that so many people knew and I didn't."

Hilda raised an eyebrow. "Are you hurt or . . . jealous?"

A breath passed my lips, but there wasn't a word attached to it. Then I swallowed and said, "A little of both, I think."

Hilda reached over to ruffle my hair again. "Well, as much as I don't want this moment to end, I should probably get inside."

I nodded passively. My mind had become a reflection of my hair: a tangled and messy knotted thing.

The next I knew, Hilda was idling at the passenger door with her bag slung across her back. I didn't even remember opening the trunk or if she had asked me to. She must have noticed something was wrong, because she asked, "You don't regret kissing me, do you?"

"No." Internally, I fought desperately to stop a flood of shameful emotions from overwhelming me. "I actually liked it a lot, and, uh . . . yeah."

Hilda grinned. "Well, I give you permission to make out with me anytime you want. Oh! That reminds me. Since we're, um . . ." She stopped herself and looked away from me.

Was she about to assume we're dating? Are we dating?! Wait—

"Remember that mall you mentioned?" she said.

"Rockridge Mall, sure. What about it?"

"Well, since you'll be grounded tomorrow, I was thinking . . . Maybe you could drive me there next Saturday?"

My heart fluttered in my chest. In fact, if that night was any indication, a long drive to the mall would be sublime.

Without thinking, I said, "Sure." Then, to distract myself from thinking about what I'd just agreed to do, I picked up my phone and shook it gently. "Maybe I can finally get you to join the twenty-first century."

Hilda's bright smile made me yearn to photographic it, so I could keep it forever. "If I do, you'll show me everything, right? I've never had a smartphone before."

I nodded. "Of course."

"Alright then. I guess I'll see you at school. Goodnight, Clarissa."

I pulled out of the driveway and headed home. Everything was fine until Hilda's house disappeared in the rearview mirror. Once I was alone in the darkness, all I could think about was what was going to happen when I got home. Paranoia began to rip my mind apart, feeding on my guilt and doubts. I had just reached the paved road leading back to Grand Forks when I pulled over onto the shoulder, put my face in my hands, and cried.

12

Little White Lies

My knees ached as I opened my eyes. I'd fallen asleep in front of my bed, and the familiar cross silently continued casting its divine judgment upon me as it had ever since my mother confined me to my room after the Chicago trip. I assumed Devon had let it slip when she called them to ask when I'd be home, but I couldn't know for sure because I had no means to talk to anyone until Monday.

Still, even with being isolated from all of my friends and only leaving my room to use the bathroom, I felt strangely apathetic about my punishment. The excitement and pure joy I experienced with Hilda still gave me butterflies. The things Hilda and I shared . . . It all felt too extraordinary for someone like me. It felt like a dream.

I even kissed her. I, Clarissa Regal Huffington, kissed another girl. Not on a dare. Not because I was drunk. Not because someone asked me to. Because I wanted to. Because it felt right. My heart raced, but it came with a lurking fear as the cross above my bed figuratively felt like a noose. Every time I thought about Hilda or the time we shared together, a rope tightened around my neck and made it hard to breathe.

Monday morning finally arrived, but I wasn't woken up by my mother screaming at me. She wasn't even home. In the night, she came into my room and put a note on my nightstand. The letter only talked about how she was at a charity breakfast and asked that I "be home promptly" after school because my father was getting back from a business trip.

"Whatever," I muttered, feeling bold in my silent rebellion as I went about my normal morning routine.

Later that day, I pulled Devon's Mustang into the student parking lot and immediately felt that something was wrong. Paranoia gripped me as I walked through the cold school hallways because everyone who typically shot me a "good morning," or at least used to give me a polite smile, didn't even look my way.

Did *Hilda tell anyone that we* . . . I swallowed, pulling my messenger bag closer to my body and trying to act like nothing was wrong. *No. She wouldn't have. She knows I'm . . . scared. Right?*

When I got to my locker, I feverishly worked my combination lock. The spin of the dial mimicked the wild and queasy way I felt inside. The sooner I got into a classroom, the better I would be.

It's Monday. That's all. People just don't want to be here. They don't know anything—unless they do. They don't! I snapped my eyes shut, fighting the invisible devil whispering in my ear. *I'm just crazy.*

I froze as I turned the corner to my locker. Devon, Max, and Matilda were crowded around it. *They're just wondering why I bailed on the party.* Swallowing my fear, I approached my three friends. Matilda quickly explained that she had seen Hilda slip something in between the slots on my locker in the morning and wanted to make sure it wasn't something that would get me in trouble.

It turned out all Hilda had left me a neatly folded note which Max demanded I show everyone for missing his party.

Clarissa,

I had a great time driving with you. I'm really looking forward to shopping this weekend. Maybe we could go to the coffee shop at lunch today. My treat this time. Finally.

Hilda

P.S. I can't stop thinking about you.

At first my friends didn't know what to make of the note, but my intentionally vague and increasingly inconsistent story only seemed to piss them off. To prove that the evening truly meant nothing to me, I made sure to throw away Hilda's note at the first trash can. It was all just an act for Matilda's sake, but I hated myself for going through with it. It even occurred to me that I should take a picture right as the paper hit the bottom of the empty garbage can. I reached into my pocket for where I usually kept my phone and found it as hollow as my heart.

Self-hatred, thy name is Clarissa Huffington.

* * *

I caught Hilda as she strode confidently down the hallway. Her body language was the complete opposite of the other day. Once she realized I was waiting by some lockers at a hallway intersection, she pointedly pretended that she wasn't looking at me, although her smile seemed to grow each time our eyes happened to connect.

Nonchalantly, Hilda approached me, wearing a subtle smile. *I can't take this away from her*, I thought. *No one is taking this away from us.* I longed for the note I had thrown away and felt like a monster.

Hilda rested her forearm on the locker above my hand and leaned forward, looking down at me. The gesture felt protective and made me want to wrap myself around her tightly. I wanted her to hide me away from the world as I told her everything about my mother and school and Matilda. Maybe she could help me.

"Morning, Fräulein," Hilda said sweetly.

I instinctively glanced around to see if anyone was watching us, then whispered, "Hilda, you can't—"

"Did you read the note I left in your locker?"

"I did, yeah. But I had to—"

"Good." Hilda pulled another folded piece of paper out of her jeans. "I have another one for you."

I hesitated to take it and instead just stared like all of its crisp edges were razor blades.

Hilda pulled the note back slightly and asked, "Is something wrong?"

No. Yes. This is all wrong. I'm not supposed to be like this, Hilda. I mean, you're gay, and that's you, but look at me. I'm just . . . me. I'm not supposed to go to underground boxing matches and watch someone I care about getting punched in the face over and over. I'm not allowed to be that person. I'm going to break your heart if we keep doing this, but I can't stop feeling this way about you. I can't take this away from you. From us. But I have to. I don't have a choice!

Hilda's increasingly worried appearance made it clear I wasn't conveying my thoughts with my silence. I snatched the note from Hilda's hand, trying to appear playful. "Sorry. I'm really tired. I was up all night pray—er, looking through all the photos I took of your match."

Hilda's genuine smile returned. "I can't wait to see them." I cringed. "We'll meet at the coffee shop, ja?" I nodded, but Hilda hesitated to leave. "There's something you're not telling me, isn't there?"

Holding back tears, I nodded. "I got grounded, so I don't think I'm going to be able to take you out this weekend."

Hilda tilted her head. "That's all?"

"There's more, but—" I broke eye contact with Hilda and held my arm. "I don't—can't talk about it."

Hilda reached out and touched my chin, probably to pull my gaze to her, but I flinched away. "Don't." *Please, if you touch me again, I'm going to crumble, and then everyone will—*

Before I could think or say anything, Hilda barked, "Fine. Goodbye, Clarissa." She stormed off down the hall, leaving me with shattered pieces of my heart. *She knew what I was about to say. She knows I'm just a stupid coward...*

I stepped forward and tried to reach out. A hand grabbed my shoulder from behind.

I turned with a hand covering my heart and found Matilda standing there. "Talk about not taking rejection well," she said with a grim smile.

Did she sneak up on me?! Wait, she must have noticed—

A wave of relief flooded into me as Matilda continued. "I'm really surprised, actually."

"Surprised?" I tugged at the unasked question as I nonchalantly slipped Hilda's new note into my back pocket.

"That she didn't attack you. You know? Given her track record."

"For the last time—Actually, it's over now. Can we just pretend Hilda doesn't exist?"

Matilda nodded. "Amen to that."

I peered down the hallway just in time to catch Hilda's eye before she turned a corner. "Thanks again for saving me from myself."

I prayed Hilda understood what I said was for her, even though she couldn't possibly have heard me.

Matilda smiled. "It's what I do, Clare."

* * *

I don't belong anymore, I lamented internally. Max hadn't even said so much as "good afternoon" to me, and Matilda was chatting with Ryan. The silence and solitude were all I ever wanted, and now I got it. *God, do they know what Hilda and I did?* They didn't, of course, but still, my breathing became frantic as I rubbed at my arms.

I glanced down at my uneaten food when someone behind me cleared his throat. "Do you have my keys?"

I turned, and Devon was standing behind me, tray in hand. His expression made it clear he wasn't going to sit with us. "Uh, yeah." I dug into my messenger bag and pulled out his keys. "It's parked in the parking lot near the exit. Sorry, I didn't have time to fill it up. I can ask my mom for an advance on my allowance and—"

Devon sighed heavily as he grabbed his keys. "Don't worry about it, Clare." Then, before I could respond, he walked away.

When I turned back to my food, Matilda was shaking her head at me. "Looks like Hilda isn't the only one you need to talk to today."

"Yeah. Actually, can we talk—"

"You know," Matilda interrupted, leaning forward, "before he picked up Kate for the party, I saw Devon talking alone with Veronica. Do you know anything about that?"

"No," I said bitterly as my fingers dug into my skirt in frustration.

"Damn," Matilda said, clearly looking for new gossip to sink her fangs into. "I was hoping you would."

Throughout lunch, I felt guilty that I'd left Hilda hanging at the coffee shop even though I promised to meet her there. Finally, I couldn't take it anymore and blurted, "Hey, Max. I just had an idea." He narrowed his eyes at me but waited for me to continue. "You know, since I, uh, kind of owe you for bailing on your party, what if I put together another party? I'll coordinate everything. It'll be like a surprise party without the surprise."

"Really?" Max said after a deep breath and a skeptical stare.

"Yeah, I'd do anything for you. Although, I could always use a hand." I looked at Matilda.

"Urgh, fine," Matilda scoffed, rolling her eyes, but I could tell she approved of the idea. "Twist my arm why don't you. Wait . . . No Hilda, right?"

I swallowed. "That's up to Max. It's his party, after all."

Max seemed to give it some thought, which was actually quite noble of him. "I'm gonna say no. Let's keep it small. Like the good ol' days. You know?"

"For once," Matilda snarked.

"Besties only," I said with a completely fake smile. "Got it."

Max smiled at me, but there was something wrong about it. "About time you did something in this friendship, Clare. No offense, but I've been feeling like I'm trying a lot harder than you are to make this work."

"We all have," Matilda echoed, nodding in approval. "It's nice to see that the old Clare is finally coming back."

"I've had a lot going on recently," I said apologetically. I wasn't sure how long I could keep pretending to be someone I wasn't, but seeing Hilda this morning made me want to hold on to whatever we had for as long as I could even if that meant lying to everyone else.

* * *

My feet dragged as I walked along the familiar sidewalks that led me home. When I got to my street, I kept walking straight instead of turning. I needed more time to think about what to say to my mother. The longer I delayed, the worse I assumed it would get for me.

Devon, the only person who I thought could help me, wasn't returning any of my texts. I even tried to call him once. Before that, there hadn't been a day that we hadn't communicated in one form or another. I was grasping at straws as I thought of something that would get a reply from him. The guilt of blowing him off to hang out with Hilda felt like I owed him more than I could ever make up for.

After walking around the block twice, I finally took a deep breath and decided to tell my parents the truth. Not the whole truth. I'd omit the part where Hilda and I kissed or how it was almost magical to watch her box, but I'd tell them practically everything else.

I hadn't even lifted my messenger bag off of my shoulder when my father called, "Clare, can you come into the dining room for a few minutes?"

"Be right there," I called back and prayed for strength.

The short, mostly one-sided, conversation went about how I had expected it to: with mother drilling into me while my father passively fact-checked my story on his laptop. What I hadn't expected was that it ended with me shouting about how much I enjoyed watching boxing while my mother literally dragged me up the stairs.

Hours could have passed as I trembled in darkness. From the yelling downstairs to the light breeze that knocked a tree branch into my window, every noise made me jump and kept me awake. I felt like I'd never be able to relax again.

I would rather feel nothing than feel like this. Please. I just . . . I can't do this anymore. I prayed to God, over and over, repeating the words in my head until it was all I could hear or feel.

Then came a knock at my door.

I rubbed my puffy, raw eyes and tried to sound like I hadn't been crying. "Come in," I whimpered, not sure if the Devil himself would walk through my door with a one-way ticket to Hell or if it would be my mother. Right then, I might have preferred the Devil.

My father walked into my room holding a plate of food, a glass of water, and my messenger bag. He seemed unsure of where to start but walked over and set the dinner on my nightstand, then pulled my desk chair over to the bedside and took a seat.

"So I think these mashed potatoes qualify as soup at this point." I could tell he was trying to get me to smile, but it didn't work. So he smiled halfheartedly. "Alright then, I'm not going to sugarcoat this. I've never seen your mother this upset before. You've messed up in the past, but this . . . This is new, for both of us. And as much as I don't want to admit it, your mother is right. You're not *you* recently. I called the school this evening. They said you're still a model student with perfect attendance and grades. So I honestly have no clue what to make of this. Because I also called that gym and they corroborated your boxing story. The receptionist even remembers you. I don't know what to do with you. Your behavior only seems to get worse. Is it drugs? Or alcohol? Do we need to call someone to help you? Should we get you some private therapy? I just need answers, Clare."

"Dad, I . . ." My exhausted tear ducts began to well again, and my tremulous voice put a worried look on my father's face. He was doing everything he could to encourage me to open up, but I couldn't tell him about the kiss. "I'm sorry." I hugged him. For all the reasons he didn't understand, I hugged him.

I flinched as he set a hand on my back, which he felt and hesitated before patting me. "Listen, I'm going to talk to your mother, and we're going to discuss your punishment. Whatever it is, try to not fight it too much, okay? Now, how about you try and get some sleep?"

I sobbed, shaking my head. "I don't think I can sleep. I'm going to try and do some homework."

"That's my girl." My dad shook my shoulder. The pain I smiled through reassured me that it would be bruised tomorrow. "But I'm betting once you have something to eat, you'll fall asleep. It's been a long day, for all of us."

Once my father was gone, I sat down in my chair to start my homework, praying that it would help me forget about my life for a while. As I leaned back, I felt a strange sensation, like something was . . . *Hilda's second note!* I nearly tore it apart because I opened it so quickly.

Clarissa,

I said I couldn't stop thinking about you in my last note. I still can't. It's only been a few minutes since I folded the last one and I'm already writing this one. I'm probably sitting in class or at work, remembering our date to Fazerrati's. (I'm counting that as our first date, by the way.) Or thinking about what you said to me in Devon's car. I still can't believe that you kissed me.

Last night was the best I've had since my mother died. I won the money I need, my dad finally opened up a little, and well . . . you know.

I want to talk to you, but . . . I can't believe I'm actually going to write this . . .

You're the best friend I've ever had, and I'd like you to officially be my girlfriend.

Hilda

After finishing the note for the tenth time, I lifted it and pressed it to my chest. It was a poor replacement for Hilda's body, but I needed something to hold. I grabbed my closest notebook and put pen to the first blank piece of paper I could find.

13

Welcome Home

I loathed sitting at the lunch table. Wishing that Hilda was sitting next to me but having to pretend like she didn't even exist made me sick. All I ever allowed myself to do was smile at her in the hallways or give her curt nods as we passed. It's what I did for anyone, but it hurt when it was Hilda. More and more, coming to school hurt me, but staying home or ditching would be unacceptable behavior, too.

Each time I saw Hilda laugh with Lin or Veronica in the quad, I wanted to scream. *I just have to endure this until we graduate*, I kept telling myself. *Just a few more months. Just a little longer. Then Hilda and I . . . Then I can be myself.*

"So what are everyone's plans for the weekend?" Max asked, somewhat facetiously, as I stared across the quad.

Devon shot me an annoyed look before he said, "Studying."

I couldn't help but look away as I fiddled idly with my food. "Sorry, I know we haven't talked since I ditched Max's party."

"Clare," Max said, reaching over to my tray. "You gonna eat this?" He held up my dessert pudding. I shook my head, looking down at my nearly untouched lunch and pushing the entire thing away from me.

"Something wrong?" Matilda said. "I swear you haven't eaten lunch in the past two or three days."

I smiled, feeling weak and drained from my constant lying. "I'm just not feeling it. Maybe this weekend I could sneak away for a quick dinner at Fazerrati's." I turned to look at Max. "You know, like the old times."

Max's face lit up, but Devon exhaled sharply. "Don't you already have plans at the mall this weekend, Clare? Speaking of which, how are you even going to pull that off? Because I'm guessing you're grounded."

I choked on my breath. "Well, I, um—"

"Wait, is this about that note Hilda wrote you?" Matilda said. "You're not seriously considering taking her to the mall, are you?" When I didn't respond, Matilda glanced down at my lunch tray, then back up to my face. "Tell me she hasn't talked you into eating vegetarian or something."

My breath hitched and my body clenched. "N-No," I stuttered. "I'm—"

"Hold on," Max said. "You're vegetarian now?"

I shook my head. "No, Max. I just—"

"You just *what*, Clare?" Max threw his hands out. "You're not making any sense, and frankly, you're acting really weird. Like, we used to talk about stuff and now you just . . . don't. And honestly, I would love to go to Fazerrati's if I didn't think you would just sit there at dinner and stare at everyone like we all made you sick." Before I could reply, he stood up. "You know what? Forget about the party or whatever. I'm done trying to get you to talk."

My chin shook, but I was too scared to follow Max as he trudged away.

Devon sighed, dropping his bag of chips. "Jesus fucking Christ." Then he got up to follow Max.

Once the two disappeared behind the science building, all eyes fell on me.

What would the old me do? What can I do to stop this painful feeling in my heart? Burst into tears with everyone looking at me? No. I can't. Mom will find out that I broke down at school and—

Then the idea struck me. Reaching across the table, I grabbed Devon's chips as if nothing was wrong. Then, as I threw a chip into my mouth, I said, "What? So Max and I got in a fight. You're all acting like this is the first time that's ever happened. Spoilers, it used to happen all the time."

Matilda smiled, but there was distinct darkness behind it.

I returned the polite-yet-false gesture, feeling like the first one of us to blink would die.

No matter how often I looked over my shoulder, I didn't see anyone following me as I walked to my locker. I tried to imagine I was being overly paranoid because of the scene I made at lunch, but nothing I did seemed to calm me down. When I reached my locker to get my afternoon block's books, I realized the door was slightly ajar.

Panicking, I threw it open and looked on in horror as everything inside was overturned and obviously rummaged through. My heart stopped beating as I looked up and down the hallway. Everyone was just walking to class like nothing was out of place. My stomach lurched into my throat when I realized that my old pencil case had been moved. The note for Hilda, which I'd been hiding under it, was gone.

Someone cleared her throat behind me, startling me so badly my shoulder slammed into my locker door. I turned, rubbing my shoulder. It still ached from when my mother had dragged me upstairs.

Matilda was standing behind me with her arms crossed. "Why are you so jumpy— What the hell happened here?"

I spun around and started rearranging everything. "Nothing. I've just been really rushed recently and haven't had time to reorganize."

"You're sure you're not missing anything?" Matilda asked.

For a split second, I swore she was the one who went through my locker. I shoved my afternoon books into my messenger bag and said, "It's fine, okay? Drop it. Also, stop following me around."

Matilda's honest and wounded expression cut me like a knife, although it only took her a second to harden herself. "You know what? Fine. Whatever all this is you're not telling anyone, I'm done. I'm done playing your utterly fucked-up guessing game. See you around, Clare."

I wanted to reach out and stop her from storming away, but I didn't because then I would have had to explain, and I wasn't ready for that. Instead, I turned back to my locker and slammed it shut, angry with myself for being such an awful coward.

* * *

Saturday's sun peeked up over the horizon as I rumbled down Hilda's driveway. Her smile, as I exited the car, made every future punishment I would have to endure worth it. The proverbial angel was on my shoulder, guilting me about feeling excited, sneaking out, and lying to all my friends, but none of it mattered. *If God didn't want me sneaking out, then he would have woken my parents up. Right?*

Hilda cheered as she sprinted down her porch to greet me. "Clarissa! I can't believe you actually came!"

My heart leaped as Hilda lifted me into a kiss. At first, I tensed up, but as I felt her holding me firmly, I naturally melted into her, wrapping my arms around her as the morning sun warmed our faces.

Hilda broke our kiss and set her forehead on mine. "Sorry, I needed to make sure you were real."

I couldn't help but grin. "Yeah, well, don't get too mushy on me. We have a lot to do today, and you better enjoy it because I'm pretty sure this might be the last you'll see of me for a while. I'm gonna be in so much trouble when I get home this afternoon. That's not even mentioning if anyone at school finds out I've been lying to them about . . . us."

"I don't want you lying to everyone, Clarissa. I want you to want this, too."

"I do," I said. "Trust me, I wouldn't be here if I didn't think you were worth it. But it's going to take me a while to tell everyone else. Is that okay?"

Hilda beamed at me. "Of course." She grabbed my hand and began to pull me toward her house.

"Ah!" I gasped as a sharp pain ran up my arm, and I tore my hand away. Hilda turned and began to say sorry when I interrupted her. "It's okay. I just slept on my shoulder wrong or something. I'm okay."

Hilda narrowed her eyes and began to say something. The front door creaked open and a mountainous man walked out of the house. Hilda's father was much larger in real life than his photo would have led me to believe. Both of his arms were covered in tattoos that I knew extended down his chest and peeked out of his collar. His chiseled face, a permanent scowl etched into it over years of boxing, looked as if smiling would forever shatter it. He gave me the slightest nod and muttered roughly, "Morning."

Trying my best to appear calm and act like I hadn't just made out with his daughter in his driveway, I said, "Good morning, Mr. Bernhardt."

The man sipped his coffee and then grunted, "Name's Ron."

Hilda jabbed her father in the side with her finger, saying

something to him in German before turning back to me. "I need to go grab my money. I wasn't expecting you so early. You're lucky I'm even fully dressed right now." I blushed, which was surely the reaction Hilda wanted to get out of me. "Be right back." With a skip, she disappeared into the house.

Hilda's father straightened up and gave me a very critical once-over. "Bruise," he said evenly.

Bruise? My blood ran cold as I quickly pulled down the shirt sleeve that Hilda had unknowingly pushed up when we kissed. "Sorry," I apologized, embarrassed that I hadn't been paying enough attention to it. "It's, um . . . It's nothing." I swallowed and looked down at my feet.

The only sound for a long time was the wind gusting across the porch as a few dry leaves drifted between us.

"It never is," Ron said darkly. "At first." Then he shook his coffee mug at me. "Coffee?"

I shook my head. "No, thank you. Actually, I was going to stop at Pleasant Grounds on the way out of town. Do you know where that is?" Another tense bout of silence followed my question, and Ron didn't look to answer me. I cleared my throat, trying to find some common ground between what felt like a Grand Canyon of differences between us. "I saw a picture of you at the gym Hilda works at. You were a boxer, too, right?"

He grunted in affirmation.

I swallowed nervously. "It must run in the family or something."

Ron's dark brown eyes narrowed at me. "Until recently, Brünnhilde has kept her boxing career a secret from me." He leaned down and got uncomfortably close to my face. "With her condition, I would not have approved. And neither should you."

I would have crumbled under Ron's combative stare had Hilda not popped out of the front door. "Okay! Let's—" she began but froze when she saw what was happening between me and her father. Then she slugged her father in the arm and started shouting at him in German. Whatever she said, it didn't sound very polite.

Not even registering that his daughter had punched him in the arm, Ron replied in German. The two looked at each other for a long time before Ron turned on his heel and walked back into their home.

I almost didn't want to ask, but I whispered, "What did he say?"

Hilda blinked at her father's back as he closed the rickety door. Then she said, in seeming disbelief, "He said . . . He said he likes you."

I shook my head. "Yeah, I'm ninety-nine percent sure you're lying to me."

"Then you should learn German," Hilda said with a grin.

"Psh," I rolled my eyes. "That'll be the day. Now let's go. I need coffee, unless you want me to be a zombie at the mall. I usually only get up this early for church."

Hilda paused. "If you want coffee, I just made some. I can—"

"No," I interrupted, not wanting to contradict what I had said to her father. "I was thinking a pit stop at Pleasant Grounds on our way out of town. For old times' sake."

Hilda cheered and held up a plain white envelope that was bulging slightly. "My treat."

I grinned. "About time, and sorry I keep ditching you at lunch. Matilda—"

"Don't." Hilda reached for my hand and pulled me close to her. "I have you right now. That's all I care about."

My heart skipped. I knew Hilda wanted me to get up on my toes and kiss her—so I did. Smiling into her silver eyes, I said, "Alright, that's enough lovey-dovey stuff. Let's go."

* * *

We weren't even in the mall five minutes before Hilda stopped me to gaze at lingerie on display in the windows of Victoria's Secret.

Even worse, she flirtily winked at me and went into the sinful store, coming out a while later with a large bag. Leaving my heart heavy with regret I hadn't followed her, and my mind burning with lustful thoughts.

Thankfully, we reached the Verizon store without further detours, but then we got hit by a different kind of roadblock. All Hilda had was cash. She could use it to buy a phone, but couldn't use the phone without a plan, which required a credit card to set up. Knowing I was on a family plan with my parents, I suggested that we just add her on to my plan, and she could give me cash to give to my father each month.

At Sephora, Hilda was nearly caught by a security guard tucking some eyeliner into one of her many bags. The perplexing part was that she still had plenty of cash to buy the stupid thing. Once we were asked to leave the store, Hilda attempted to justify her actions to me by saying the eyeliner was going to be for me, and she didn't want me seeing it during checkout. My frustration with her quickly turned to sympathy. She even promised to never steal as long as we were dating. I considered it a great victory for both of us.

Soon we were face to face with Matto's Film & Photography, and despite me explaining I didn't have any money, Hilda dragged me inside. Once the smell of film hit my nostrils I had relaxed. It wasn't long before I was buzzing between displays, explaining everything to her.

Once I was done talking, which admittedly was probably for too long, Hilda asked, "If you could have anything here, what would it be?"

"I guess, if I wanted to keep even a shred of my credibility as a photographer in the twenty-first century, I would pick"—I pointed up at a Nikon D3300 sitting on its box behind the counter—"that." The camera was marked at 399 dollars and came with a lens, a perk that a lot of higher-end cameras lacked. "I've dreamt of owning a Nikon, but the only way I could ever afford one was if I got it used. But they're so good that nobody ever gives them up, and at the rate I'm going I'll never own one before I start college."

After hitting four more stores, we finally pulled up to Hilda's house around five—much later than I had intended—but my phone had been surprisingly silent. It wasn't a good sign, but with Max and Matilda thinking I was grounded, I shouldn't have expected anything from them. My mother, on the other hand, was probably too furious to be bothered. She would be waiting for me. Each second that ticked away was another day I would be grounded, not that I cared anymore. The memories of today were the perfect mental cushion for my impending isolation.

I cleared my throat, pulling Hilda's attention away from her phone. "We're here."

Hilda looked around. "Sorry, I was trying to get this to work. I think I liked your profile on Twitter? The heart is red now. That means I followed you, right?"

"No, that just means you liked that tweet." I looked around and didn't see her father's truck anywhere. "Your dad's not home?"

"Doesn't look like it. He might have taken the truck to get fixed." Then she tapped something on her phone. "Tsk! I didn't mean to do that. Dammit, how do I go back?"

Seeing how frustrated she was, I reached over and took her hand. "Hey, it's okay. As my uncle would say, 'Rome wasn't built in a day.'"

Hilda squeezed my hand. "Sorry, it's just . . . I want to be good at this, but it's a lot all at once. Do you want a surprise?"

"Sure?"

Hilda unbuckled her seat belt and reached into the back seat. As she rummaged through all her bags, she said, "There are actually two. One is small, and one is large. Which do you want first?"

Starting to feel giddy like it was Christmas morning, I replied, "Uh, the small one?"

Hilda nodded but didn't stop her search. "Ah-ha! Okay, close your eyes and hold out your hands." When she peeked over her shoulder, her eyes narrowed at me. "Clarissa, close your eyes!"

"Ah, sorry!" I snapped, shutting my eyes.

Hilda grabbed my wrists, making me jump slightly, although I kept my eyes shut. Then she began to move my hands. "Okay, hold out your hands like this. There. Ready?"

With my hands pressed together, palms up in front of my face like I was receiving Communion for the first time, I said, "Okay, I'm—"

Something substantial and square landed in my hands. It was plastic. Not square, really, but cubic, and oddly contoured. Then my thumb ran over the familiar lip of a film feed slot.

"Hilda!" I gasped as my eyes shot open.

The click of a shutter closing and the sound of whirring gears was all I heard as I looked directly at the front of a Polaroid OneStep. The picture Hilda had taken was already working its way out of the feed.

"This will be my masterpiece!" Hilda smiled as she pulled the camera away from me to retrieve her prize.

Still a bit shocked, I asked, "You didn't buy this, did you!?"

Hilda raised an eyebrow as she began to shake the developing polaroid. "Ja? I didn't steal it, if that's what—"

I quickly snatched the photo out of her hand. "Don't shake it! It's a misconception to shake polaroids. It can really damage the film."

Hilda ruffled my hair before placing the camera on my lap. "You're seriously the cutest when you get all . . . What's the word? Upset?"

I looked at the photo and blushed. *Wow.* Hilda went back to sorting through her bags in the back seat.

After looking through the viewfinder and generally checking out Hilda's camera, I sighed. "I can't believe you got this. I'm totally going to steal it from you."

Hilda, who seemed to be hiding something behind her back in the passenger seat, raised an eyebrow. "What do you mean, Clarissa? That's for you, and"—she whipped what she was hiding behind her back around—"so is this!"

I gasped as Hilda revealed a factory sealed-box of a Nikon D3300. "You didn't?!"

Hilda grinned. "I totally did. Remember when I told you I got lost looking for the bathroom? I lied. I waited until you left the camera store, then ran back in. The man who sold this all to me was very helpful. He even showed me how to put some film in the OneStep. I think it's time you had your first professional—"

I thrust myself forward, pressing my lips onto Hilda's. Eventually, I broke the kiss just long enough to unbuckle my seat belt.

Hilda gasped and set the Nikon box down on the dash. My hands moved of their own accord. I did anything I could do to feel closer to her. I ran my hand down her chest, feeling every contour. When I reached the end of her shirt, I moved my hand under it and started working my way back up. I felt her tense up as I ran my fingers along her tight abdominal muscles, then her labored breathing as I reached her chest and the elastic of her sports bra.

I hesitated, but Hilda gave me a small nod, and I forced my hand under the barrier. We continued to make out as I moved my palm over her breast. Sensations of warm skin, cold metal, and her tongue in my mouth nearly overwhelmed me. I could feel her heart pounding on my palm. I could smell her shampoo as her hair brushed my cheek. I gave Hilda's right nipple ring a playful tug, the effect of which made her break our kiss and moan my name softly into my hair.

As if being able to read my thoughts, Hilda pulled back, breathing heavily, her face flushed and her silver eyes filled with want. She said something in German that was so soft and full of yearning that I just whispered, "Yes." I didn't understand the words, but I felt the intent. I was ready.

Hand in hand, we raced up to Hilda's room, where we rapidly discarded all of our clothes, both cameras and a still-developing polaroid forgotten on the dashboard of my mother's car.

* * *

With a soft groan, I opened my eyes to the sound of a cell phone vibrating somewhere nearby. Still groggy, I reached out and I pulled the phone to my face. My vision came into focus just in time to see the number of missing calls from my mother click from eleven to twelve. A flood of adrenaline gripped me as I also noticed the time, nearly eight o'clock. My hands shook as I scrolled down the list of notifications. All of my friends and family had been trying to reach me for the better part of the evening. My heart caught in my throat as I slowly turned my head away from my phone to the half-naked woman sleeping soundly next to me.

Memories of how Hilda hastily threw comforters and blankets on the ground filled my mind—to make things more comfortable for us since her bed was a military cot and not very conducive to . . . sex. The realization blossomed like a flower in the chest. What Hilda and I had done was soft and beautiful and practically the opposite of everything I had ever imagined it to be. Watching Hilda's chest as it rose and fell filled me with a sort of serenity but also a strange dread.

We weren't married, but we . . . Did this count? Was what we did . . . Would God care that my first time was with Hilda? Was Matilda right about being sent to Hell for loving someone—

I snapped my eyes closed so tightly that it hurt and scolded myself for even thinking about that. I was stupid for letting it get this far and too busy helping Hilda to even realize what it meant for me—what it meant for my future. *Our future?*

It felt like I couldn't hold a breath in Hilda's room, where I was surrounded by foreign weightlifting equipment and unfamiliar furniture. I needed fresh air and space where I could . . . just be alone with my thoughts.

I swallowed a sob because I knew my own home wasn't that place either. After everything I had done, my mother likely wouldn't even let me through the front door, but I couldn't stay with Hilda. If I were around when she woke up, I wouldn't even know what to say to her.

As quietly as I could, I got dressed. "I'm sorry," I whispered to her at the door. Then I realized I left her half-exposed to the air. With a goofy smile, I tiptoed back over and pulled the covers up around her.

Hilda shifted ever so slightly but didn't wake up.

I leaned down and kissed her soft lips. The warmth was washed away with the cold stinging of tears.

14

What Comes After

My emotional range shifted hysterically as I drove home. One minute I was crying because I left Hilda alone with no explanation. *Something only a selfish coward would have done.* The next minute I was shouting and punching the steering wheel because it felt like the only way to push out all of my self-loathing. I wouldn't be able to hide whatever I was feeling for Hilda from anyone, least of all myself. The line was crossed, and I just needed time alone to process what it meant for me.

I hadn't even taken a step into the house when my mother came careening out the living room. "Clarissa Regal Huffington, you better—" She stopped dead as I awkwardly tried to balance all of Hilda's bags while shutting the door behind me. "What's all that!?"

I started to make my way to the stairs like nothing was wrong. "I went to the mall with a friend today. Don't worry. I didn't buy anything. All this stuff belongs to her." I prayed that if I treated the situation like it wasn't a big deal, my mother would only punish me for what she knew about.

"You think that's why I'm so upset?!" my mother barked. "Your father is down at the police station, filing a missing person's report for God's sake! Nobody has heard from you all day! And now you show up—"

"Stop it!" My words cut through the air like a knife. "I went to the mall, Mom. The mall. You're acting like I drove home drunk or something." I yearned to bite down and say nothing else. *No. You want a fight, so you're getting one.* "You don't get to stop me from having a life!"

"You think—"

"I'm still talking!" I shouted, startling my mother. "I'm done following your insane rules just because you think you're always right. Let me tell you, if I ever made my daughter feel like you make me feel when you throw me upstairs and lock me in my room or when you burned all my photos—! I never want to be like you. Ever! I'd rather be dead."

The expression on my mother's face flicked between sickened and furious for several long seconds before she slammed her teeth together. My heart thundered in my chest, but my mother wasn't the only adult in the house anymore. *What I did isn't a sin! And if it is, I'd rather be condemned to Hell for being with Hilda than live one more day under you!*

My mother seethed something incoherent, and her eyes lit up with an unholy rage. Her hand shot out toward me, catching me by surprise.

I cried as my mother's nails dug into my forearm. I jerked my hand back and slammed the bags into the side of my mother's face with a loud *thud*. She tumbled forward, throwing me back into the front door. The stained-glass cross above us shattered and sent prismatic glass raining from the heavens.

We were both breathing heavily. My mother held her head and shrieked when she scanned the ground. I pushed past her and stumbled up the stairs. I didn't want to look over my shoulder, but as I did, my mother was just standing there.

She had herself propped on the coat rack and looked to be on the verge of tears, just staring at the broken pieces of glass scattered on the floor.

Tears stung the corners of my eyes when I saw my mother so weak and defeated. Remorse and grief cut my soul, but I swallowed and tried to find my previous courage.

At the top of the stairs, I turned and said, "You . . . You don't get to hurt me anymore."

After shutting my door and locking it, I took a seat at my desk, realizing then that my laptop was gone. With a sigh, I leaned back and wondered what else she might have gone through and taken. *Not that I have anything to hide—at least not physically.*

Thoughtlessly, I reached into my pocket and pulled out my phone. Looking at my lock screen, I wondered if Hilda was awake yet or how she'd react to me calling her. I owed her an explanation. I just couldn't formulate any words that sounded right together, except the five that I wanted to use. For a long time, I just stared at the unsent words "I think I love you" with my heart at war with the wooden cross hanging above my bed.

The rush of heavy footsteps ascending the stairs pulled me away from my phone.

The door handle rattled, and I grinned like a petulant child.

Oh come on, Mom. You need to try harder than that.

My mother roared as she banged on my door. "You open this door right this instant!"

"Clare," my father said. "We just want to talk."

"I'm fine, Dad, but really, I'm tired. I'll talk about this tomorrow, okay?"

My mother's fist hammered on my door again. "You'll open the door or I will have your father break it down!"

My father lowered his voice, although I could hear everything he said. "Mary, please. If Clare needs space, we should respect—"

"No," my mother hissed back. "Roger, she attacked me and broke the—"

I rolled my eyes and said, "I can hear you, you know? I'm just going to sleep. I promise."

There was more whispering, but my parents spoke quietly enough that I couldn't hear them.

After a short conversation, my father cleared his throat. "Okay, Clare, if you promise you're going right to sleep and you stay in your room all night, we'll respect that. But tomorrow you have a lot of answering to do. Is that understood?"

I sighed loudly. "Yeah, Dad, that sounds great."

* * *

I woke to the sound of a power drill. Dawn was just breaking and all of Hilda's shopping bags were on the floor. The realization that yesterday wasn't some sort of beautiful dream hit me right as the doorknob to my door detached and fell to the floor. My bedroom door swung open, and there stood my mother, dressed for church but looking like she hadn't slept. My father was nowhere to be seen. He probably wasn't even awake yet.

The expression on my mother's face told me she wanted to either crucify the first person that she saw or expected Satan and me to be chatting about mundanities. When her dark gaze fell on me, I shrugged and shook my head, not sure what she wanted from me anymore. She started wailing and demanding answers.

I didn't have anything to say to her. So I said nothing.

* * *

My footsteps echoed throughout the lifeless interior of Saint Christopher's because my mother and I had arrived before the ambient choir music started playing. She was stopped by one of the nuns, who was surprised that the two of us were there. I took the opportunity to lie and tell my mother I needed to use the bathroom. *Thanks for that trick, Hilda.* I rushed toward my uncle's office, praying that he was awake and had the time to speak with me before mass started.

My closed fist hovered an inch away from the door to his office. With a gulp, I knocked twice.

"Come in. You'll find no locked doors here on Sunday," Uncle Nick's cheery voice called out.

I took one final deep breath and opened the door.

"Clare?" Uncle Nick said, somewhat perplexed. "I'm going to assume you're not here to help me fold pamphlets like you did when you were a little girl. Is something the matter?"

"Kind of," I said weakly as I thoughtlessly ran my hand along the burning scratch marks my mother had left in my arm. "I need to talk to you."

My uncle happily gestured to either of the two chairs in front of him. "Come, sit, sit."

"I'd rather stand," I said nervously, unsure of how my uncle would react to what I was about to tell him.

My uncle hummed and then seemed to nod to himself. "I can see something's really upset you. If you'd like, we could treat this as a confession. Anything you say here can't be repeated. It's forever between you, me, and God."

That made me feel better, if only slightly. "I don't know where to start," I confessed.

"Well, generally at the beginning, but I'm open for you to start anywhere you want."

I took a deep breath, trying to center myself before I dropped my bombshell. "I have this friend," I muttered, almost choking on the cliché. "She did something. With another girl, I mean. Something—" *Don't say sex, don't say sex.* "Intimate." I winced.

"Ahhh," Uncle Nick said, nodding. "Does your friend feel guilty then?"

I gulped. "Yes, kind of. Not exactly. It's not guilt about what she did. It's everything else. You see, my friend has had to lie to all of her friends to protect herself from . . . herself. Sorry if this isn't making any sense, but it's just . . . my friend is scared and doesn't know who to trust anymore because she's not sure how all her friends would react if they found out she had been lying to them about . . . stuff."

"Ah, to be young," he said as he leaned back in his chair. "Okay, let's start with some easy questions. Does the other girl, the one your friend was intimate with, does she feel the same way as your friend?"

"No, she's . . ." I closed my eyes and prayed for strength. "Gay." I was barely able to get the word out of my mouth. My uncle didn't speak right away, and his round face didn't react how I suspected it might. He just kept his jovial smile and seemed to be thinking about what to say. Fearing the worst, I spluttered, "My friend didn't know that at first, of course. She only found out recently."

My uncle nodded. "Do you know if your first friend, the confused one, regrets the decision she made?"

"No," I responded too quickly, seeing my uncle raise an eyebrow. "But, uh, the two have been close for a while. I think it was kind of . . . inevitable."

Uncle Nick hummed, deep in thought again. "Has it just been the one time? Do you know?"

I chewed on some words, trying to muster up the courage to ask the real question. "They kissed before," I said and then took a sharp breath. "Is what they did a sin? Is my friend going to Hell because she feels this way about another woman? Because her first time having sex was . . . She didn't know what it meant for her . . . How it would make her feel . . ."

My sudden outburst seemed to catch my uncle by surprise, but only for a moment. He put his index fingers on his lips and shimmied them about as he pondered. After a moment, he pointed them at me. I'm sure he didn't mean it, but it looked like he had a divine gun aimed at me, its holy ammunition set to split me in two while I waited for his answer.

"To answer your first question, no, being intimate with someone of the same gender does not immediately make someone gay, or a lesbian, as this case seems to be." He chuckled to himself. "Adding to that, sometimes people get confused, Clare. Humans are fallible, and we often make mistakes. Sometimes this means we mistake one feeling for another. For instance, some people who are unsure of themselves or are cowardly find solace in those who are confident and bold. These feelings of companionship or camaraderie can easily be confused with those of physical affection or even love."

The first invisible bullet must have hit me square in the heart because that certainly sounded like Hilda and me. *Was all this just confusion? Was what I felt for Hilda . . . not real?*

Leaning forward and tapping fingers on the edge of his desk lightly, my uncle loaded the next round. "The theological answer to your second question is a bit more nuanced. I don't want to get deep into it, but I'll say this: the laws of the Old Testament were rules for the Hebrews to follow because they needed to atone for original sin, Adam and Eve. When Jesus came down from Heaven and willingly sacrificed Himself on the cross, it was to forgive everyone of that sin so that all people could have a clean slate, so to speak. Now there are, of course, many interpretations of what exactly that 'clean slate' entails. Some people think one thing. Others believe something different. Such is the error of human interpretation of the Bible, I'm afraid."

I wasn't sure if I had dodged that bullet or if it hit me like the first. Either way, I dared to ask, "W-What do you think?"

My uncle leaned back and seemed to relax. "Ah, yes. The crux of the matter at hand. Truthfully, it doesn't matter what I think."

I blinked in disbelief, swearing I felt strands of my hair move as a stray holy bullet whizzed past my face.

Uncle Nick brightened, his cheeks rounding like two small cinnamon buns. "What matters, and what you must take away from this, is that it doesn't matter how anyone else thinks or feels. What matters is your personal relationship with God. He loves everyone, the saint and the sinner, the rich and the poor, the confused and the sure. That's the power of His love for His children. For you. Now it's my personal belief that you can't be a good Catholic without first being a good person. Looking at others not to see if they have more, but to see if they have enough. You've been that kind of person as long as I've known you, which, might I remind you, has been your entire life." He reached behind himself to grab a box of tissues and set it in front of me.

I blew my nose, not even realizing I had started to cry.

Uncle Nick stood and walked around his desk, opening his arms wide. "Now bring it in." I leaped into him, and after a long, soul-cleansing embrace, he pulled away gently. "It sounds to me like this friend of yours is finding out who she is. So, 'To thine own self, be true,' as Shakespeare once wrote." *Hilda.* I felt more tears come. My uncle patted me on the back and continued. "Maybe your friend just needs time to reevaluate who she is. No small task, I might add."

Although I feared the answer, I sobbed and asked, "How long?"

My uncle shook his head. "Wish I could tell you. Some people take hours. Others, years. Some spend their whole lives searching for who they are." He gently rested his hands on my shoulders. "I will say that knowing you, it shouldn't take too long. A few complications along the way perhaps, but"—he stopped and eyed me very brightly—"you wouldn't want to keep us all waiting forever, now would you?"

I gasped. "You—"

"Clare, please. Just because I'm mostly ears and belly doesn't mean I don't have eyes."

I hugged him so tightly that I feared he might pop. "You won't tell Mom, right? Or Dad? Please." My sobbing was muffled by his shoulder.

When I pulled away, his big jolly face said everything. "Oof!" he grunted as I hugged him again. "Shh. Shh. It's okay."

After a few more seconds, he broke the embrace. "Now, if I know your mother, she's probably searching every nook and cranny of our hallowed halls for you." He grinned foolishly. "Am I right?"

I nodded. "I'm sorry. Let me grab one more tissue."

My uncle waved his hand as he gathered some papers off of his desk. "Don't be ridiculous, Clare. You stay back here until you're ready. I'll find your mother and let her know we talked. I won't go into details, of course, but I suggest you spend this morning in prayer. If this really is who you are, you must be sure. This choice will affect the rest of your life."

"What if it's not a choice?" I asked my uncle as he tried to pass me. "What if I'm just like this?"

"Right, my apologies." He cleared his throat and got a serious look in his eyes. "When you die, you will stand before God, and he will judge you. It's not for me—or anyone else on this Earth, for that matter—to tell you what the outcome of that judgment will be. I'm only here to guide you, but the path is yours to walk. Have faith. Choice or not, it's you, and you alone, who will shoulder the responsibility of your relationship with God. If you feel that this is the path he's set for you, then walk it with your head held high." With one more grounding shake of my shoulder, my uncle moved around me and left the room.

I looked up at the cross hanging behind my uncle's desk and whispered, "I'm okay like this, right?"

God didn't answer, obviously, but I did feel a strange serenity. Layers of shame and guilt seemed to fall off of my shoulders. Still, I felt like a jerk for how I'd been treating my friends, but I vowed to the cross to spend the rest of the year making it up to them.

I sat down, wondering how I was going to spend the next few hours of my life, other than replaying my day with Hilda on loop. As I relaxed, something rectangular in my back pocket felt uncomfortable. As I reached back, the realization that my mother hadn't taken my cell phone away hit me like a truck.

I quickly navigated to my newest contact: "Hilda's Awesome New Phone." *Please answer. Please . . .* With a deep breath and heart aflutter, I pressed the call button.

On the second ring, someone picked up but didn't speak right away.

"H-Hello?" I said nervously.

Hilda replied, although her voice lacked its usual force. "Hey, Clarissa."

I nearly jumped out of my chair, recognizing a familiar sniffling noise coming from the other side of the line. "Wait, are you crying right now, Hilda?"

"N-No," Hilda stuttered, "I just—I didn't ruin everything, did I?"

"Of course not, Hilda. I . . . Listen. We need to talk about us, about yesterday and last night."

I could almost feel Hilda gulp. "Okay. I'm sorry that—"

"Stop," I interrupted. "None of what's happening is your fault."

There was a long pause. "I don't understand. What's happening, Clarissa?"

I placed my hand over my face, stupidly forgetting that Hilda had no idea what epiphanies I'd had since I snuck out of her house. "Sorry, I'm not making much sense right now. I get that. I just wanted to tell you that leaving your house when you were still asleep was really messed up, and I feel like such a jerk. And . . .

I like you, Hilda. I like you a lot. So much that it scared me. I mean, it still scares me, but I think you're worth it." There was a dead silence, so I checked to make sure we hadn't been disconnected. "Hilda?"

Hilda giggled, but I think she started to cry again, too. "It's like a dream to hear you say that, Clarissa."

I smiled, even though Hilda couldn't see it. "I know. It feels like it, right?"

Hilda cleared her throat. "I hope you didn't get into too much trouble, because I already have our next date planned."

I blushed and bit my lip like Hilda was some hunky heartthrob on a movie poster. "I'm intrigued about this new date, too, but I'm in a lot of trouble, actually. I don't think I'll be going out anytime soon." Not wanting Hilda to dig into what I just said for fear of her showing up at my house and whisking me away, I added, "You'll actually never guess where I am right now."

"Church?"

I sighed. "God, is it that obvious?"

"No, I can hear the music in the background."

"Huh?" Then I realized that I, too, could hear the choir music. "Ugh, I'm so bad at this."

"Bad at what?" Hilda inquired.

"Being smooth or whatever. I don't know." I sighed again. "But I talked to my uncle and, uh, he knows that we're, uh . . . together now."

"Of everyone you could have told, you told him about us first? Why?"

"I trust him, and he actually had a lot to say on the subject. It was all good, too." *Though I doubt Mom will ever see it that way.*

"It was?" Hilda asked, beckoning me to continue speaking.

"Yeah, it was . . . nice. So, um, you left all your makeup and stuff in my car. I had to tell my mom the cameras were yours, too, because if she thought any of that was mine, it would've all ended up in the fireplace."

Hilda gasped. "What did you say? The fireplace?"

"Yeah, my mom goes off the deep end sometimes. God, just saying that out loud makes me flinch. I'll explain more when I find out after mass just how much trouble I'm in. Also, I forgot to thank you for the cameras. So, you know, thank you."

"Your mother—"

"Don't. I don't want to think about her right now."

There was a long pause.

"I miss you, Clarissa."

"I miss you too, Hilda."

Neither of us hung up right away.

"Clarissa, I—"

"Please, if you're going to say what I think—"

"I think I'm falling in love with you."

Another bout of silence followed, agonizing and long, as I prayed that I could just say four words back to her. "I-I'm sorry, Hilda. It's just too much right now. I . . . You're the best friend I've ever had, but I can't . . . I can't say that yet." I pressed my lips together as I held my breath, waiting for Hilda's response.

"I . . . I need you to answer a question for me. What are we?"

"Well." I smiled, wiping a tear away from my eye. "I can tell you we're a little past casual dating."

"Are you my girlfriend?" Hilda asked bluntly.

"Yeah," I said softly.

"Good," Hilda said in that special way only someone with her accent could. "Because if you said no, I was going to cry until you took me back."

I laughed at the absurdity. "Yeah right. More like the other way around."

"So," Hilda said. "How are the cameras?"

Considering my uncle's words about taking as much time as I needed, I skipped mass and spent the rest of the morning on the phone with Hilda in the small office. Somewhat embarrassed, I admitted to her that I hadn't even opened the Nikon or touched the OneStep.

15

Rejections and Realizations

The storm clouds that covered the sky in gray and black did little to dampen my spirits on Monday morning. The colors of the world outside my body might have been muted and dreary, but inside, I felt like it was the warmest summer's day, and I was nearly bursting at the seams with buzzing prismatic energy. I finally understood why the LGBTQ flag was a rainbow.

As I had done for the better part of four years, I walked along the window pathways of Saint Mary's toward my locker, yet everything had shifted. The umbrella-carrying students, the decorated schoolroom doors, the flyers on the walls—they all had an ethereal familiarity that I'd never noticed before. There was a sharply distant feeling to everything as if the whole school had taken a deep breath and was waiting to exhale.

Packing my messenger bag with all the things Hilda and I had purchased at the mall was a chore. My history and geometry books were tragically left at home, so I needed to borrow copies when I got to class, but it was a burden I happily endured.

The question of whether I was gay, bisexual, or simply in love was the most dangerously enticing thought I'd ever had. Hilda gave every thought on the question a new context. My whole life needed to be recontextualized. I didn't even know where to start. Or how to start. Every time I would begin, my thoughts always strayed to something new that needed to be considered. Old memories needed to be refiled and sorted. Late nights spent with friends in the hills around Grand Forks in Bible camp. Having Matilda and Veronica sleep over and trying on bras while we talked about boys. Max. Literally, all things regarding Max needed to be sorted with the finest-tooth comb I could muster.

Even with my brain processing things as fast as it could, Hilda was ever-present in my thoughts. I couldn't wait to tell her about the master plan I'd concocted. I felt as though there was an invisible sunbeam being cast down on me from the heavens. Against my better judgment, I had stealthily tweeted from my dad's laptop between brushing my teeth and breakfast. The world had to know how great I felt. I needed to share the brightness somewhere, and Twitter seemed as good a place as any.

I saw Matilda leaning on my locker right when I turned the corner, so I mentally prepared myself for the worst but gave her a smile and wave as I walked over. I hadn't even said good morning when she started in. "For someone who was supposedly grounded all weekend, you're all sunshine and rainbows."

I bristled because Matilda sounded like she knew something more than she should have. "Good morning," I said, trying to sound like it was no different than any of a hundred other mornings we'd spent together.

Matilda kept her dangerous edge. "I saw your tweet this morning, too. Did you win the lottery? Remember, we promised to share."

I couldn't help but giggle. "I don't remember agreeing to that, but listen, I owe you an apology. I've been a real jerk recently, and we haven't really talked about it."

Matilda's judgmental look softened a bit. "Really? I mean, it's about time. Your mother literally dropped by my house yesterday looking for you, which means you snuck out, and before you say anything, I already talked to Max and D, who both also got a visit from your mother. I would have blown up your phone, but after you didn't respond to me the first two times, I assumed your mother had it."

I scratched the back of my head. "Yeah, sorry. Like I was saying, I kind of—"

Matilda's eyes immediately narrowed. "You didn't take Hilda to the mall, did you?"

"I . . . went to the mall, yeah. I also totally didn't lose my virginity, either, but you know. Crazy weekends, am I right?"

Matilda's jaw hung open like someone had just unplugged her from reality.

Not sure how to follow that bomb up, I opened my locker to put the door between us. "Also, what if I told you I got not just one but two new cameras?"

As I started moving books around to make room for clothes, makeup containers, and cameras, Matilda appeared in my peripheral vision. "Who cares about your stupid cameras!? You—" Her voice dropped to a whisper. "You had *sex*? With who? Where? Clare, you can't just say that shit and then change the subject."

I glanced over at her, but only to acknowledge that I'd heard her before I went back to playing Tetris with my locker. Admittedly, I was a bit pissed that she also brushed off my camera acquisitions. "Can't I? Because I'm pretty sure I just did."

Matilda shook her head. "You're being strangely vague about all this, Clare. I mean, it's not like—" She stopped dead when I pulled out the iconic black and pink lingerie bag and shoved it into my locker as quickly as I could. "Wait! Was that—"

"Hold this for a second." I shoved my OneStep into her chest, which served to get it out of my way but also had the added benefit of shutting her up.

Turning the camera over in her hands, Matilda gasped. "Wait, you weren't joking about the cameras, but how could you afford—"

I slammed my locker shut and turned to face Matilda. With a very, very watchful eye, I said, "Will you keep your voice down? I didn't want to tell anyone, but someone broke into my locker a while ago, and they must have known what to look for because they only took one thing. I just don't want anyone knowing what's in here right now. Okay?"

"So you lied to me when I asked what was wrong the other day. Someone did go through your locker."

My mind skipped. "I, uh—" *But if it wasn't you, then . . .*

Matilda held out my OneStep. "Seriously, Clare, talk. You need to explain this to me because I'm getting seriously worried about you."

With a dash of Hilda's confidence, I plucked my camera out of her hands and snarked, "I said I was sorry about that, didn't I?"

Matilda crossed her arms cantankerously. "Okay, no. There's no way anyone we know would buy you lingerie, other than maybe Max, but I know for a *fact* that he was home all weekend. You and I are having this conversation. I mean—" Again, she lowered her volume to a whisper. "You had sex. You!"

I shrugged. "Sorry, Matilda, class starts in five, and that wouldn't even scratch the surface of what's going on in my life right now."

Matilda snorted out her frustrations. "Fine. Lunch then."

"Sorry, I have plans for lunch." I waggled my eyebrows to imply that I would be busy with someone. Silently and with a great deal of satisfaction, I noted that Matilda was momentarily speechless.

"Wait, but Max—Clare, don't tell me you're dating Hilda!"

That stopped me in my tracks, but I didn't let my smile fade at all. "Listen, if my parents let me, I'll call you tonight. Promise. But I need to get to class. Stantin, remember?"

Matilda grabbed my arm as I turned to leave. "Just tell me it's not Hilda. To my face. Tell me that you didn't . . . do it . . . with her."

I swallowed, staring into Matilda's hazel eyes and realizing that she was actually pretty attractive—well, she would have been if she wasn't staring daggers at me.

"It's not." *It's not not her.*

"Thank God." Matilda sighed, hanging her head. "Anyone but her."

I was a bit surprised that she didn't seem to care about the gender of the person I was dating. The problem, seemingly, was entirely about *who* it was, which begged the question . . . "What about Lin? What if I told you I was dating Lin?"

"I take it back." Matilda snorted. "Any other two people."

I wanted to press further but felt like my luck was already running out. "You do not realize now what I am doing, but later you will understand."

Matilda cocked an eyebrow. "Am I supposed to understand what that means?"

A smile stretched across my face. "John, chapter thirteen, verse seven."

* * *

When Hilda rounded the corner of the hallway across from where I was seated, my heart jumped. Her right hand was wrapped in white gauze, but it looked more padded than the previous times. A thousand questions popped into my head. I started to stand, but then I saw Lin turn the corner and I froze. I watched Lin admire the view of Hilda's panties sticking out of her jeans as she leaned down to open her locker. My fists clenched with jealousy and I exploded off the hallway bench.

Lin saw me approaching and returned to her normal, resting bitch face. "Huffington," she said.

Hilda looked up from digging around in her locker. "Morning, Fräulein."

I tried looking back up at Lin but caught myself admiring the same view that she had.

"Better pick your jaw up off the floor, Huffington," Lin said evenly. "Lest everyone figure out you two are dating."

Dread crept behind my deadpan stare as I tried to gauge how much Lin knew.

She rolled her eyes when I looked to Hilda for any sort of confirmation. "Yeah, no. You wish Bernhardt was that shitty of a person. Nobody looks at someone the way you were looking at her just because. Those were bedroom eyes. The 'I've seen you naked' eyes. But mostly, you were silently screaming, 'Don't fucking touch my girlfriend, bitch.' And I gotta say, I admire that, Huffington. Who knew you had balls?"

I looked around wildly to see if anyone had overheard our short conversation, but my actions probably did more to bring attention to us than what Lin had said.

Lin shook her head. "Jesus, I take it back. But don't worry: your big secret is safe with me. For Bernhardt's sake, not yours. I want that to be clear. So you get one chance." She held a finger in my face. "You get one fucking chance to not screw this up."

Hilda shut her locker and stood. "Lin, that's enough."

With a heavy sigh, Lin dropped her hand away from my face. "Whatever. Don't say I didn't warn you, Bernhardt."

When Lin was gone, Hilda gasped, reaching out for my clawed-up arm. "Oh my God, Clarissa. What happened?!"

"Don't." I pulled away and rolled my sleeve back down all the way. "Like I told you on the phone, my mom kind of freaked out yesterday."

I could see the worry on Hilda's face. "Should you talk to the school counselor or—"

"It's not that bad," I said, trying to block out images of what Hilda might do if she knew the truth. She just didn't understand my mother. Nobody did. "What about you?" I said, changing the subject and nodding to Hilda's bandaged hand. "That looks pretty bad."

"It's fine." Hilda held out her hand and wiggled her fingers. Then she booped my nose with her index finger. "See."

I did my best to pretend that I hated it, but I was blushing anyway.

* * *

Pleasant Grounds was busier than usual, probably due to the dismal weather. On the one hand, having more people around meant that Hilda and I could blend into the crowd as long as we sat somewhere secluded. On the other hand, we were more likely to run into someone we knew. Thankfully, we found a small table for two all the way in the back, and that was where I started to offload all of the things I had brought to school.

I shoved the large Victoria's Secret bag across our table while we waited for our drinks. "Here's all your, uh . . . underwear. I didn't look at it. Promise." Tragically, the truth was that I desperately wanted to peek but just hadn't had the time. *Was it the angel or the devil? Or something else entirely?* My stomach twisted with delight.

Hilda giggled as she crammed all the stuff into her new backpack, which I also brought with me. "If I were you, I don't think I could have stopped myself. But since you didn't, maybe one of these lunches we could sneak away and—"

I interrupted her by clearing my throat and thrusting a small bag filled with her makeup supplies into her chest. "Here's all that makeup I borrowed," I said a bit louder than normal, hoping anyone who might have overheard Hilda would think she was talking about that and not the other things.

Lastly, I pulled out a small black bag and held it out. "I don't even know what's in here. When did you pick this up? Another time you went looking for the 'bathroom'?"

Hilda smiled but didn't reach for it. "No, I got those at that store you refused to go in."

I scoffed. "It was a smoke shop, Hilda. Do I look like a stoner to you? I mean, what would you even buy in there anyway? It's not like you smoke."

Hilda shrugged deviously. "If you're so curious, why don't you take a look?"

Glancing in the bag, I saw two clear plastic boxes. Too curious to stop myself, I reached in and pulled one out. Beyond the plastic was a set of hoop-shaped earrings with swirled rainbow orbs on either end.

Earrings? What would Hilda need with—

The realization hit me like a bolt of lightning from the heavens. I threw the set of nipple rings back into the bag and clenched my fist to close it, fearing someone around us might have seen.

Hilda burst into laughter as my face reddened.

Still unable to look her in the eyes, I muttered, "You're such a jerk."

She reached across the table and took the bag out of my hands. "I'm not the one who made the first move."

I cleared my throat. "You're not making this very easy for me."

My anxious words only seemed to make Hilda more eager as she grinned. "Good, I don't like easy things. I like complicated."

"Well then, you'll love this idea I had last night."

Hilda raised an eyebrow. "Oh? I think the bathroom is empty."

I didn't get the implication at first, but then it clicked. I rolled my eyes, hiding the fact that I was barely able to stop myself from taking Hilda up on the offer. "What I was saying was, since you need some help in your classes, and I'm grounded, I thought we could meet up after school and study."

"Study," Hilda echoed, only with air quotes and a yearning gaze, but once she thought about it for more than a few seconds, her smile evaporated. "Wait, how can we meet after school? You're grounded."

I nearly shouted. "That's the best part, Hilda. Nobody goes to the library downtown, at least nobody who goes to Saint Mary's. I can totally ditch my elective class after school. I just need to have a talk with Sister June about it, but I'm sure she'd agree. I was even thinking about getting my bike all fixed up. Then I could even use it to go between there and your work. We can cram on your breaks, and I can hit up the library afterward to print your assignments and stuff. Or, heck, you could come with me, and we can do some extra studying there. The library is the one place my parents will let me go, even when I'm grounded, so it all works out." Hilda seemed to doubt that my plan would work out. "What? Is something wrong?"

"No, it's a good plan. But when I'm not working, I need to train for Golden Gloves, remember? I will be late some nights."

"Yeah, duh! Hilda, I'm taking so many hard classes right now even I'm having a hard time keeping up. I'll need these late nights just to maintain my current GPA. As long as my grades never drop and I'm always at the library to get picked up, I don't think my parents will suspect a thing."

I could see the conflict behind Hilda's eyes as she tried to keep her expectations in check. "Is the library open so late?"

"No," I said with a Cheshire grin, "but the Starbucks across the street is open until eleven, which, conveniently, has everything I would need to study: coffee, Wi-Fi, and more coffee. So even if it gets late, I can just tell my parents to pick me up there. Am I a genius or what? Even my mom won't deny me my cell while I'm at the library, in case of an emergency. I swear, with all the time I've had alone in my room, I've thought this through. I honestly can't find any flaws, and believe me, I looked."

Hilda looked down into her coffee, deep in contemplation. For a few moments, I thought she wouldn't go along with my plan. Then she looked up and smiled. "Okay, I'm in."

"Great! We can probably start later this week. I just need to clear it all with my dad. I mean, the parts he gets to know about."

Hilda set her mug down and held out her unwounded hand. "I can't wait."

I looked down at her outstretched fingers. Instinctively, I peered around to see if anyone from school had come in during our conversation. Seeing me scout around made Hilda sheepishly retract her hand back to her coffee. Then she muttered, "Sorry, I'm not trying to rush you. I just—"

I shook my head, trying to raise her spirits. "I get it. My girlfriend should have the right to hold my hand in public." I briefly brushed the back of Hilda's bandaged hand. "Soon, I promise."

16

Amelie

Rain pattered on the long glass windows of the library as I looked through my physics textbook. Hilda had stopped her training session early; that was uncommon, but I was happy she decided to join me in our usual secluded section of the Grand Forks Public Library. The way Hilda aggressively typed away on the computer in front of her made me think that sometimes she would rather be in a boxing ring than doing homework.

I was about to ask what was bothering her so much when my phone buzzed.

Dad: *I'll be outside in 5.*

I sent my phone's predicted "Okay" as an answer, then poked Hilda. "Hey. My dad's almost here. Want to take a quick break? I don't think anyone's going to come by."

Hilda's head fell forward, and her shoulders dropped. "Not right now. I need to finish this before they sell out."

Curious as to how Hilda's homework could "sell out," I looked over at her screen. She was halfway through filling out some sort of online order form. "What's that?"

Hilda sighed. "I'm buying a ticket for a concert I want to see."

A bit wounded she hadn't mentioned this to me, I asked, "Oh, uh, should I get a ticket, too?"

"No." Hilda snapped but then gritted her teeth and appeared conflicted. "I don't know. Listen, we need to talk."

I put on a smile and tried to ignore the familiar tone Hilda had in her voice. "We do? What's wrong?" The obvious way she looked at me made me press into my chair.

Seeing my reaction, Hilda softened somewhat. "Clarissa, you know I love you."

Hearing those words made my heart melt, but I couldn't help glancing around to make sure nobody else overheard her.

That made Hilda groan. "I can't keep doing this. I just . . . I hate seeing you hide in a book each time someone walks by or even looks at us. I hate that I can't talk about my feelings for you openly. I hate to watch you pass in the hallways at school and pretend I don't want to reach out and hold your hand or talk to you about how my morning was. I hate that you go all the way around the school campus just to meet me at the coffee shop and you don't even show up."

I choked. "I'm trying—"

"I know, Clarissa, but I can't be a secret. I need to be . . . I need to be open about who I am. I want us to be open about this. If you can't . . . then I . . ."

I was so scared, but I felt compelled to speak. "Are you breaking up with me?" The stillness between us was too much, so I quickly added. "Please, don't—"

"Amelie and I met at a mutual friend's birthday party. I didn't know it at the time, but she was dared by someone to kiss the tallest person at the party. I think most people had assumed it would be a boy. Well, it wasn't."

I froze. Hilda never brought up her past relationships. It hurt being forced to face the truth that Hilda had dated other girls before me. I started to shake because if she broke up with me, then I felt I wouldn't be strong enough to come out on my own. That all the progress I was trying to make would be for nothing.

I swallowed and forced myself to ask, "Why haven't you told me any of this before?"

"I knew I liked girls before she kissed me, but I didn't know I could love them until afterward. I thought I'd never need to kiss anyone else again. I was so taken with her that I came out to my parents that night. After my last class of the day got out, I would run across town just to see her because we went to different schools. Most days, I wouldn't make it in time to see her before she got on the bus. Sometimes I did, though. I asked her to be my girlfriend the summer before last. She was friendly, smart, and she made me laugh like I thought nobody else could. She had this ability to make friends with anyone she met. Like you."

"Then you moved?" I knew that wasn't the case, but it was all I could do to quell the fear building inside my body.

Hilda sighed. "No. Unlike you, Amelie loved the attention we got when we were together. She liked people staring at us when we walked around Berlin holding hands. She liked that I was tall, even back then. When she learned I could fight, she liked that, too. But I don't think she ever liked *me*, and I was too blind to realize that."

A soft "oh" was all I could muster.

". . . The day after my mother died, I went to a party. I wasn't invited. I just went. I couldn't be home or at the hospital anymore. I knew Amelie was going to be there because I had seen her say so on Facebook. I really needed her. I just wanted someone to hold me. I wanted her to tell me everything was going to be okay. Well, she was there, along with some boy I'd never seen before hanging all over her. I asked what was going on and . . . the boy asked me who I was." Hilda leaned forward, and her tone was sickening. "That's when Amelie tried to pretend we weren't together. Like all that time we spent with each other . . . Like it wasn't special. She pulled me aside and said because I was a girl she could also date boys and that she hadn't even bothered telling anyone at her school about us, not even her parents." Hilda tapped her chest and seethed as quietly as she dared. "Then she offered me to one of her exes. Apparently, he and I would 'hit it off,' and I would 'like having sex with boys if I just tried it.'"

I moved to console Hilda.

"I hit her."

My hand froze in the air between us as Hilda stared down the empty row of bookcases, anger and regret plain on her face. She swallowed and seemed to force herself to continue talking. "I hit her boyfriend, too. He tried to . . . They didn't know anything about fighting. It wasn't fair. I didn't mean to." She opened her mouth to continue, but only a sad, painful sigh emerged.

The silence that fell between us felt like it lasted for hours.

Hilda closed her eyes and took a deep breath, and when she opened them again, she locked her gaze onto me. "I didn't have many friends. I've never had many friends. My whole life, nobody has really cared about me. They just want to know how tall I am or why my eyes are so strange or why I dress like this. Trust me, I get it. I'm different. When I moved to America, I wanted to fit in for once in my life. I just wanted to be like everyone else. I wanted a phone. I wanted clothes that fit. I wanted to pretend that I'm just another girl and blend in. It's not so much to ask, ja? When you first invited me to eat lunch with you, I was so happy. I was happy because you were that person I dreamed about being and you wanted to hang out with me." She sobbed. "I've tried to give you time. I've tried so hard. But I can't keep going like this. It hurts too much. I thought . . . I thought 'soon' meant sooner."

Forcing my way through my own fear, I finished reaching out and cradled Hilda's cheek. Right as she began to lean into me, a familiar voice called out. "There you are! I've been calling you and—"

Spinning around, I nearly fell out of my chair. My father was standing behind me, and I wasn't sure what was worse: the fact that my father had seen me holding Hilda or the gutted look on Hilda's face.

My dad walked over and eyed us suspiciously. "What's going on here?"

I looked over to Hilda, hoping she would answer, but she only crossed her arms and waited for me to speak. "Nothing," I said with a smile.

My father seemed skeptical. "Nothing, huh?"

I nodded. "Yeah, I just randomly bumped into Hilda here tonight and she . . . uh, was telling me about some relationship drama."

My dad chuckled lightly. "Trouble in rock-n-roll paradise?"

Hilda chewed on her lip as her eyes darted between my father and me. "No," she said so coldly that I was stunned by it. "I was telling Clarissa about my ex-girlfriend from Germany."

My dad sprouted an uneasy smile. "Oh, um, I didn't know you were, uh—"

"A lesbian?" Hilda finished and then threw out her arms. "Isn't it a little obvious?"

My dad laughed, trying his best to ease some of the tension. "I never like to assume. You know us old people. We're so out of touch with what's 'hip' these days." It was cringe-worthy that my dad called being gay 'hip' like it was a teen trend he'd seen on a magazine headline. "Well, come on, Clare, get your things. If we're late for dinner, your mother is going to ground both of us."

Hilda and I didn't talk as I hastily packed up. She didn't even acknowledge me when I said goodbye, and her eyes looked so heartbroken that I wanted to run over and kiss her. But I didn't—couldn't. *So much for progress . . .*

* * *

Hilda broke up with me, I repeated over and over to myself as I stared at my plate of untouched food while my parents talked to each other.

Then I heard my father say Hilda's name, and I looked up. "What?"

My dad seemed a bit caught off guard. "I was just telling your mother that we ran into Hilda at the library." I opened my mouth to speak but was cut off by my father. "As I was saying, she seemed distraught about something to do with her ex-girlfriend in Germany."

"Well, that answers that," my mother said. "I knew she was a homosexual. Normal people don't dress like that. All that about 'clothes not fitting her,' I knew it was a lie. Anyone can find properly fitted clothing if they have half a mind to look. It's part of their culture, I think."

The cold, dormant blood that had filled my veins since I left the library came back to life. "What's wrong with being gay?" I asked casually. "Doesn't God say to love everyone equally?"

My mom straightened up in her chair. "I never said anything was wrong with being gay, but people like her . . . They're not good people. I can't even imagine all of the things that girl does for 'fun.' I'm guessing most of it is illegal."

My dad cleared his throat and spoke more calmly but no less to the point. "Imagine if someone caught you talking to Hilda tonight as I did. In the wrong context, comforting your friend could have looked very, um . . . I mean, taken out of context, it almost looked like—"

"What did it 'almost' look like, Roger?" my mother asked.

Everything they said was wrong. As they talked, I kept looking between them, hoping one or both of them would suddenly burst into laughter and say, 'Could you imagine if we were really like that?' Then a laugh track would play, and the sitcom that was my life would roll credits. I waited, but it never happened.

"You were touching her face?" my mother asked, finally turning her attention back to me.

I blinked, already feeling my willingness to fight deteriorate. I was just so tired—so tired of trying hard to be the perfect version of myself for everyone. My selfishness had already ruined the only loving relationship I'd ever had, and without Hilda to guide me, I couldn't come out. I wasn't strong enough to be who I was alone.

"It's like Dad said. I was just trying to make her feel better. It didn't mean anything. Now, may I please be excused? I have some homework to do."

My father looked down at my plate. "Did you get enough to eat?"

"Yeah," I lied as I pushed away from the table. "I might snack on leftovers later, but I need to"—*run!*—"finish an essay."

My parents looked at each other, but by the time they turned around, I had already turned my back to them.

* * *

Nothing I had ever experienced prepared me for the week of school after Hilda broke up with me. If that was what I made Max feel like, then I owed him a bigger apology. I felt myself drifting into an ocean of emotional disconnection. I was so exhausted, not from want of sleep, but for trying so hard to be someone I knew I wasn't. I was trying to simply exist. Wherever I needed to be, whoever I needed to be, that was what I forced myself to become. I was almost upset at how all my friends went along so easily with my new game of pretend. In fact, I came to the realization that I should probably stop calling them my friends at all. None of them cared about me. Otherwise, they would have figured it out. Now we were just people that were polite to each other to keep up appearances.

Max had moved on and left me behind. Devon's jovial spirit returned, too, and I was forced to accept that he'd found a new best friend in Kate. We never got to talk about me or Hilda, which was now a moot point. Matilda had basically stopped talking to me at all since I never cracked when it came to dating Hilda, and she must have held it against me. Maybe I was overly cynical about everything, but I was kind of happy. It was really nice to see everyone else get a happy ending as school came to a close. I'd live on there, trapped in Grand Forks, having had one brief window of my life when I was truly happy and . . . in love.

On Thursday, Matilda practically exploded as she slammed her tray onto the lunch table. "I assume you've all seen it!?" Max, Devon, and a few others near the end of the long table looked over. "Look!" Matilda pulled out her phone, unlocked it, and spun it around on the table for everyone to see.

There was a picture of Lin and Hilda at a heavy metal concert. The logo on Hilda's shirt matched the tickets she was buying at the library. Lin had her hand wrapped up around Hilda's torso, gripping her left breast so tightly it was pulling her shirt down enough to expose the front of Hilda's sports bra. Lin's other hand was making horns with her index and pinky fingers. She looked like she was having the time of her life.

Hilda was making an identical gesture with one of her hands while her other hand held a drink of some sort. A white piece of tissue paper was sticking out of her right nostril, and I could see the blood it was absorbing. Despite that, Hilda also appeared to be having a great time at the show. She'd gotten her hair cut and even dyed the tips of the long side pink. Or Green? It was hard to tell because the lighting of the photo was so bad. If I had taken that photo, it would have been better. I would have been in it. Hilda and Lin were glistening with sweat as a crowd of black garb and leather studs surrounded them.

Matilda sat back and smugly waved at her phone. "I. Am. Always. Right. Say it. I'm waiting."

"Whatever," Devon said evenly. "So Hilda and Lin are together. I don't see why you care so much. It's not like it's a big deal."

"It's a huge deal! Do you have any idea what this means?! I was right the whole time about Lin! Remember last year I said she was gay! Hilda, too. I called that from a mile away."

I couldn't help but snigger. It widened into a chuckle. Then it turned into a full-blown laugh as I bent over forward. It was the only real emotion I'd felt since Hilda and I broke up.

"What's so—" Matilda began but stopped for some reason.

I was about to say, *It's complicated*, indulging my own dark humor when a shadow was cast on my back.

Lin stood there, her eyes locked on Matilda's phone. She was holding a black trash bag in one hand and a wad of money in her other, but I couldn't focus on anything but her disgusted expression.

Over Lin's shoulder, I saw Hilda standing in the middle of a hallway. It was easy to spot her because of her dyed hair, and she seemed to be having an intense and animated conversation with Kate and Veronica, who both seemed to be trying to stop her from walking over.

Matilda snorted, pulling my attention away from them. "Funny, we were just talking about you, Lin."

"Who gives a fuck?" Lin said, dropping the trash bag onto the ground next to me. "Here's your shit, Huffington."

"W-What?" I stuttered, feeling my back painfully press into the table.

"W-W-What?" Lin mocked, getting up in my face. "Fuck you!"

Max stood up. "Hey—!"

"This isn't any of your fucking business," Lin chided. "Now sit down before we both do something we regret." Then she looked back at me and narrowed her eyes. "You're fucking pathetic, Clare. Don't try and contact my friend again. She's done with your shit."

As Lin stormed off in Hilda's direction, I noticed that most of the quad had gotten wind that something was happening at our table, and all conversations had vanished into whispers.

Max, God bless him, held up a hand and announced to all the onlookers, "Nothing to see here. Just Lin being a total bitch. Nothing new." A few people laughed, but most people kept glaring at me.

Matilda was the first to speak. "Why does Lin have a trash bag of your stuff? And who is this 'friend' that she was talking about?"

My mouth opened, but then someone asked, "Oh my God! Were you dating one of Lin's friends? Who—" Then another. "Is that how you got those new cameras?"

Devon held out a hand. "Guys, cut it out. Let Clare—"

"So you lied to everyone? What the hell Clare!?"

"Seriously, just let her—"

"Of course it's Hilda. Who else could it be—"

"Wait, you're gay?"

Something inside me snapped, and all the rage, guilt, and fear warring within me vanished. As politely as I could, I stood up. I smiled at all my friends, then respectfully excused myself. The very second I turned a hallway corner and couldn't see anyone, I ran.

* * *

Nobody tried to follow me. Or maybe they did. I wasn't sure where I was even going until I ended up at Saint Christopher's. Time passed absently as I sat with my legs pressed up to my chest on the small balcony overlooking the church, quietly sobbing. I didn't want my uncle or someone else to come to find the source.

"Hey," a warm voice from behind me said.

I turned, sobbing in disbelief as Veronica stood at the top of the staircase.

"V-Veronica?" I stuttered. She was wearing a light-blue long-sleeve turtleneck with her signature bright smile and red hair around her shoulders.

Veronica nodded gracefully. "I know you probably don't want to hear this right now, but you have the whole school in somewhat of an uproar. Devon has formed a small posse to track you down. For better or worse, I can't tell."

"How'd you know I'd come here?"

"It seems like forever since I've been here. You know my parents still ask me to accompany them? I think one day I will, but it takes time." She reached into her purse and held out a small packet of travel-sized tissue papers.

"Thank you," I said as I ripped open the package and blew my nose. "I'm sorry. I'm a mess right now."

Veronica gestured to a space on the floor across from me. "May I?"

I nodded. "I'm . . . I'm sorry," I said, trying my best to stop sobbing. "Not about this. About the pictures."

Veronica shifted elegantly as she sat. "For what it's worth, I never blamed you. I was just mad and . . . upset that I had done something so stupid. But I accept your apology."

I hugged her. It made her stiffen, but she soon relaxed and rested a hand on my back. After a while of letting me cry on her shoulder, Veronica stood and offered a hand to help me up, too. We looked silently out into the nearly empty church.

"You're going to miss class," I finally managed to say between sobs.

Veronica giggled so lightly that it barely even registered. I missed that about her. "Like you, I don't have a class after lunch. You see, I have this tall friend in crisis and would be remiss if I didn't help her. Oh, look, there she is now."

Tall? I snapped my attention to each entrance as I scanned wildly for Hilda. When I was sure her pink tips weren't anywhere to be seen, I turned and realized Veronica was just shy of an inch shorter than me.

"There she is," Veronica smiled brightly. "Surprised it took her so long to find herself because she's been right here the whole time."

Tears began to run down my face again, but I couldn't help but laugh. "You're horrible."

"Maybe. Now tell me, are you and Hilda together?"

I dropped my head. "Hilda broke up with me. She wants me to come out, but I can't. My parents will . . . I just can't."

Veronica hummed softly. "I won't pretend to understand, but I think I can relate a little."

I sniffled. "You can?"

Veronica nodded. "Forgive me, this is a poor analogy, but once someone has seen you naked, that's all they ever seem to see. Plus, having Devon dump me because everyone else has seen me naked made me feel very . . . isolated. People look at me differently. Occasionally, I still feel naked, even when I find someone staring at me. It's . . . very unpleasant, to say the least. Devon's never explained why he broke up with me, but I think he felt responsible for everything and couldn't figure out how else to approach it."

"Yeah," I whispered, knowing that wasn't even close to a good enough response. My heart ached for all the suffering Veronica must have gone through alone. "I can't imagine. That must be awful."

"Well, I mean, I hope you can imagine a little bit." Veronica snickered. "I mean, you've seen Hilda's birthday suit, right? Could you ever not see it anymore when you look at her?"

"When I look at Hilda, all I see is—"

"Love?"

I choked up and tried to speak as well as I could without crying. "It used to be that. Now . . . I don't know anymore. When my dad learned about Hilda being gay, he told my mom and together . . . together they acted like it was the worst thing on the planet. Like Hilda had some disease or something. I'm so scared that they'll treat me like that, too. Like I was some sort of criminal. She already thinks Hilda is such a bad influence on me. If she knew that we've been together, I'd—" My throat closed.

Veronica did her best to hide a smile. "Well, I did hear Hilda enjoys beating people with her fists and buying her way through her homework. But those are only criminal offenses if both parties aren't consenting."

I tilted my head. "Huh? Buying her way through homework?"

Veronica raised an eyebrow. "Oh, you didn't know? I had assumed you were one of the people she had been paying. I know she pays Lin and Kate." She broke eye contact with me. "Perhaps I've said too much."

"I had no idea. I wished Hilda had told me. All those nights . . . She must have been pretending just to spend time with me, and I've been—"

Veronica's phone buzzed in her purse. "Excuse me."

As Veronica typed away, I couldn't stop myself from asking, "Do you know if Lin and Hilda are together? I saw a picture of them—"

"As far as I am aware, they are just friends. As for the photo in question, if it's the same one I've seen, they had been drinking heavily. Lin was talking about it this morning. I believe one of Hilda's coworkers was also attending that show and brought some alcohol with him, which, I believe, our two friends shared exclusively."

I smiled and blew my nose again. "That's good."

"So this is where the pity party is happening," Lin interrupted venomously as she climbed the last step. "This balcony reflects your personality perfectly, Huffington. It's so small and worthless you can hardly see it, yet somehow, it finds a way to lord itself above everyone else."

I looked over to Veronica in disbelief. "You texted Lin?"

Veronica shrugged sympathetically. "Believe it or not, I think you two should talk."

Lin walked over and joined Veronica and me on the cramped balcony. Nobody spoke for a long time.

Veronica eventually sighed and said, "Lin, please."

Lin crossed her arms. "What? I told Huffington that if she fucked up, I would be there for Hilda."

Veronica slammed her foot down, the sound echoing through the church. "Enough. You of all people know what Clare's going through right now. Help her. Please."

She's standing up for me. Like a friend.

Lin swore under her breath and seemed to finally recognize that I existed. "Fine. What's wrong with your pathetic ass this time, Huffington? Other than the obvious."

I swallowed my fear. The first two people other than Hilda to hear my next words were Lin and Veronica, the last two people on Earth I expected to tell face to face. "I'm in love with Hilda."

Lin rolled her eyes. "I said other than the obvious, didn't I?"

My courage faltered but I pushed forward. "I just can't do it in public. My mother, and everyone else . . . It's too—"

Lin reached into her pocket and thrust a piece of crumpled paper into my chest.

I grunted and tried to grasp the paper. When I looked down, I realized it was the note I had written Hilda, the one that was stolen out of my locker. I gasped. "You were the one—"

"Duh," Lin said. "My sister taught me how to open any locker before she graduated. That note is pretty fucked up, Clare, even for you. All that shit about keeping your relationship a secret is selfish, ignorant, and—"

"I'm trying—" I spluttered, trying to stop myself from bursting into tears again.

Lin rushed forward and grabbed me firmly by the shoulders. "Fucking stop crying like a pathetic child!" Veronica moved to intervene, but Lin shoved her off with an elbow. "No! She needs to hear this." Lin's nostrils flared as she gripped me tighter. "Clare, you're acting like a selfish bitch, and I won't stand here and listen to you cry about how hard your life is. It's always 'me, me, me' with you. Do you have any idea how many nights Hilda's called me and just talked about how hard this has been for her? How many times did she ask if you came out? A hundred? A thousand? Did you not get the fucking hints!?"

Fear took over, and I looked over the balcony, unable to confront Lin's aggression head-on.

She grabbed my jaw and forced me to face her. "I wasn't finished. I had to beg Hilda to go to see Testament with me, and only after she was drunk did she still fucking bitch about how badly she wants to be with you. And yeah, I told her to break up with you, and I convinced her to let me give you all that shit you left at her house, but it was for her own good. I don't care if Hilda hates me for what I did, but being with you was poisoning her, and I couldn't stand it any longer. You don't get to ruin Hilda's life!"

Lin let me go, but she didn't shove me or anything. She just . . . fell away. "You don't owe it to anyone to come out, and I get that you're scared. I was, too. But frankly, you're a fucking baby. Either come out and be with Hilda or don't. Constantly fucking with her like you did with Max all these years is a bitch move and I won't stand for it."

"But—"

"I'm not going to sugarcoat this, Clare. I don't think you deserve her." Lin's teeth snapped together, and she turned away and wiped at her eyes. "But if you really love her, you'll do what's right." At the staircase, she stopped and said, "I hope I helped, or whatever."

There was a stunned silence as Veronica and I listened to Lin's footsteps echo down the stairs.

Once we couldn't hear anything anymore, Veronica turned to me, shock still apparent on her face. "Clare, I'm so sorry. I didn't—"

"She's right," I said, unsure of who I was speaking to. Myself? Veronica? God? Did it really matter? "How could I be so cruel to someone I love so much? How could I be so scared of me?" Pressing both hands against my heart, I looked up at Veronica. "Is that crazy? Am I crazy?"

Veronica's sympathetic smile was all I needed, but she shook her head. "You are a great deal of things, Clare. Crazy doesn't make the top fifty. You want to see crazy?" She reached down into her turtleneck and pulled out a simple golden cross on a thin gold chain. "If you could tell Devon I started wearing this again, I think he'll understand what it means. If he doesn't, well—" She shrugged.

"I'll tell him."

Veronica stuffed the gold necklace back into her shirt, and after a thought, a bizarre grin overcame her.

"What's that look for?" I asked.

"It's nothing. But since you asked, I guess I'm a little envious of you."

I gasped. "Me? Why?"

"You're in love, and I suppose, if you're gay, that means you'll never have to deal with the vast puzzle box that is the male intellect ever again. I'm honestly a little jealous."

The joke was terrible, really terrible, but we both laughed anyway. We talked for a bit. All of the little things made my big things seem less daunting. The past few months had been filled with such seemingly impossible questions that it was nice to feel grounded again.

Veronica nudged me. "I can stay if you'd like, but I really should be going."

I sighed. "Honestly, we should both get going, but I still need some time alone, if that's okay."

Veronica nudged me with her elbow. "You don't have to ask me if that's okay. Take all the time you need. I'll do my best to cover for you, and I'll talk to Devon. If you'd like, I can even collect your homework—" Her phone buzzed, and her eyes widened upon seeing the screen.

"What's going on?"

Veronica smiled as she began to type a reply. "What's your next step? If you don't mind me asking."

I took a deep breath. "I think . . . I'm going to find Hilda and confess everything to her. Then I'll tell everyone else."

"Simple," Veronica said with a hint of sarcasm. "Two things before I go. God forbid, but if the worst should happen with Devon, Matilda, and Max, you're always welcome to eat with me at lunch. Secondly, I totally didn't just get a text from a certain someone who's also searching everywhere for you. Almost assuredly, I didn't just text them back, letting them know that you're going to meet them at their work. I mean, who would even do that?"

I ran over and hugged her. "Thank you so much."

Veronica gave me one final squeeze. "See you tomorrow. Hopefully." She crossed her fingers. "And be strong. If you can get through a lecture from Stantin, you can do anything."

By the time I cleaned myself up and scrounged up enough courage to move forward with my plan, there was still one thing missing. I pulled out my phone and ignored the massive wall of notifications. I needed something: proof I was still me, that I hadn't changed, that I had been me my whole life. Tapping the camera app, I held out my phone and took the worst selfie ever. As I went to delete it, a new notification appeared on my screen.

Veronica Lancer: *Go out the back. Quick. Your mother is here, and she's looking for you. I'm stalling as best as I can.*

* * *

My throat tightened as I placed my hand on the rusted doorknob of Mick's Gym. I promised myself that I would still go through with everything, even if Hilda rejected me.

"Hey, kid," Richard called as I entered. "Wasn't expectin' to see you here." I followed his curious gaze back into the gym and saw Hilda furiously pacing the side of the boxing ring, staring at her phone. "I'm assumin' this ain't no coincidence."

"I love her," I said hoarsely over the knot in my throat. After a quick grunt, I reiterated proudly, "I love Hilda."

Richard scratched his chin, looking confused. "'Course y'ah do. Is this some kinda joke, kid? Cuz I ain't gettin' it."

My face flushed, and I felt a little ridiculous. *Was I so transparent?* I hid my embarrassment behind a smile. "Yeah, kinda. Can I go back?"

Richard nodded. "Yer always gonna be welcome here, kid."

As I approached Hilda from behind, not wanting to spoil my big entrance, Richard roared. "Bernhardt, check your six!"

Hilda whipped around so hard she nearly dropped her phone. "Clarissa!" she gasped. "You—"

"I love you, and I'm sorry I made you wait to hear it. I'm sorry you had to cry because of me. I'm sorry I made us hide our relationship. I hate how we have to be apart at school. I hate being scared to be myself and feeling ashamed about how I feel about you. And if you'll still have me, I want you to be my girlfriend again."

Hilda opened her mouth, but I kept going. "Not like before, either. I want everything. Handholding in the hallways, slobbery make-outs behind the gym at lunch. I want to take you out on so many dates that you get sick of seeing me. Not to mention all the pictures I'm going to plaster over social media. I swear I'm going to cover my entire room, floor to ceiling, and I don't care if my mom burns them all again. I'll take so many it won't matter. But mostly I just want you back . . . please."

Hilda continued to stare at me like a deer in headlights, so I shouted, "Everyone, I'm gay! And I'm in love with this beautiful woman right here." I pointed straight up at Hilda's face and looked around to see that I had the attention of everyone inside the gym.

Richard walked over to me and said, "And I thought I was the loudest person here." Then he pressed a gentle hand into the small of my back. "Now, what are you waiting for, Bernhardt? Poor Clarissa here just put her heart on her sleeve. Be a cryin' shame if you didn't say somethin'."

"Ja," was all that Hilda said, and it was the softest and most beautiful thing I'd ever heard escape her mouth.

Richard grunted. "Good enough." Then he shoved me forward.

I stumbled, but Hilda was there to catch me. With one hand wrapped around Hilda's shoulder and the other around her waist, I held the awkward embrace Richard had forced me into.

Looking up into Hilda's steelie eyes, I whispered, "I love you, Hilda."

Hilda straightened me and took a step back, giving me a hard once-over. "Louder," she said.

"What?" I gasped.

Hilda waved to the gym. "I know you love me. But I want everyone else to know it."

Licking my lips, I shouted, "I love you, Hilda!"

"Again!" Hilda yelled back.

"I love yo—"

Suddenly, Hilda dipped me back, and our lips melted together.

Richard cleared his throat, interrupting the best kiss of my life.

"Y'all done yet? Believe it or not, I'm tryin' to run a fuckin' business here."

I brushed the pink tips of Hilda's hair as she stood me upright again. "I like this. It's really . . . you."

Hilda's hand found mine, stopping me from combing her hair. "Thanks. You'll never guess what it matches."

Richard snorted. "Ha, that's a good one, Bernhardt. I'll remember that."

I blushed, but something caught my attention. Over Hilda's shoulder, standing just inside the doorway of the gym, was my mother. It was so implausible that I had to shake my head to make sure I wasn't hallucinating. Worse still, by the horrified look on her face, she had heard and seen everything.

17

Forced Out

"Clarissa Regal Huffington!" my mother screeched. "What is the meaning of this!?" She stalked toward me, teeming with disgust, her shrill voice reverberating off the sun-bleached posters.

My whole body was frozen, and I couldn't think. "Mom, I . . . You . . . How?"

As she marched, my mother held her phone above her head. "I've been watching you. Your father was brilliant enough to set up some sort of phone tracking. He thought it wouldn't be needed, but I knew! I knew it was only a matter of time before . . . What is this? Who are these people?"

Richard reached out his hand. "Richard Longstreet. I run this gym with Chris here. We—"

"Does running this 'gym' also mean you harbor delinquent high school students and degenerate homosexuals?" my mom snapped. Richard's cautious smile turned into a thin line. "I get the feeling I know exactly the kind of business you run here, Mr. Longstreet, and I won't stand here and have my daughter be coerced by you or your agenda!"

I took a step forward. *No, you can hurt me, you can make me feel like trash, and you can lock me in my room, but nobody talks to my friends like that.* "Richard has nothing to do with this, Mom. This is about me. This is about who I am."

My mother narrowed her eyes at me and hissed, "No, it isn't. You think I don't know my own daughter? I don't know what these people have been telling you, but you're done listening. And you." She pointed at Hilda. "You should be ashamed of yourself. Come, Clare. We're leaving."

Hilda stepped up next to me and threaded her fingers with mine. When I looked up at her, she only nodded, letting me know I was going to be okay.

With Hilda next to me, I felt invincible. "No," I whispered as I gripped Hilda's hand so hard that I felt like I was about to break her fingers. "No, Mom. Hilda and I . . . She's my girlfriend, and I want to stay here."

My mother turned around, deaf to my declaration. "I wasn't asking—" She stopped dead because she noticed our hands.

Shaking from head to toe, I announced, "Mom, I'm gay."

My mother burst out in hysterical laughter. Then she pointed at me. "You're not gay. You don't even know what that word means. These people . . . Can't you see what's going on here? I mean, look around you for God's sake."

Chris and Richard exchanged a quick look, but before they got any ideas, I said, "I'm staying here with Hilda, and you can't make me leave."

"Oh?" My mother bit. "We'll see about that!"

I closed my eyes and clenched my whole body, bracing for impact, but . . . it never came.

"Yeah, 'bout that." Richard's voice cut through the air, and when I opened my eyes, he was standing between my mother and me with his arms crossed over his chest. "Yer gonna wanna take a good look around you before you thinka setting a hand on anyone in my house."

Following my mother's eyes, I saw that everyone in the gym had stopped whatever they were doing and were all staring. Not at me, but at my mother. Each seemed more massive than the last, and all looked freaking pissed. Chris stepped up and held an arm across Hilda and me in a protective manner. That was when I realized he wasn't protecting us, he was stopping Hilda, who looked absolutely livid. When I looked down at our hands, she was the one shaking and squeezing my hand, not the other way around.

Worry gripped me, and I set my free hand on Hilda's shoulder. "It's okay."

"It's not," Hilda spat, "It's—"

"Hilda," I said softly, which finally got her attention. "You can be upset later, okay? But right now, I need you."

"Yeah, save it for the ring, Bernhardt," Richard said, then glared at my mother. "Now, I don't know nothin' about no 'agendas' or 'delinquents' or anythin' like that, but I ain't too keen on the way you're actin'. So get the fuck outta my gym. And I don't ever wanna see yer face in here again."

To her credit, my mother didn't back down and pompously sneered, "You can't do this. That's my daughter." When nobody moved, my mother took a step back. "You can't do this."

Richard tilted his head. "I'm gonna start countin'..."

My mother swallowed. "I'm... I'm calling the police." A few seconds later, the front door slammed shut, and my mother was gone.

Richard rubbed his chin and turned to us. "You two okay?"

Everything had happened so fast—it was *still* happening fast. I tried to get a grip, but I just .... I just ...

Hilda's voice pulled me back to reality. "Clarissa, are you okay?"

I took a deep breath. "I think so. That was a lot. But I'm okay." I squeezed her hand. "We're okay, right?"

Hilda gave my hand a reassuring squeeze while Richard snapped his fingers at Chris and pointed to something. "Good, 'cause we gotta get you two the fuck outta here."

I tried to understand but couldn't. "What? Why?"

Richard chuckled. "Believe it or not, you both ain't supposed to be outside of school right now. Truancy officers and the like. There's also probably a couple laws 'bout keeping a mother from her daughter by way of mass intimidation. But they can't find you if you ain't here—"

Startled that he was probably right, I asked, "What about you?"

Richard laughed. "Us? Kid, I appreciate the sentiment, I do, but this rust bucket's been through much worse. One old windbag ain't gonna blow this house down."

Chris thrust a visored motorcycle helmet into my chest, and I grabbed it with both hands without thinking. Then he asked me, "Have you ever ridden on the back of a motorcycle before?"

I shook my head.

Richard shooed me toward the back entrance. "First time for everything," he said.

"What about Hilda?" I turned to see Hilda rushing into Chris and Richard's office.

Chris laughed as he followed me like a bodyguard. "Do you really think we're going to separate the two of you after all that? Who do you think is going to drive?"

I looked back to see Hilda already emerging from the office with a set of keys and a helmet of her own.

Outside, I mounted the back of Chris's Harley Davidson and wrapped my arms tightly around Hilda. Chris double-checked that everything was in order before he gave Hilda a knock on her helmet. "Drive safe, stay under the speed limit, and take the corners easy." Then he turned to me and gave me a thumbs-up. "Hold on tight."

Hilda turned the key and kicked the bike to life. The motorcycle roared forward, and I closed my eyes. My grip on Hilda's waist tightened. As we drove, I heard police sirens pass us but didn't dare to look. I had Hilda, and I never wanted to let go.

After what felt like hours of riding a rollercoaster, Hilda cut the engine, and we stopped moving. Finally, I peeled my eyes open, wondering where Hilda could have taken us. The view of Saint Mary's had never looked so inviting but also foreign. Hilda had parked us on the sidewalk right next to the flagpoles.

By the looks of things, the afternoon bell had just rung, and students were filing out of the buildings.

Hilda put out the kickstand and leaned the bike over. I almost lost my balance, but she caught me, saying something that sounded like "careful," but it was muffled by her helmet.

I removed my helmet and took what felt like my first real breath in a long time. "Why didn't you ever tell me you had a motorcycle license, Hilda?"

Hilda, having taken off her own helmet, gave me a devious look. "Clarissa, I—"

"Oh my God," I interrupted, gasping. "You don't have one."

Hilda shrugged. "No, but a couple times Chris has let me drive back from Chicago. There's no one on the highway that late—"

"Just a couple times?!" I scolded. "You . . . We . . . God, what am I going to do with you?"

Hilda smiled as she set both of our helmets on the bike. "I could think of a few things . . ."

By now a small group of students had begun to stare at the strange sight of a motorcycle in the middle of the sidewalk—or, probably more accurately, the two people standing beside it.

Hilda must have seen me glancing around and said, "You should probably—"

"No," I interrupted and reached out for Hilda's hand. "I'm not going to hide the way I feel anymore. That being said, I should get home before my mom does. I don't know what's going to happen, but if I just come to school crying every day for the next month, you'll know why."

Hilda jolted me toward her and then pressed me into her so I couldn't escape. "If your mother makes you cry, even for a second, I'm coming over to save you. Nothing will stop me from getting to my girlfriend. Ja?"

A dark part of my mind strayed to the fact that my mother would say literally anything to make me feel guilty, and therefore cry, but hearing Hilda call me her girlfriend again made it better. "Okay, but you have to promise that if I'm a mess for a while, you'll keep dating me."

Hilda spun me around, sandwiching me between her and the motorcycle. Then she said something in German. It was smooth and soft and everything I needed to hear, even if I didn't understand a word of it.

I grinned. "Yup, I still don't understand German."

"Maybe you'll understand . . ." Hilda leaned down as I pushed up on my toes, and we kissed.

After we finally managed to stop, Hilda asked, "Do you want me to be there when you talk to your family?"

I shook my head. "No. This is something I need to do alone. They need to understand that this is about me and not something you, or anyone else, forced me into. I'll be okay. Promise."

"Okay." Hilda pressed her forehead gently against mine. "I love you."

"I love you, too."

* * *

By the time I arrived home, I was drained, having had my fill of hoofing around Grand Forks. I stared up at the cardboard covering what remained of the glass cross above my front door. The second I opened the door, I would face my father. The old station wagon was absent from our driveway, so I assumed my mother was still out doing God knows what. Probably screaming at Richard and Chris. Thoughts of the worst possible outcomes had been swimming in my mind since Hilda mounted the bike and drove back to work. I sent a silent prayer to God as my hand slowly reached out for the handle on my front door.

As I closed it behind me, Dad curiously poked his head out of his study. "Mary? Clare?! What are you doing home so early?"

I heaved a sigh. "It's a long story."

"Well, you better start explaining. Also, why did you add this phone line to our account?" He disappeared into his office and came out a second later, holding a bill in his hand. "I called the phone company today to dispute this extra charge, but they said you authorized a fourth line on our account. And you also purchased a forty-five-dollar concert ticket using the new number?"

"Where's Mom?" I asked nervously, wondering just how much my father knew. Not much, judging by how mildly he was treating me.

"I don't know." He raised an eyebrow. "Why are you here? Did something happen at school?"

"Yeah, kinda. Can we sit down?" I didn't wait for him to answer before I made my way to the dining room.

My dad followed, clearly a bit miffed at my behavior. I pulled out a chair for him and took the adjacent seat while I explained the additional phone line.

"So that's it," I said. "Hilda's been giving me cash, but I've kind of been spending it on coffee. Sorry."

My father sighed. "I wish you would clear things like this with me before you just run out and did them. It's not serious this time, but you can't keep this up. Your mother's at wit's end with you as it is, and though I see you're just helping Hilda, your mother isn't going to like this. Speaking of which, I think she was planning on picking you up." He pulled out his phone.

Fear spiked through me, and I tried to reach out to stop my father from calling my mother. "Wait, Dad—"

My father held up his finger, stopping me as we both listened to the phone ring. My heart stopped beating when, on the third ring, my mother must have picked up. Immediately, I heard yelling on the other end of the line, although I couldn't make out what my mother was saying.

My father sat up and adopted a concerned look. "Mary, wait. Slow down. Clare? She's right here. She walked home . . . The police? Honey, slow down. No, she's fine. Mary, what's going . . . Please, I don't understand—"

The familiar double beep in the middle of my father's sentence signaled that my mother had hung up. For a long time, my father stared at the screen of his phone. When he looked up at me, it sent a chill down my spine. "What have you done?"

* * *

When the front door opened, my gaze locked on the hallway, and I centered myself for the battle to come. My mother burst into the dining room. She quickly bore down on me and did something that I wouldn't have expected in a million years. She kneeled and gathered me into her arms for a hug. Stroking my hair, she said, "Thank God you're safe! I thought those people had done something to you!"

I was stunned. "I'm . . . I'm fine, Mom."

Exasperated, my father asked, "Can someone please explain what's happening?"

My mother stood back up and took a deep breath. "You remember Hilda? Well, it turns out that she somehow—"

"I'm gay," I interrupted, locking eyes with my father and praying to God he understood the gravity of what I had just said.

Of course, my mother just groaned. "For the last time—"

"Yes, I am, Mom," I stood up to meet her. "You can't just pretend this isn't happening or ground me until I change my mind. I'm gay, and you don't get to tell me otherwise!" I felt like a prisoner who'd finally been released from an indefinite sentence. All of the guilt and shame that had held me down so long fell away and left me . . . stronger.

My mother, still ignoring me, waved and said, "You see, Roger? This is exactly what I was afraid of."

I snapped my teeth together and shouted, "Will you stop and look at me for two fucking seconds!? This is who I am. I'm still your daughter. I'm still me. I'm just a—"

"Don't say it," my mother hissed. "Don't you dare say—"

"Lesbian. I'm a lesbian, Mom. And if you can't deal with that, then I guess you're just the bitter old woman that everyone thinks you are."

My mother's face contorted in frustration. "And what about tomorrow? Or next month? A year from now? Were you secretly a lesbian all these years you've been dating Max? Why now? What suddenly happened to make you think you're gay? I'll tell you what, you met that degenerate Hilda and her 'friends' down at that filthy gym. Do you think we don't get it? We understand peer pressure. We were teenagers, too. Hilda's got you all mixed up so you can't tell right from wrong."

Hot air shot out of my nostrils. "Stop trying to blame this on Hilda! I would still be gay even if I never met her. And sure, I'll admit, it would have taken me longer to figure it out if she hadn't been in my life, but you're treating it like a decision."

My mother scoffed. "Isn't it?!"

I nearly screamed in agony, wanting to rip all my hair out. "Do you think I would ever want to feel this way if I had a choice? Do you have any idea how scared I've been? How ashamed I was? The guilt, it hurt so much that I thought I would never be able to feel anything ever again!"

"That's God!" my mother roared. "That's God telling you that what you're engaging in is—"

"Shut up, Mom! I talked to Nicholas about this, and he said God would still love me even if I fell in love with another woman. He said the only thing that mattered was my personal relationship with God. And right now"—I swallowed, restraining a sob—"if either of us is going to Hell, I think it's you." I searched my mother's horrified face for a long time, praying to find even an iota of empathy or understanding. When I saw nothing change, I hung my head in defeat. "I can't do this anymore. I can't pretend to be someone I'm not. Ground me. Take away everything. I don't care." I unceremoniously tossed my phone and apparent tracking device onto the table. "I'm done fighting with you, Mom."

My father finally stood, wedging himself between us. "Now, let's not put the cart before the horse. Clearly, we all have a lot to talk about, and we should do it as a family. We should listen and try to be as understanding as—"

"Roger, you can't seriously think—" my mother protested.

"Mary," my father interrupted, holding his hand up. "I'm not sure what to think right now, but if Clare thinks she's . . . gay . . . then we owe it to her to hear her out." He looked to me, but I could tell that he was a bit out of his element, even if he was keeping it together a thousand times better than my mother. "Clare, you understand this isn't something you can take back, right? This decision is going to follow you for the rest of your life. People will treat you differently, in ways that you, or even I, can scarcely imagine. You might not get a job. You might be turned away from great career opportunities. Do you understand that? This is serious."

I nodded, doing my best to appear like I had already considered that.

My father took my mother's hand and said, "Your mother and I understand that imitation is the sincerest form of flattery. Trust us. We get Hilda's appeal. She's 'gothic.' She's athletic. She's 'cool.' But like your mother was saying, just make sure she's not confusing you . . . or even coercing you into something you don't fully understand."

I shook my head and sighed. "I know what I'm doing. Hilda and I have been dating for almost three months. Each time you would drop me off at the library, I ran off to meet up with her."

Shock washed over my mother's face before she asked, "Have you . . . Have you had—"

"Sex?" I interrupted. "Yeah, we have. Lots of it." After that, I knew I should have left it alone, but I added, "Hilda actually took my virginity."

My mother's expression soured into something that was equal parts repulsed and disappointed. I might as well have said that Satan himself tattooed the number 666 on my lower back. No, it was worse; it was like I told her I was gay and I'd been having sex with my girlfriend for almost three months.

My father had the common sense to keep his expression mostly neutral, but he narrowed his eyes slightly. I couldn't tell if it was concern or something else. My mother shouted, "I won't hear another word of this! Go to your room and don't come out until I say so!" When I didn't move, my mother ordered, "Now!"

Hearing that commanding tone made horrible memories rush into my mind, but I held myself firm. I was tired of trying to explain myself, of being war-torn and constantly fighting with my mother's unquestionable authority.

With a deep breath, I said, "Fine, but I'm done arguing."

When I reached the doorway leading to the hall, my father called out to me. I turned back to see my mother crying quietly into my father's shoulder. "Aren't you going to at least apologize?" He looked so worried and unsure of what to do. I had never seen him so vulnerable. He always knew what to do to make things right, but not this time.

It took everything I had to summon the strength to speak without falling apart. "I'm sorry I yelled, and I'm sorry I've lied about dating Hilda. But that's all. I'm not going to apologize for who I am." Then I turned on my heel and walked to my room.

* * *

I stirred to life under my thick blankets as a bright sunbeam broke through the curtains of my bedroom window. Yawning, I rubbed my eyes and tried to focus on the clock that replaced my phone on my nightstand. My eyes widened in horror as I realized I was almost an hour late for school.

Throwing off my bedsheets, I frantically rushed through my morning routine. After brushing my teeth, I ran down the stairs but couldn't find my messenger bag. I walked into the dining room thinking maybe I'd left it there, but then I remembered I'd left everything at school the day prior when I ran off during lunch.

Oh God, I hope someone I can trust picked up that trash bag Lingave me at lunch.

Nearly out the door, I saw something unfamiliar sitting on the dining room table. It was a neatly folded note with my name on it. The familiar handwriting told me it was from my father.

I'll get the bad news out of the way first. Your mother has looked into special places that specialize in specific cases like yours. I've talked her out of it for now, but she seems determined to at least explore that as an option. I don't know what she will do if you continue to press your boundaries, so please, tread carefully for the next few days.

In all probability, you're going to start some sort of therapy, though I'm still trying to work out the details.

The good news is, until your mother and I figure out what to do with you, you're under house arrest. And for the love of God, please, I'm begging you, stay put for once.

As far as the school is aware, you're taking an extended leave of absence for a family emergency.

Love,

Mom & Dad

As I continued to read, my once-familiar and welcoming house transformed itself into a dark and grotesque place. A place where I wasn't loved or even wanted. I was standing in a prison, and escape was my only option. I crumpled the note and threw it across the room. As I looked around the large dining room, every nerve was on high alert. It felt like a group of people could burst in, throw a bag over my head, and whisk me away. *Never to be seen again.*

Hesitation and fear wracked my body as I slid open the living room window. Slipping out of it, I ducked into some hedges and watched the street for any sign of movement. After she'd tracked my phone, I wouldn't have put it past my mother to ask the neighbors to watch our house in case I made a break for it. When I didn't spot anyone looking out of their windows or any cars coming down the street, I sprinted down the sidewalk.

A few blocks away from home, I finally slowed down and started to think. I didn't have any money or . . . anything really. *Should I go back? What if Mom came home by now? What if she—*

"Miss Huffington?" a stuffy but gruff man's voice called out.

Startled, I nearly tripped backward, having thought I'd been caught. With a hand pressed against my heart, I looked over and saw Mr. Stantin standing by the open trunk of an SUV in the driveway I was crossing. His eyes were puffy and his nose a bright shade of red. He began to speak but coughed into his hand. "Listen, I don't know how you found my address, but if you're looking for an extra credit assignment to make up for missing class, you're barking up the wrong tree."

I blinked, still in shock. "I'm not . . . Why aren't you at school?"

He coughed again. "Why do you think? Now, what are you doing here?"

I swallowed. "My parents are forcing me to take an extended leave of absence for a family emergency." While Stantin ran a critical gaze over me, I thought of something. "Um, Mr. Stantin, could I use your phone, please? I left my cell phone at home." When Stantin didn't move, I added, "It's a bit of an emergency."

Stantin sniffled, reached into his pocket, and held out an older-generation iPhone. "Here."

With Stantin hovering less than two feet away, I manually input Devon's number. It went to voicemail, so I quickly tried it again. *Please pick up. Please . . .*

On the third ring, someone answered, but I didn't let them speak. "Hey, it's Clare. Come pick me up on the corner of First and King." I lowered my voice to a whisper and turned away from Stantin. "Please . . . I need help." Before Devon had a chance to answer, I hung up. With a sigh, I did my best to rally my spirits before turning back to Stantin and handing him his phone. "Thank you."

Stantin seemed to hesitate before taking back his phone. "Is there something going on I should know about, Miss Huffington?"

I kept my smile, doing my best to portray that I wasn't running away from home without a plan. "Not really, it's, uh . . . It's just a misunderstanding that's kind of gotten out of hand."

Stantin didn't seem to believe whatever I was faking. His gaze fell to my arm, which I hadn't realized I was digging my own nails into.

Then I noticed Stantin hawkishly scan left, then right, checking the street. His voice dropped so only I could hear it. "Miss Huffington, are you in any danger? Do you need me to call the police?"

I shook my head but felt my smile break. "No, but—" I swallowed, trying not to cry. "Can you stay with me? Until my friend picks me up. Please."

* * *

"And that's what happened yesterday," I confided, wiping a tear from my face. "It just . . . I'm scared of what's going to happen. How could my parents do that to me?"

Stantin's usual expression had turned to one of concern as he rested a hand on my shoulder. What little composure I had left evaporated as I sobbed. "Running from your problems never solves them. I ran away from home when I was your age and joined the army. Taught me a lot, but I always regret I didn't make things right with my folks before they died. Make sure you don't make my mistake, okay?" I swore I heard him add "for me," but the screeching of tires and the roaring of an engine made it impossible to tell.

I turned to see Devon's Mustang whip around the corner, leaving dark black skid marks on the road. The car flew down the street and screeched to a halt in front of Stantin's driveway.

Devon jumped out of the driver's seat without even bothering to turn the car off. "Clare, what's wrong? Are you . . . Mr. Stantin?!"

Stantin coughed into his hand. "Mr. DeVille, good to see you're skipping class, too."

The pure bewilderment in Devon's expression made me smile.

* * *

Shutting the passenger door to Devon's car, I took a deep breath, not even sure what to do or where to go. Devon slid into the driver's seat and just started driving.

I asked, "Wait, where are we going?"

Devon looked upset and seemed to ignore my question. "I can't believe you."

"What?"

"You told Mr. Stantin you were gay before you told me! I mean, don't get me wrong, I figured it out months ago . . . but still! How dare you?"

My heart skipped, and I stuttered, "Y-You knew?"

At a stoplight, Devon turned, giving me an egregious look. "About you dating Hilda or you being gay? Because I'd be a pretty shitty best friend if I hadn't put both together."

I turned away but kept Devon in my peripheral vision. "Why didn't you tell me?"

Devon rolled his eyes. "Are you seriously asking me why I didn't tell you that you're gay?"

"No." I swallowed. "But it would have been nice to know you knew."

"Everyone knew," Devon said, and when I turned to gasp at him, he continued. "I mean, come on. You're about as subtle as Max is when it came to dating Hilda. Did you think nobody noticed that the same days you snuck off to meet with your 'friend' just happened to be the same days Hilda wasn't at lunch, either? Also, all of our study nights suddenly stopped because you were 'grounded,' but somehow you kept getting straight A's." He tilted his head at me knowingly. "Nobody is that dense. Even Max figured it out. The only one who doesn't believe it is Matilda, but we all think she's just in denial."

"Why . . . Why didn't anyone say anything?"

Devon blinked in disbelief. "Lin cornered Max and told us that if we confronted you, it could really hurt you. She said you needed to 'come out on your own terms.' The last thing Max and I wanted to do was hurt you, so we kept our mouths shut."

I made a mental note to give Lin the biggest hug on the planet. Then a thought occurred to me, and I couldn't help but grin. "I can't believe you got Max to keep his mouth shut."

Devon shrugged. "I mean, he still cares about you, Clare. Maybe more than anyone else." My spirits dropped, but Devon seemed to catch them. "Hey, if it's any consolation, I'm pretty sure he's going to forgive you. After all, you and Hilda gave him quite the show the other day."

"Excuse me?"

Devon pinched the bridge of his nose with one hand as he drove. "Clare, you can't have your girlfriend drive you back to school on a loud-ass motorcycle while everyone is getting out of class, park on the sidewalk, then proceed to make out with her and expect your relationship to be a secret. Max said it wasn't a very hesitant kiss, either. He described it to me in vivid detail. Several times." Devon pretended to vomit. "Seriously, it was gross." He quickly caught himself. "I mean, hearing about your kiss, not the . . . well, you know. You're like my sister. I don't think—"

I reached across the car and put a hand on his shoulder. "Hey, it's okay. I knew what you meant."

Devon sighed. "So you want to talk about what's going on and why you were at Stantin's house?"

I took a deep breath and began to recount my story again, and as I did, it felt a little easier. There were parts where I still cried, but overall, it was better.

18

Hilda & I

Devon shook his head as we hit downtown. He was just driving without a destination as we talked, which was perfect. I was too distracted by recounting everything to really care where we were going. I was just glad to be away from home and with someone I could trust. At a stoplight, he turned and said, "Your mother is completely insane."

I sighed. "Maybe, but I don't really want to think about my mother right now. I feel so . . . lost. I need a plan."

"A plan?" Devon repeated and seemed to think for a moment when an idea must have struck him. "I got it!"

I began to ask, "You got what?" But before I could finish, Devon slammed on the brakes and turned the steering wheel hard. The tires of the Mustang screeched across the road as Devon threw us into a wild U-turn. When we were facing the opposite direction, he slammed on the gas, rocketing us forward.

Finally catching my breath and steadying my heart, I yelled, "Don't you think I've had enough heart attacks today!?"

With a twinkle in his eyes, Devon merely smiled. "I got a plan."

* * *

Hilda's father must have seen the plumes of dirt left by Devon's car because he was watching us ominously from his porch as we parked.

Devon cleared his throat as we walked up, whispering to me, "You sure we got the right house, Clare?"

I looked at the barren landscape surrounding us. "I've only been here a few times, but it's not like there's anything else out here."

Devon seemed hesitant but nodded as we walked up to Hilda's father. Ron looked like a statue of an angry biker with his arms crossed. He was clearly waiting for one of us to explain what was going on.

I was exasperated from having to explain my situation for the third time, so I cut straight to the important part. "Good afternoon, Mr. Bernhardt. I—"

"It's Ron," Hilda's father gruffly reminded me.

I bit my lip. "Ron, sorry, I-I need a place to stay."

Ron asked, "Both of you?"

Devon replied before I could. "No, just Clare. It's a long story."

Ron exhaled and narrowed his eyes at us. "Give me the short version."

I gulped, trying to think of where to start when Devon jumped the gun. "Clare's mom wants to send her away to some sort of messed-up camp because she's gay."

I looked over at Devon, slack-jawed.

Devon shrugged. "That's the short version, right?"

When I looked over to Ron, his lips had become a hard line, and it was impossible for me to gauge what he was thinking.

Without warning, he leaped forward at me. I nearly screamed, but I realized he was only hugging me. He placed his giant hand on the back of my head and pressed my face into his chest. "I'm so sorry."

Naturally, I wrapped my arms around him and squeezed back, whispering, "Thank you."

Devon interrupted, holding his phone and scratching the back of his neck. "I don't want to interrupt, but, uh, there's more people on their way here."

Ron stepped back and grunted. "I'll make some coffee." Then he set his hand on my shoulder and looked me in the eyes. "If you need me to call anyone—child protective services, the police, some family out of state maybe—you let me know." Then he held open the front door and nodded for Devon and me to come inside.

As I took a seat at the strange dining room table that didn't seem to match any of its chairs, Devon sat across from me and chuckled. "So this is Hilda's house. Not how I imagined it at all."

I shook my head and looked around, practically for the first time. All the walls were barren save for the occasional cuckoo clock, and none of the furniture matched. I also didn't see any technology from this century, including a television.

I ran a hand down my face and sighed. "What am I going to say to everyone? I mean, Max—"

"Hey!" Max's familiar voice shouted from behind the front door, startling both of us. "I heard my name taken in vain. Now someone open this door before I kick it down."

I ran over to the door, and as my hand reached out to grab the handle, I heard Hilda say, "Just open it, Max! It's never locked."

The door flew open, and Hilda charged past Max. Our eyes locked and she grabbed me in a tight hug that I never wanted to end.

"Clarissa," she whispered into my ear so warmly that I nearly melted. "I'm so glad you're safe."

I smiled. "Me too."

As I stared into Hilda's bright eyes, I heard a familiar but very out-of-place voice call out. "Can someone *please* explain what's going on."

I turned to see Lin and Veronica walk in as Max held the door open.

"Lin?" I gasped.

Lin looked like she wanted to say something but bit her tongue. Veronica bowed slightly. "Afternoon, Clare."

I was stunned that everyone was just standing there normally while I still had one arm wrapped around Hilda's waist. The silence grew, but Max, God bless him, said, "So, uh, are we supposed to start talking, or are you?"

Lin immediately slugged him in the shoulder. "What the hell is wrong with you? Were you raised in a barn?"

Max rubbed his arm and fired back. "What the hell is *your* problem? Psycho."

I burst into laughter, which brought everyone's attention back to me. "Sorry. You're right, Max. I owe you all an apology."

Lin muttered, "I bet that's the first time anyone's ever said that out loud."

Snorting, I continued. "But I think you'll want to hear the whole story." I did my best to keep my smile from waning as I gestured for everyone to take a seat at the mismatched table.

At least by this point, I had gotten pretty good at telling people about how my mother had been treating me all year, plus about the note and how it all ended up with everyone converging at Hilda's house.

When I looked over to Lin, she stood up abruptly, nearly knocking her chair over. "Fuck," she swore to nobody in particular. "Fuck!" she said louder and punched the table so hard it shook.

"What's wrong?" Veronica and I said simultaneously.

Lin spoke through gritted teeth. "This is all my fucking fault. If I hadn't been such a bitch to you, you never would have had to—"

"Stop," I interrupted and waited until she looked at me before I continued. "I was going to have to come out eventually, and honestly, I think you did me a huge favor by pushing me. Seriously, Lin, don't blame yourself."

Lin mumbled something like "alright" as she sat back down, but I could tell she was still beating herself up.

Max tugged at his earlobe. "Well, I guess that means it's my turn then. Clare, you lied to my face. A lot. And it's been really awkward for me to keep sitting with you at lunch when you don't run off to meet up with your 'secret friend,' but . . ." Max added air quotes to emphasize my cringe-worthy behavior. I squeezed Hilda's hand under the table, bracing for the worst. "Even with all that, I can't stop caring about you. As a friend, I mean, like . . . you know." When I looked up, Max's goofy smile warmed my heart.

"Are you sure you don't care?" I asked as I looked around to all of my friends. "None of you care that Hilda and I . . . that we're together? It doesn't bother you?"

Max hit his forehead with his palm so forcefully it slapped, then he groaned, "Oh, now she asks if we care." He looked around the table and pointed out the door. "No, Clare, everyone here just ran out of school mid-period because we wanted to sit here and insult you. Who do you think we are? I mean, other than Lin, of course."

Lin punched him in the arm again. "You are a colossal ass. Did you know that?"

I teared up with joy. "This is . . . It's perfect. Thank you, everyone."

A loud and low grunt came from my right, and everyone turned to see Hilda's father standing in the doorway to the kitchen. "You three." He pointed at Max, Lin, and Veronica. "There's a bedroom upstairs. Last door on the left before the bathroom. Bring every box in there down here." When nobody moved, Ron's voice grew dark. "I wasn't asking. Get moving."

My three friends fumbled over each other as they rushed to follow orders.

Hilda gave me an unsure glance before she began speaking to her father. "Papa—"

"You there. You're Devon, right? I hear you're a bit of a mechanic."

Devon offered a half-hearted nod. "Yes, sir."

Ron snorted. "Come with me and we'll see if we can get my truck started."

Confused, Hilda turned to me and asked, "What's going on?"

"I don't know," I said.

"Papa, why are we moving Mom's things?"

Ron grunted and nodded at me, the only person still sitting at the table. "Clarissa is moving in with us for awhile."

Still a bit dazed, I stood in what would become my room. Around us, our friends moved boxes and cleaned cobwebs. Not one of them allowed either me or Hilda to lift a finger, which was a bit frustrating, but then Hilda pointed out that I should start planning where to put my furniture once it was all there. It was a good distraction.

I pointed at the wall across from the door. "I think I'll make that where I set up my collage. Maybe I'll even paint it black so everything really stands out. What do you think?"

Hilda hummed. "If you do that, then you can put your bed here, and we can sleep against the same wall." She walked over and thought about something. "And you can put your dresser here and your desk here."

I sighed, trying to imagine how I would comfortably get dressed in such a cramped space or where I would even put all my clothes with such a small closet. "That's gonna be a little tight."

As he carried a box out of the room, Max snarked, "That's what she said."

I rolled my eyes. "God, I wish Matilda was here. She would know how to—" I stopped and looked at Hilda. "Wait, where is Matilda?" I could immediately tell Hilda knew something that she wasn't telling me. "What's wrong?"

Hilda chewed on her lower lip. "Are you sure you want to hear this?"

I mentally braced myself. "Yeah."

Hilda shrugged. "Alright, here it is: Matilda thinks that I seduced you into thinking you're gay."

I smiled, trying to keep our conversation light. "I mean, she's not necessarily wrong."

Hilda scowled. "Clarissa, this is serious. We both know that's not how it works, and if we play into that notion, it will get worse for everyone like us. Max and Devon have both tried to talk to her about it, but I get the sense that Matilda wants an explanation from you."

I reached out for Hilda's hand. "I'll talk to her. I promise. I'll make her understand."

Hilda pulled me in close to her. "Don't do that. If Matilda's really your friend, she'll understand. You can't force people to accept you. It never ends well."

I wrapped my arms around Hilda's neck. "How are you so good at this?"

"That advice came from Lin, actually. Also, I've been out a lot longer than you have."

Max walked back into the room, interrupting our kiss by saying, "Yeesh, get a room, you two. Oh, wait." The three of us laughed. Then he pointed and beckoned Hilda over to him. They whispered back and forth, and I couldn't make out anything until Hilda gasped.

"What? Are you serious?!" Before I could ask what was going on, Hilda turned to me and said, "We'll be right back, Clarissa."

A few minutes later, Hilda walked back in, holding something behind her back.

"What's going on?" I asked as she strode confidently toward me. "What are you holding behind your back?"

"Oh, you mean this?" Hilda slowly revealed a box with my unopened Nikon camera.

I leaped forward, snatching the box from her. "How?!" I didn't bother waiting for her to answer before I looked around for a place to open it, but having no furniture, I sat down in the middle of the room. As I began to rip open the packaging, I prayed that the battery came partially charged so I could start taking pictures right away.

Hilda took a seat next to me. "Max has been keeping everything you left at school in his truck. He's been waiting to give it back to you, but you weren't at school."

I finally got the box open and started sorting the pieces neatly around us. Once the box was empty, I forwent the instruction manual and tested myself by putting the camera together on my own.

Right as I slid the memory card into place and was all set to take my first photo, the familiar click of a shutter went off, which was strange because my finger wasn't anywhere near the—

Then the whirring of gears made me look up.

Devon, Lin, and Veronica were all standing around Max, who was holding the OneStep Hilda had also purchased for me, a fresh polaroid rolling out of the feeder.

I gasped. "Max, you didn't!?"

Ignoring me, Max pressed a snobbish finger into his lips and gesticulated pompously with the polaroid. "Now, what to call this?"

Hilda answered first, her love of Shakespeare warming my heart. "Much Ado About Nothing?"

Veronica was next. "The Two Lovers."

Devon scoffed. "The Most Complicated Photo Ever Taken."

"Hmm," Max droned. "What about Lesbians for Life? Too on the nose?"

Lin appeared to be on the verge of vomiting. "You all sicken me."

Feeling like I needed photographic retribution, I lifted the Nikon to my eye and flicked on the power. "Two can play at this game!"

"Quick!" Devon yelled as I adjusted the focus on my lens. "Everyone, do something stupid!"

"That must come as second nature to you and Max," Lin quipped right as I clicked the shutter button . . . and I must say, it felt good. Real good. I could get used to this Nikon.

I pulled the camera away from my eye so Hilda and I could review it together. Max had knelt and was flexing his arms inward like a strongman, his cheeks puffed up with air. Unbeknownst to him and Lin, standing in the back, Veronica had given them both bunny ears, though her soft smile betrayed complete innocence. Devon was looking exaggeratedly offended by Lin, who had the middle finger of her right hand nearly shoved in his face.

"It's perfect," I said, mostly to myself, feeling more at home at this moment than I had in a long time.

Everything was great until Hilda's father appeared behind everyone in the hallway. He surveyed what was happening and then took a deep breath. "It's going to be dark soon. Let's get this over with."

* * *

For what felt like the first time ever, I strode up the walkway of my parents' house and felt completely fearless, although with all my friends waiting on the sidewalk and Hilda beside me, it helped my bravery.

Once Hilda and I got to the front door, I reached out but stopped midway and pulled my hand back.

"It's okay, Clarissa. We—"

"Shh," I interrupted, knowing what was about to happen. "Wait for it . . ."

As if on cue, the front door swung open. "Clarissa Regal Huffington!" my mother roared. "Start packing your things—" She stopped abruptly when she saw Hilda standing next to me. "You! What are you doing here?"

I watched Hilda glance back at where everyone else was waiting patiently. "That depends, Mrs. Huffington."

My mother raised an eyebrow and then bit her words so hard I swore I felt a slight shock wave. "Depends on what?"

I took a deep breath. "If you're sending me away, then I'm going to stay with Hilda, and I'm taking all of my stuff with me."

I watched my mother closely as she processed the information I'd laid before her. "Oh, it's just that easy, is it?" she jeered.

I squeezed Hilda's hand for strength. "Yeah, Hilda's dad actually said it's fine."

My mother laughed. "What about after you graduate?"

I felt unexpectedly gutted that my mother seemed to give me up so quickly. Had she really not cared about me all these years? Was I always just an accessory to her, like a handbag or a fancy necklace? Something she owned but only acknowledged in passing or when appropriate?

My mother continued, even as a wave of pity for her washed over me. "Do you really think you'll get into college without my help? You think you can afford that alone? She can barely afford clothes that fit for Christ's sake! You don't know anything about the real world. You've never had a job. You don't know what it's like to have nothing. If left to your own devices, you'll just take pictures for twelve hours a day. Your father and I have provided everything for you your whole life, and this is how you repay us? With this . . . this ultimatum?!"

"I'm not going to argue with you anymore, Mom. You stopped listening to me years ago."

"What are you talking about?" my mother barked. "All I've done since school started is listen to you rave about how you're choosing to disrespect everything your father and I worked so hard for. How you're taking your life and throwing it away. This is a choice! You're choosing her over us! Over your family! Over G—"

"You're not giving me any other options!" My words hung in the air until Hilda let go of my hand and gripped my shoulder, pulling me closer to her. In that moment of safety, all of my anger left me, and I spoke plainly again. "I'm done, Mom. Hilda is going to help me pack right now, and I'll be gone before dinner."

My mother, her expression twisted in loss and disbelief, didn't move from the doorway. I felt sorry for her. Not in a pitiful way, either. I liked to think she was trying to understand but just couldn't. I wanted to help her, but we both knew that she just wanted to be mad. I was going to let her, but I was done being angry.

Some semblance of control returned to my mother as she said, "She's not allowed in this house."

For a moment, I thought Hilda would challenge her, but she actually stepped back, letting my mother have this small victory. The action made me nearly beam with pride. "Clarissa, I'm going to tell everyone what happened."

"You'll do no such thing!" my mother snapped, reaching for my arm. "This matter is to remain—"

Hilda moved like lightning, sliding in front of me and knocking my mother back with a shove to her collar bone.

Standing tall with a disgusted tone in her voice, Hilda said, "Don't touch Clarissa unless she consents." Then she snarled, "You hear me?"

My mother faltered, retreating into the house with both of her hands on her chest and looking absolutely weak and mortified. Without a word, she turned and ran into the dining room, not even bothering to close the door behind her.

I sighed and ran a hand down my face. "That didn't help, Hilda."

Hilda muttered something in German through gritted teeth, but there was one English word that I understood clearly: "monster." I shook my head, trying to focus. This wasn't the time to be upset or frustrated; I'd had my fill of those emotions. Reaching up, I ran my hand through Hilda's hair, but it didn't seem to relax her at all.

Gently, I whispered, "Thank you." I brushed Hilda's pink-tipped hair out of her face and rested my hand on her cheek.

Hilda took a deep breath and nodded before she headed back to the sidewalk.

* * *

A lot of my possessions were staying behind; that quickly became clear. I hadn't even finished stuffing a quarter of my dresser into one of the three duffle bags I used for summer Bible camp in years past when my dad cleared his throat in the doorway.

I didn't even bother glancing up. "Hey, Dad."

I felt my father move into the room. "Your mom told me what happened. Got a sec?" He sounded sincere, but I didn't stop packing. "You're really doing this, then?"

I sighed. "I don't have any other option. Mom—"

"You know she'll come around, right? It's just a shock. That's all." My father moved to set his hand on my shoulder but hesitated, turning it into a fist and lowering it to his side. "I know it's hard right now, but we'll get through this. There's no reason to run away. We're a family. We can figure this out."

Better to run away than get sent away. I touched his shoulder. "Thanks, Dad, but I can't. I'm done fighting with Mom about . . . everything. I can't deal with her trust issues anymore, questioning everything I do. You both always told me to grow up." I looked around my room. "I guess this is it. Actually, I need to talk to Mom."

My father cleared his throat. "What about? She's locked

herself in the kitchen, and she's on the phone with Nicholas. If it's serious—"

I shook my head. "I was just going to ask if I could take my laptop with me. It would be nice for homework."

"All that stuff is in our closet. I'll go grab it for you. But—"

The doorbell rang, cutting my father off.

I moved around him. "That's probably Hilda wondering what's taking me so long. I'll get it."

When I opened the door, Hilda's father was standing there with a scowl on his face. "We don't have all night. Where is your room, and what's coming with you?"

My father interrupted my response; I hadn't even realized he followed me downstairs. "Hello, I don't believe we've met."

"We haven't," Ron said gruffly.

Seeing that he wasn't going to get a handshake, my father withdrew his outstretched hand. "So Clare's going to stay with you for a little bit." The way my father said that made it sound like I was going for a weekend sleepover or something. "From what Clare tells us, you take a very hands-off approach to parenting. Can I trust you'll take care of my daughter?" Ron's only response was a slight tilt of his head, his eyes briefly darting to me. My father took a heavy breath, clearly growing tired of the silent treatment. "What makes you think you're even capable of taking care of a second daughter? You're barely a father to your own, as I understand it."

The sudden insult made me gasp but didn't seem to bother Ron at all, who said, "I was raised to believe that actions speak louder than words." Then he nodded at my arm. "Clarissa, you mind rolling up your sleeve for me?"

I gulped, but I slowly peeled back the sleeve of my shirt. I didn't even realize my hands were shaking until I'd fully revealed the discolored claw marks my mother had made. My father's eyes widened.

Ron took a long and intense breath, giving my father a grave look. "Now, let's address your concerns. Firstly, my Brünnhilde has held down a job all year while taking some of the hardest classes Saint Mary's offers. In what little free time she's had, she started her semiprofessional boxing career and is well on her way to making the U.S. Olympic team in time for Tokyo. Her grades may not be perfect, and she skips class more often than I'd like, but there ain't anything wrong with a kid being a kid every now and then. And yeah, I'm a shitty father. I'll be the first to admit that. But the thought never crossed my mind to kick my daughter out on the street because of her sexual orientation. Not once." Hilda's dad stepped through the doorway and pulled up both his sleeves, revealing his completely tattooed arms. "Now this next thing is important, so I really need you to pay attention. I don't know if it's *you* or your *wife*, but the next person to lay a hand on Clarissa without her permission is answering to me."

My father stammered. "It's not—"

"I don't care," Ron interrupted. "I'm going to help your daughter move out, and if you try to stop me, my first call will be to child protective services and my second will be to every news station and newspaper in a hundred miles." I watched as my father's face went white. "Yeah, Brünnhilde told me you work downtown at city hall. It's an election year, isn't it?" Without waiting for an answer, Ron turned to me. "What's ready to move?"

I pointed up the stairs. "My room's right there. It's the only room without a door." Ron's lip twitched, and his hands curled into fists, so I spoke faster. "My desk and chair. Start with those. They should be easy. Just empty everything onto my bed, and I'll sort it in a minute."

As Ron stalked past us, my dad ran his hand over his face. "Clare, I can't let you go live with that man. He's—"

I set a reassuring hand on my father's shoulder. "It'll be fine, Dad. I'll have Hilda and—"

"Us," Devon cheerfully interrupted as he, Veronica, Lin, and Max all walked up to the porch. Behind them, Hilda was lifting a dolly out of the back of her father's pickup.

My father smiled forlornly at all my friends. "Hey, Max, Devon, Veronica, and, uh . . . I don't believe we've met." He offered a hand to Lin, but she just folded her arms across her chest.

"Yeah," Lin sneered. "That's not gonna happen, asshole."

I winced slightly at Lin cursing at my father, who dropped his hand again. "I can see you've made some very interesting friends recently, Clare."

"That's right," Lin continued in her rudely sarcastic tone. "I'm just a fucking bucket of sunshine and rainbows. Ask anyone."

Devon nudged Lin, and asked, "You don't mind if we help, do you, Mr. Huffington?"

My father shrugged, and even though he was smiling, I could tell he was doing his best to treat the situation like it wasn't hard for him. "Sure, come on in."

* * *

Everyone had stuck around while they waited for me to give them a task. The two exceptions were Lin, who seemed on high alert and rarely left my side, and Hilda, who was stranded outside on the sidewalk the whole time, although maybe both were for the best. Packing my room had devolved quickly into a complete mess of trying to organize people more than things. Once the major pieces of furniture were loaded into Ron's pickup, the rest went into piles and then into boxes. I'd sort everything out once we got it all moved. This was the quickest way to leave and not have another altercation with my mother.

With my room almost empty, I heard a familiar but very unsettling voice echo up the stairs. I walked over to the banister and looked down to see Matilda standing just inside my front door. Her arms were crossed and she was talking with Veronica.

Part of me wanted to run away and pretend I wasn't home. Another part of me wanted to fly down the stairs and fling myself at her and beg for forgiveness. Thankfully, after some internal consideration, I just called down, "Matilda! Hey, I'm up here."

When Matilda was about halfway up the stairs, Veronica called up, "Take your time. I'll keep everyone busy outside."

Matilda and I stood awkwardly in my room. The dust outlines and pressure marks left by my furniture were the only sign that it had once been a bedroom.

I wasn't sure where to start. Thankfully, as Matilda looked around, she said, "You're really doing it, aren't you?"

I nodded. "Yeah. Also, I wanted to—"

"I know." Matilda said, avoiding eye contact with me.

"But I—"

Matilda whipped around. "How could you, Clare!?" I was shocked to see tears welling up in her eyes. "I thought I was your best friend."

I stuttered, "Y-You were." Afterward, I realized that was the absolute worst thing I could have said.

A fire ignited behind Matilda's eyes, and it seemed to burn all her tears away in a blink. "Yeah, emphasis on *were*, right? I mean, did you think it was funny when I helped you through all your break-ups with Max? Am I just your fucking emotional punching bag? Or were you secretly getting off watching me when we would change together for parties? Or when we tried on each other's clothes?"

I gasped. "What?! No. Never. Matilda, you're my *friend*. I just didn't mean to hurt you, and you have to believe that I never thought about you like that."

Matilda seemed to chew on her thoughts. "Hilda was your friend too, and look at how you two turned out. This may come as a surprise to you, but I'm not looking to be converted or whatever."

"Why are you suddenly treating me like some kind of pervert

just looking to get into your pants? The only reason I didn't approach you sooner is because of how you've been treating Hilda at school. I mean, you basically put on a parade when you found out Hilda was gay. How was I supposed to come out to you then?"

Matilda narrowed her dark eyes at me. "I don't like Hilda because she's a fucking bitch, Clare! It never had anything to do with her being gay. Yeah, I made a big deal about it, but only because I called it a mile away. Do you think I'm some kind of bigot or something?"

"You just said that you didn't want me 'converting you.' How else am I supposed to interpret that?"

Matilda's eyes darted away from me and held there. "I thought we shared everything with each other. But you lied to my face. That's really messed up. I feel betrayed. And don't start with me about 'how you didn't know at first.' Trust me, I've heard that excuse from everyone already, and I don't buy it. But you want to know the worst part? I think some part of me always knew you were a lesbian, but I was in denial or something. I didn't want to lose my best friend, because if you were gay, then we might not be able to share everything we used to." I opened my mouth to counter and say that nothing would have changed between us, but Matilda held up a hand. "It's dumb, but I think that's why I pushed you and Max together. I just wanted to protect you."

"I never asked for your protection," I said, coming off more indignant than I wanted. "And I'm sorry. Trust me, I wanted to tell you. I wanted to tell everyone, but—"

"But what, Clare? Too busy ditching everyone at lunch or being 'grounded'?" Matilda turned and started to leave. The old me would have stood there and let her go, but after the way things had gone, I wasn't going to.

I quickly ran around her and blocked my doorway. "Stop. I want to make this right. You mean a lot to me and I don't want to throw all that away just because I'm not hiding who I am anymore. Please."

I saw the conflict behind Matilda's eyes. Then she softly choked out, "I-I'm sorry, Clare. Maybe one day I'll forgive you. But that's not today. Can you move?"

I hesitated. I wanted to fix it so badly, but I remembered that I shouldn't try to force anything on anyone. Dropping my head away from her and stepping aside, I said, "I didn't mean to hurt you."

Matilda paused as she passed me, but her gaze was fixed forward. "I know, but you did."

Shortly after Matilda left, I found myself standing on the porch again, this time with my father in the doorway. A weary smile rested on his face as we watched my friends make sure everything was secured in the back of Ron's pickup.

"Not exactly how I had expected this to go. For some reason, I had this great dream of your mother and me helping you move into your college dorm. Guess that's all out the window now."

I smiled, trying my best to be encouraging. "What are you talking about, Dad? I'd love for you and Mom to help me move into a dorm, but I need to get into college first, which might take a while considering, you know, everything that's happened. Maybe I'll take out some loans or something. I'm not really sure." I scratched the base of my skull. "I'm kinda new to this whole 'being an adult' thing."

My father nodded, but I could tell he was struggling to keep himself from faltering. "You're growing up to be such a wonderful young woman. I just . . . I wasn't ready for it to happen so soon." After a long pause, he added, "You'll always be welcome here, Clare. Right now, it's just . . . a difficult time for your mother. She'll come around."

I sighed. "I want to believe you. It's just . . . when Mom wants to listen—I mean really listen—I'll be willing to talk to her."

My father reached into his back pocket and pulled out my cell phone. "It'll be easier if you have this. I took the tracking app off of it, and I'll keep Hilda's number on our plan until you and, uh, your girlfriend can get your own plan. Is that how I should say it? A coworker said to say 'partner,' but that sounds like those old spaghetti westerns we used to watch when you were young. Remember those? We would cuddle up in front of the fireplace on cold days and watch them." He chuckled, but it was strained and filled with regret. "Sorry."

I hugged him. "You're doing fine, Dad."

Hilda walked up to us, trying to not interrupt the moment. "Clarissa, we're ready to go."

I stepped sideways and opened the hug for her to join. "Want to get in on this?"

Hilda paused until my dad beckoned with his hand. "Come on in. I should probably get used to this, right?"

Hilda beamed at my father as she joined us, and as we hugged, I overheard her whisper "thank you" into his ear.

Once our hug was over, my dad stepped away from us, unable to hold back his tears any longer. "You take good care of my daughter, Hilda. Don't let her stay up past midnight or she turns into a terror in the morning. She's not allergic to anything that we know of, other than her mother's broccoli casserole, but then again, who isn't?" He tried to laugh but neither Hilda nor I followed suit.

Hilda must have seen how hard this was for my father, because instead of pulling me closer to her and away from him, she said, "Clarissa and I will be around. It's not like I'm moving her to Germany with me."

My dad shifted uncomfortably and looked at me. "Clare, I-I know this might be too much, but if you make it to church this Sunday, I think it would mean a lot to your mother. You don't have to talk to her, just . . . make an appearance, you know?"

Some part of me wanted to stay and fight it out with my mother, but I wasn't that person anymore. The truth, not only about who I was but who I could be, was liberating.

I pulled away from Hilda and hugged my father again. "I know, Dad. I'll try."

At the sidewalk, I turned back one last time. My father was still standing on the porch. My mother had come out, but she wasn't looking at me. Her head was buried in my father's shoulder.

Praying they understood that I meant it, I shouted, "I love you."

19

The New Normal

I opened my eyes to an unfamiliar ceiling. In a moment of panic, I sat bolt upright. I looked out into the surreal sea of moving boxes and overstuffed camping luggage. It took me a few seconds to realize that it was my ceiling. In my new home. With Hilda.

"Guten Morgen," Hilda said with a yawn as she sat up. The blankets dropped to her thighs, revealing her bare chest. I had been too exhausted to even put panties on the night before, leaving me completely in the buff under the covers. We hadn't even done anything; I just needed to be close to her, and she was all too willing to cuddle my stress away until I fell asleep on her.

"Morning," I said as I bunched up some blankets to cover myself.

I was distracted by Hilda's glinting piercings just long enough for her to catch me staring.

"Guten Morgen," she repeated in a slightly more sultry way.

I fumbled along the side of the bed for my bra and panties, but Hilda stopped me. Then she eased into my back and cuddled closer. I felt the bare metal—and what they were attached to—press into my back.

"Shhh," Hilda cooed. "I heard my father leave just a few minutes ago."

I looked over my shoulder at Hilda's tired grin.

"Don't. Move." Then Hilda's pink-tipped hair disappeared under the covers.

* * *

My breath was labored as I lay on top of Hilda. "God. Can you please wake me up every day like that?"

Hilda snickered. "I thought you'd like that."

I rolled off her but couldn't stop myself from wrapping my arm around her stomach. "I loved that." With my other hand, I smoothly brushed her hair away from her face. "I love you."

"I love you, too. But you have a long day of unpacking, and I need to finish my homework. We can't spend all day in bed."

"As much as you'd like to?" I asked, pouting playfully. In reality, I was still completely drained from the move and struggling to come to terms with the fact that this wasn't just a fabulous dream.

"If boxing has taught me anything, it's that practice makes perfect," Hilda said and gave me a peck on the forehead before she sat up and stretched.

Some prudish part of me still averted my gaze when Hilda was fully nude, but I kept her in the corner of my eyes as we searched for her underwear. "Here." I picked up her panties and held them out.

"Ah! Thanks. Do you want the first shower? I need to run to my room to get clean clothes."

"You go first. I still need to find my clothes. I packed so quickly I don't really know where anything is, let alone my toiletries."

At the doorway, Hilda stopped and turned. "Clarissa, can I tell you something?"

"Huh?" I said, still a little overwhelmed.

"I'm really proud of you. I don't know if I would have been strong enough to do what you did."

"You're just being modest."

Hilda shook her head. "I'm serious. You're really amazing, and I think you made the right decision."

I blushed with pride. "Thanks. I needed to hear that."

"Now, get to work!" Hilda stuck her tongue out at me right before she disappeared down the hallway.

I was on my third box when Hilda came in holding a plate piled high with eggs and steaming bacon. Her hair was wet, and she was wearing tight black shorts and a thin gray crop top that did nothing to hide her piercings. "Coffee is still brewing. My father forgot to change the filter."

"I didn't think I owned so much stuff." I sighed as I flopped on the bed, already defeated. "All this had been so easy to pack. Why is it so difficult to unpack? Both of those piles over there need to go to Goodwill or something. I haven't worn any of that since junior high." I stared up at the wooden ceiling, thinking that maybe it wasn't such a good idea to haphazardly move *everything* I owned in a single evening. Lin's idea to label everything as we threw it into boxes might have been the right call.

A slice of bacon suddenly dangled just above my mouth, and I playfully bit into it like a shark as Hilda tried to rip it away.

Hilda gave the half slice of bacon she was holding a pouty look before she finished it.

When she reached for another piece of bacon, I said, "Alright, go get your textbooks."

"Huh?"

"You said you had homework to do, right? Well, I'm not going to let you keep cheating your way through high school. If someone finds out, you'll actually be expelled."

Hilda frowned. "But—"

"No buts! I'm not going to college alone. You'll be coming with me even if I have to drag you kicking and screaming." My voice softened a bit. "I need you. I can't do this alone."

Hilda took a deep breath, resigning herself to her fate. "Well, if you put it like that, I guess I'll be right back."

I couldn't have been more pleased with how the events of the morning unfolded, except for the fact that I still had no idea which moving box held my underwear and toiletries.

* * *

"Have you talked to your mom since you moved out?" Max asked as he, Hilda, and I all walked into Saint Christopher's with the rest of Max's family trailing behind us.

I scanned the front of the congregation and immediately spotted the backs of my parents in the front row. "No, but I think I'll wait till after mass."

This ground was as neutral as it got between me and my mother. Some part of me hoped that she would be more willing to listen here, given that a week had passed since I moved out, but it was a fool's hope.

Once the sermon concluded, I walked down the main aisle toward the altar as people milled around and headed back to the main exit. I felt the eyes of people I'd known my whole life follow me like I was nude or wearing some sort of awful dress. It probably didn't help that Hilda, in her usual metalhead attire, was following closely behind. She seemed to understand how stressed I was and never reached out for my hand, even though she probably wanted to.

"Hey, you two," my dad said, trying his best to act like nothing was out of the ordinary.

I hugged him right away. "Morning, Dad."

When I broke the embrace, I noticed my mother eyeing me coldly. "Well," she said. "Do I get one?"

I hesitated, but we eventually hugged. It was awkward for both of us. The devil on my shoulder whispered to me that the only reason my mother even asked for a hug was to keep up appearances among the congregation, but I mostly ignored it.

Once we were finished the quick embrace, my mother took up her usual tone. "Good morning, Hilda. How are you today?"

"Good." Hilda smiled but seemed to look over my mother's shoulder as she said it. "The sermon was nice, too, although still a little dry."

Uncle Nick chuckled as he walked out from behind a curtain, where he was clearly trying to eavesdrop. "Was it now? Well, I'll try and spice it up next time. It's so rare that we have nonbelievers here. I admit, sometimes, I fall into a routine." He opened his arms wide and eyed both of us expectantly. "Who's first?"

I began walking over, but Hilda made a break for it, so I had to skip to match. If my uncle's center of gravity weren't in his belly, the middle-aged priest would surely have collapsed backward as we fought to hug him simultaneously.

"This is what I'm talking about!" he announced gleefully as he wrapped one hand around each of us and squeezed. "Didn't I always say we Huffingtons are huggers?"

Hilda grabbed the small of her back and pretended she was hurt. "Ja, but next time, not so hard. I need to work out later."

Uncle Nick playfully slapped his belly. "Me too, but I get the feeling only one of us is going to follow through with it. Now, how's my favorite family doing?" He looked at each of us with an honest smile, pretending he had no idea.

"Life's been . . . strange," I admitted after a short silence. "I still don't know if what I did was right." I looked at my parents, hoping they'd understand. "Moving out, I mean. Not the other thing. I'm still gay."

Uncle Nick set one hand on my shoulder and one hand on my mother's. "Can I pull the two of you aside for a moment?"

My father and Hilda shared a worried look as my uncle gently ushered us away.

A short walk later, we were in one of the many dim prayer rooms in the back. Tiny tea candles stood atop a padded bench that ran the length of the small room.

My uncle exhaled. "So usually I wouldn't be so forward, but I think this situation demands a little more rod than carrot. Mary, despite your best intentions, I'm just going to say it: you're stubborn, and if you continue on this path, I believe it will only end in disaster. If Clare is truly committed to this new path, and I have faith that she is, then it's only God who is allowed to judge her. From what I've been hearing, you've been acting rather Old Testament when you should be turning the other cheek."

My mother released a long sigh but eventually nodded. I supposed that was the best I could have asked of her.

Uncle Nick then turned to me. "Now, I think Clare is a fine young woman, and she's going to take lessons away from you that only you could teach. The bad, maybe, but overwhelmingly the good. The good, most importantly."

I butted in. "Yeah, in fact, I've been forcing Hilda to do her homework all week and told her I would drag her to college with me—kicking and screaming if I have to."

My uncle smiled. "You see? Already ahead of the curve. I think Clare has you to thank for that kind of attitude."

"And so much more," I added, looking at my mother, whose painful expression hid so much. "I know you love me, and I know I didn't turn out how you wanted but . . . I'm still . . . me."

My mother's lip quivered as she fought to maintain her composure, but she remained silent.

My uncle clapped once. "On that note, Clare, you have to

understand, change—especially sudden change—can be a shock to any relationship, even strong ones. Sometimes that change takes more time for one person to process than others. At times like this, patience and understanding must be held in the highest regard. Do you understand?" I nodded, and my uncle sighed in relief. "Now, I'm going to ask both of you to light a prayer candle for the other and do your best to forgive and look forward to the relationship you'll grow from here."

Once my uncle had left, we did as instructed and walked back out into the nave in complete silence.

Hilda and my dad were talking as we reformed the small circle.

"What happened?" my dad and Hilda asked in near unison.

My mother looked at me and swallowed. "Nicholas just wanted to speak with us. He was very insightful, as always."

I did my best to smile. "Yeah, it was nice."

"Clare," my mother said with a stern look. "You have to understand this isn't . . . Hilda is not the kind of person who I imagined you being with. Regardless of her gender."

I shrugged. "Eh, she's not so bad, once you get to know her. Still, I got my work cut out for me. She can be a real punk sometimes."

My mother gave Hilda a passive-aggressive look. "I'm sure."

I sighed, trying to think of something to say. Then it hit me. "Oh, Hilda and I applied to a few colleges last night, and we're going to keep at it when we get home, too."

My father seemed genuinely shocked and then smiled. "Oh, that's great! Which ones?"

Before I could answer, my mother said, "How do you expect to pay? College is expensive—"

"Mary." My father set a hand on my mother's shoulder and gave her a very pleading look. In return, my mother exhaled and nodded to me, as if to apologize.

I wrapped an arm around Hilda's waist. "We'll figure something out. Hilda actually qualified for Golden Gloves up in Chicago. So in a few weeks, we'll be heading up there. If she places well, she could be scouted for the U.S. Olympic team, not to mention maybe get a few scholarships. Right now, we're both hoping for UC Berkeley. Hilda's dad has some friends out there who we might be able to rent a room from. But even if that doesn't work out, we'll have each other. Wherever we end up."

My father nodded somberly. "That's good to hear. Just keep us updated, okay?"

"Of course, Dad." An awkward silence fell on us, so I added, "I guess we'll see you next Sunday?"

"Or before," my father insisted. "We can do dinner sometime this week. We'd like to know about your move and, well, everything. Maybe you could stop by after school one day. Hilda, you're invited as well, of course."

I saw my mother struggle to keep her mouth shut, so I said, "Maybe. We're both studying for finals, so it's going to be a lot of long nights. I honestly don't know if we'll have time, but we'll try."

My mother astonished me when she said, "I'll try, too."

At the sidewalk, my heart soaring, I turned and looked at Saint Christopher's in the mid-morning sun. I squeezed Hilda's hand, and she wordlessly squeezed back as we stood there.

It was me.

It was us.

It was love.

Thank you for reading!

Connect with Ophelia:
Twitter: twitter.com/Author_Ophelia
Facebook: https://www.facebook.com/opheila.alexander
E-Mail: authoropheliaalexander@gmail.com

CPSIA information can be obtained
at www.ICGtesting.com
Printed in the USA
LVHW052020230621
690958LV00017B/2096